All God's Children

To Bonnie,
You know that lake and I hope you get a kick out of the "weather" and Muskegon features! May you recognize your heart & soul as God's beloved! Like Cal came to know. Love,
Betsy P. Skinner

All God's Children

Betsy P. Skinner

DEDICATION

For "P"
and my Muse

Copyright © 2019 by Betsy Skinner.

ISBN: Softcover   978-1-7960-7226-6
        eBook   978-1-7960-7227-3

All rights reserved. No part of this book may be reproduced or transmitted in any form or by any means, electronic or mechanical, including photocopying, recording, or by any information storage and retrieval system, without permission in writing from the copyright owner.

This is a work of fiction. All of the characters, names, incidents, organizations, and dialogue in this novel are either the products of the author's imagination or are used fictitiously.

Any people depicted in stock imagery provided by Getty Images are models, and such images are being used for illustrative purposes only.
Certain stock imagery © Getty Images.

Print information available on the last page.

Rev. date: 11/18/2019

To order additional copies of this book, contact:
Xlibris
1-888-795-4274
www.Xlibris.com
Orders@Xlibris.com
803743

Cast of Characters

Church Officers and Members

Moderator	Thomas Dreiden	Myrtle Dreiden (wife)
Treasurer	J. B. Johnson	
Trustee	Tendal Harris	Margaret Harris (wife)
		Connie (daughter)
		David Somers (Connie's fiancé/husband)
Clerk	Nancy Dobbs	
Missions/Outreach Chair	Gunther Dobbs	
Music Committee Chair	Kathy Yost	
Search Committee Chair	Smit Rother	
Christian Ed Director	Lilly Smith	
Organist	Gertrude Rudders	
Church Secretary	Dalia Crumpett	
Pastor	Rev. Calline Simpson	
	Sorrel Dixon (love interest)	
	Elizabeth Cromwell (fiancé)	
	Billy Dixon (son)	
	Martha Beckman (Billy's fiancé)	
	Bob and Joan Simpson (Calline's parents)	
	Bingo (Calline's dog)	
	Patty Fritz (Calline's best friend)	
	Bessie-Geneva (Calline's deceased great-grandmother)	
	Sister MarieTherese (M.T.) (Calline's spiritual director)	

Other Members

Alexis Grimsley	Richard Kellogg Grimsley (husband)
Helen Mellbridge (deceased)	Willomena Brainard (daughter)
Rachael Connors	George Connors (son) Gloria Rigley (sister)

Neighbors & Others

Vee Morgan	Young teen
Miss Becky	Proprietor of Miss Becky's Eatery
Peter Vanderlaan	Candidate for Music Director/Organist
	Randy Campbell (husband)
Mims Smith	Organizer, The Lemonade Stand
Melinda Suarez	Mother of triplets
Wonder-Full Counselor	Mysterious Stranger
Mr. Johns	Micky and Ricky (sons)
Officer Jensen	Crime Scene Investigator

CHAPTER ONE

THERE ARE MANY things that church ministers should do, and some things that would be best left alone. The Reverend Calline Simpson knows this. Standing at the sliding glass door while her boxer, Bingo, relieves herself, she weighs the should dos and the leave alones, worrying that the scales are tipping to the latter. "Time to come in now!" she calls to the dog, whose frantic spurts and spins always bring laughter. Not so amusing are her thoughts of last night: how Sorrel Dixon, church fundraiser extraordinaire, asked for a spontaneous meet-up at Curley's. How, in spite of feeling bone-tired, in a forced refreshed voice, she said, "Sure!" and felt excited. How he told her, "I wanted to tell you in person that I'm sad you aren't doing Elizabeth's and my wedding. I'd prefer to have you bless this thing, but Elizabeth wants to marry in the Keys." How his "this thing" reference to his marriage seemed offhanded, and she liked this. How holding his gaze scared her.

How she felt heat rise to her neck, then in a forced, even tone, she said, "Sorrel, it's so thoughtful of you to consider my feelings about officiating your wedding. I offer you every blessing for your special day." How, after announcing this lie, she rose from her chair as if she'd just sat on a tack, clumsily tripped on the chair leg, and was out the door before her coat was buttoned, and it was already in the teens.

"Lord, bring me back to right now," she prays, as she opens the slider to let Bingo in. She turns to face the sienna photograph of her patron saint, her circuit riding great-grandmother, Bessie Geneva. The pastor of High Dunes First United Congregational

Church finds it comforting to confer with her Grand's image, as crazy at it seems. Grand would understand the challenges of leading a church in ordinary times, but what of now, when the place is anything but the peaceable kingdom? "How did you do this, Grand? You traveled by horse and buggy, husband and kids in tow, preaching your heart out. Like tiny tots, the people wanted all of you." Calline pours a cup of dark Java and watches the sun's first beams cast white stripes across the lawn. She listens.

"Get a kitchen timer."

Why not? she thinks. Calline looks for the timer she uses on the treadmill, which currently serves as an extra clothes hanger.

"Set it for five minutes. Five minutes; you can handle anything for five minutes, lovey. Then go for another five, and the next thing you know, you're off and running."

Calline rubs the back of her neck to flatten the hairs raised when she's sure it's Grand whose channeling. In haste Calline finds the timer by the toaster, and sets it exactly for five minutes. "*Tick-tick!*" She fixes her usual Tyson sausage patties and buttered rye toast. She takes an extra dollop of butter for good measure. *Bbbrrriiinnnggg.* She sets the timer for another five while she cleans dishes and dresses. Her favorite size-sixteen cotton jumper and turtleneck rub in places they didn't last year. The extra pounds aggravate her, but her resolve to decrease fat and increase greens is shot. Christmas is coming, so forget it for now.

"I promise, I'll lose the extra 30 . . . okay, 40," she declares to her reflection. Looking at herself square-on is something she does only out of necessity since the accident, ashamed she's over 40-years old and has never let on to anyone in the congregation why she limps. But, in order to apply the Chanel her dad gave her mother when they were dating, and a touch of color on her lips, she must look at herself square-on, eyeball to reflected eyeball.

"This is because of you, Sorrel Dixon." She dabs the perfume under her right ear. It perplexes her why this man, so long in her "just friends" category, has entered a new chamber in her heart. Twelve years since her divorce, no serious romance has come her way. This one, Sorrel Dixon, is the one who feels right, just as her conscience clangs, *leave it alone*.

Recently, she confessed to her best friend, Patty Fritz, "Sorrel and I have been with each other in all kinds of compromising situations—on youth camping trips, fundraisers, organizing rallies, you name it. I never felt anything but a sort of kid-sister feeling. Why now?"

"It's the forbidden fruit syndrome, you crazy woman," Patty opines. "But, truthfully, I think you're distracting yourself to dodge the general ennui and the anxiety about things stirring at church." Patty, her closest confidante since seminary, hears her friend's every woe, wonderment, and now, wickedness. Little gets by her, as far as Calline's inner workings go. Good friends know their subject. Of late, Patty knows hers way more than tolerable.

"Now that Sorrel is getting married, suddenly he's the apple and I'm Eve?" Calline sighs, persisting lamely. "He's never with Elizabeth at church functions; in fact, he seldom speaks of her."

"Out of sight, out of conscience? Is that your rationale for pursuit?" Patty teases, with tinges of serious warning. "There's the Code, need I remind you dear one?" Patty chides with mercy.

"He apologized to me last night because I'm not performing their wedding. In truth, I'm relieved. Lately, Patty, I feel like Bingo tugging at the leash to run free." Calline sighs.

"But when you let her off the leash, what happens?"

"She runs into traffic, usually," Calline remembers the near miss when a car skidded to a halt, almost catching the dog under a front tire. Imagining her beloved Bingo nearly dying without her restraints was no encouragement to lose hers around Sorrel Dixon.

Calline settles into her father's worn leather library chair facing the fire place. Logs smolder and hiss from last night's blaze. Every morning after prayers, she fondles the corners of the pages of her calendar. Notes scratched like chickens with ink on their toes jam into eleven months. Calline turns to the twelfth. What renderings will she, her journal, and her congregation encounter in December, 1987 and beyond?

In the stillness, she is aware of an ineffable ache in her spirit. Was she bored, lonely, love-sick? All of the above, perhaps. She can ignore these sensations, numb them, but they return, like children who repeat and repeat their pleas until those in charge answer. Or not. *But, still, there's this calling, and so much yet to do,* she hears.

It was in her last semester at the University of North Carolina when she announced, "Mom, Dad, I think I'm going to theological school."

Joan and Bob Simpson feared her daughter's life would be like her great-grandmother Bessie Geneva's. "The gospel's hostage you'll be. No time to be mother, daughter, wife." Breast cancer plagued Joan during the years of Calline's studies and claimed her life three days after Calline's graduation from Yale Divinity School.

Her compelling call would beckon her onto a path, as onto a gauntlet of resistance and hostility. Search committee chairwoman, Rachael Connors, overseeing the search for High Dunes FUCC's thirteenth pastor and first woman, leveled with Calline, "It's not all hunky-dory here, the idea of hiring a woman and all. Will you consider anyway?" Even with the exodus of folks refusing to accept her, enough "yeas" on the anonymous voting ballots emboldened Calline. She needed a job, she needed to prove to herself, and to her God that she could echo with the same conviction, the declaration of the faithful across the millennia: "Here I am Lord, send me." Even if it was to a place on a main highway to what seemed to her like nowhere.

As if stress, longing, and a hurting left knee weren't enough, the pastor's conscience rattles itself every time she thinks of The Code: no clergy-parishioner fraternization, period. Why, she prays, does her resolve to resist entanglement with Sorrel Dixon weaken now, like her resistance to all things sweet and doughy?

"Amen," she whispers, chews the crust of a third slice of buttered toast, and bundles for the cold walk to church. She can be at the front door of the building in no time if she trot-limps—through her neighbor's yard, across a leaf-blanketed garden, and over a boxwood hedge that surrounds the church parking lot. Today, the wind drives hard off the lake, forcing her to pull her turtleneck over her chin and the collar of her dad's Navy pea coat up around her ears. The kitchen timer *tick-tick-ticks* in the coat pocket. Sure enough, she's off and running, just like Grand said.

CHAPTER TWO

AT FIRST ENCOUNTER, the sheer size of Lake Michigan stunned the new minister. For weeks after moving to the little shore town of High Dunes she watched for the tides, and sniffed the air for the distinct scent of ocean, where she had spent summers as a child. But this was a lake, not an ocean, and it was a formidable summer magnet, drawing people to play in the fickle sunshine that lingers until ten. Men, women, and children, all powdered with sand, queue at Fat Jack's for ice cream. Ephemeral are summer's pleasures, nibbled away by shorter days and the cold. Apart from the lake and Evan Van Reuters, High Dunes' founder, the town might be just that: a wall of high dunes made jagged by capricious winds and erosion. On the first Friday in March, the schools let out and businesses close to celebrate Van Reuters' legacy of almost two hundred years.

Calline tugs at the church's main entrance door, spared from the fire that took the first building. One hundred thirty-two years earlier, Congregationalist missionary, Reverend Nehemiah Smith, rode into town with moral zeal and pent-up libido. A convert spied The Reverend laying hands on a church founder's wife. Shortly thereafter The Reverend Smith was found hanging from the bell clapper. That night, the building caught fire and was razed by dawn. Reverend Smith is seldom mentioned unless someone asks why there's no belfry in building number two.

The massive door and its handle are as big as the sentiment behind keeping the cumbersome thing. "My great-grandfather made that doorknob, and he probably sawed the wood for the door," Richard Kellogg Grimsley growls. He and his wife, Alexis, write the biggest check and hold it over anyone who contests their will on just about anything. Watch out, because the agenda at hand will surely provoke Alexis, whose voice is loud and influential. Richard, who salutes his wife, will stand at attention.

Except for the lack of a belfry and the addition of square footage, building two replicates the first almost to a tee. Four Corinthian columns support the portico, where folks enter into a stone-tiled foyer to change into inside shoes in inclement weather (which it usually is) and hang coats. A bronze plaque bearing the names of the eleven founders hangs over a long oak bench in the foyer. Folks sit to switch boots to shoes, chit-chat about the game or their kids, and spare not a little breath for the latest gossip.

The second building's additional square footage allows for a chapel, two classrooms, and an administrative office; each are a bit cramped, but functional. Daylight and moonlight spill into the sanctuary through the big beveled-glass panes, the imperfect glass pocked by tiny bubbles and swells. An ornate crystal chandelier hangs dead center, its presence so formidable, people avoid sitting underneath for fear that it will lose its grip. Except for the gaudy light fixture, the sanctuary reflects Puritan austerity: hard wooden pews, worn wide plank floors, no stained glass, and a pulpit with simple churchy carvings. Calline thanks God that only two steps are required to get to her sermon manuscript. Her knee could not take the original Puritan-styled pulpit, a skyward-spiraling preaching perch resembling something like a high diving board with rails.

The preacher and lector peer over fifteen rows of pews divided by a central isle, enough seats for 250 worshipers, the founders' vision for church growth. Recently, though, velvet ropes cordon off the back five pews, leaving plenty of places for the congregation that swells in the summers and recedes in the winter. Attendance has plateaued as of late and, given the recent stirrings of unrest, no telling what.

Calline strips from hat, coat, and scarf, anticipating the secretary's daily antics. "Dalia, you here?" Secretary Dalia Crumpett reminds Calline of her Aunt Nettie's potbellied pig. Dalia came to the job, not unlike a pig might to a dysfunctional family that couldn't refuse exotic, innocent and cute, the irresistible prelude to awkward, messy, extravagantly under worked, and anything but suited for church domesticity.

"She's unfit for the job," Moderator Thomas Dreiden complained at the recent Governance meeting. "We've enough going on here that is troublesome, without the complaints about Dalia. Her shrills over the phone and the other god-awful quirkiness she brings aren't helping our image." This complaint was a stretch for the usually upbeat and affirming Thomas.

"I agree," piped in Tendal Harris, senior trustee. "Mea culpa. I let the trustees 'yea' her in. She begged for the job. You know what she does to get her way. We thought we could rehabilitate her, you know." Tendal blushed, embarrassed he was part of that decision.

"I make a motion we keep her until we get through Advent and Christmas. After we hire Gertrude's replacement at the organ, then we make our move," suggested Tendal. All heads nodded and a unanimous vote "for" carried. Dalia would be out the door, squealing to everyone, no doubt. Until then, Reverend Calline would pray for patience, tolerance, and kindness, her fickle triumvirate of virtues.

"Cal, Sorrel called. I told him you were giddy to talk to him," Dalia announces as soon as the wind slams the door behind Calline.

"Dalia! You used the word *giddy*?" Her irritation with Dalia has no bounds.

Dalia files a chewed nail and gives that *I know about you two* wink. "I know, learn diplomacy, you always say. I have to look that word up again." Then, that oink-like giggle that galls the Reverend no end.

"Well, look it up again, and *again* if necessary!" Calline huffs, and limps to her office. She lights a candle on the table in the corner of her tiny space. A lost bet between her predecessor and his secretary afforded Dalia the office intended for the pastor, and left Calline with the diminutive space. Like roots of a root bound plant, each object of the pastor's work and sentiment has a place. A secondhand overstuffed chair jams next to a three-legged table where the candle blinks light into a musty corner. The tools of her trade—concordances, lexicons, commentaries, Gospel parallels, and theologians along the conservative-liberal spectrum: Barth, Neouwen, Ruther, Cone, Daly, Fuerri, and others—squeeze together on shelves that once stored the custodian's cleaning supplies.

A yellow V.W. pulling up to the mailbox draws Calline to the window. "Is that what I think it is? Someone in a car I've never seen before just left a package in the mailbox. Dalia!"

"Yep. What's the matter?" Dalia's symphony of flushing and gum popping require Calline to yell, a tone she uses more often lately.

"A yellow VW just came and went. A tall silver-haired woman. Check the mailbox, would you?"

The bathroom door slams, then the front door. Dalia, remarkably quick on her feet, returns with a legal-sized envelope, handling it like one of her mother's fresh-baked pies. Calline rips it open. "Good Lord, it's Helen Mellbridge's handwriting. And here she is, dead and gone. That woman wore silence and sadness like an extra layer of skin. Nobody could get her to talk." It was just the day before yesterday that Calline tried to urge the dying woman to release the burden of something she hinted at but never shared. "Maybe this is a posthumous confession of some kind," Calline says to the envelope.

"You done the eulogy?" Dalia blows a bubble the size of a ping-pong ball, letting it shrivel over her bottom lip.

"Working on it; big gaps, though. Maybe this will help." Calline shuffles the pink watermarked pages, and stares blankly, thinking.

ALL GOD'S CHILDREN

Dalia runs to answer the phone, plopping into her chair, kicking the floor to set herself spinning; the receiver coil wraps around her. "Whee!" she squeals. "First Church, it's the church for me. And you?" she announces to the, no doubt, unsettled caller.

"Cal, it's for you. Sorrel," giggles Dalia from the next room.

Unnerved, Calline pulls her knees to her chin and wraps herself into an old mohair shawl her mother bequeathed.

"Sorrel!" she says a bit soprano. *Please dear God, don't let him detect one ounce of anything.* Her stomach roils and her cheeks warm.

"Cal, I have a favor to ask. Billy's coming home from school and I'm working on finishing touches at the connubial home. Could he stay at your place for a night or two until the dust settles?"

Sorrel's reference to his marriage irritates her. She lets so much bug her these days. "My place is a mess, but he could come tomorrow, I suppose." Calline hates herself for answering so quickly and clears her throat nervously. *Shoot, Sorrel's not stupid. Just where to with this man so good and wise, funny, and keenly in tune with the Spirit?*

"Elizabeth and I are getting married," he announced to an intimate few at a recent gathering at the Pub. His friends seemed happy enough. Calline feigned delight and congratulations, imagining how disappointed and shocked the others would be to know her struggle over this man who occupies her dreams with growing intensity.

"Sure, Sorrel. Tell Billy I can't wait to see him." She means this. She loves Sorrel's son as her own. Being with him would lift her spirits. Being with him connects her to Sorrel.

"One more thing, Cal. Stewardship voted last night to make 'High Hopes for High Dunes—FUCC' the fund raising theme for this year." They both laugh, knowing if anyone can high-hopes the church, the charming Sorrel Dixon can. "Can you meet to discuss details? Tomorrow, Curley's?" Sorrel is not flirting, he's just doing church and this is fine by the reverend, even if they just met last night; her butterflies are confused.

"Fine, tomorrow at eight? Curley's," says Calline, changing her schedule posthaste, nervous to see him again so soon. Gingerly, she places the phone down and strokes the soft tattered shawl, thinking about that new pale blue top cut a little lower than she would usually allow, but it sure looks great with her eyes.

Dalia steps into Calline's tiny office and pulls her torn cap to her chin. It recedes to the level of her brows, dyed orange-red to match her hair two, or was it three, colors ago? "Cal, I'm having lunch with Mother." Calline grabs her left knee when rising to stand. "That leg of yours seems to be bothering you more than usual." Dalia is capable of concern.

"It's always worse when the cold sets in and when I'm . . . oh, never mind." Calline never complains of the pain and insists on the secrecy of why. "Bye, love. Hi to your mom." Feelings of affection for Dalia come to Calline like a sudden breeze. Perhaps she could forgive the quirky woman her shortcomings, because when she focuses on them she feels a kind of inexplicable hopelessness. *Romans 5 is it? Something about how hope is always possible when God's love enters our hearts,* she thinks. She limps to the kitchen to heat some Earl Grey. She thinks probably it would be best to set the timer for another five minutes while she reads on the tea bag, "Like this tea bag, we are made stronger by being in hot water."

CHAPTER THREE

THE LETTER OF her dear deceased friend, Helen Mellbridge, rests on the little table next to Calline's office prayer chair, a musty-odored faded red gingham number she inherited from a friend at seminary. A candle sends a spiral of smoke, almost strong enough to set off the smoke alarm. This letter may send off sirens of its own. Calline stretches to reach for the ringing phone.

"Cal, it's Jack." Jack Riggs is third generation director of the oldest funeral home in High Dunes. "We have the Mellbridge funeral set at your place. Tomorrow. Three." Jack Riggs barks like a five-star General and this persistent tone peeves the minister.

"If you don't give me more time to sort things out enough to justly honor one of the pillars of this congregation, Jack, I'll tell about the time you dropped the ashes bag of Howard Manley on that blustery afternoon by the lake. How his poor blind widow stood and wept as most of Howard's remains landed on her shoulders and hat."

"Not likely, but good try. Three tomorrow, firm." As usual, Jack is unfazed. And Calline won't salute, even if Jack almost always gets his way.

She'll take Helen's letter home to read there. No distractions. Billy should be coming early afternoon. Limping home, cradling Helen's letter under her coat, Calline shakes her keys to single out the one to 476 Oak Place. Bingo's head pops up and disappears at the four-paneled glass-paned front door streaked with dog saliva. The key clicks in the door and the muscular dog pushes her way out, hysterical to greet. Calline raises the envelope to avoid the slobber flying from the dog's flues.

"Whoa, Bingo. Out you go. Here, take this." Bingo settles with her ripped rabbit toy out back. Calline goes straight to the dog's chair, and settles to devour Helen's letter.

Dearest Friend Calline,

You and treasured friends of my beloved High Dunes First United Church have often wondered and asked why I've seemed so, well, so—melancholy. And reticent to tell.

Without further prelude, here it is. When I was fourteen, one of Daddy's field hands raped and impregnated me. Shamed, Mama and Papa sent me off to Aunt Joan's for the term of the pregnancy. I was so lonely and frightened. My aunt said a nice couple was coming to take the baby as soon as she was born. Before the couple arrived, I, with Willomena (my name for her) in satchel, escaped. Days later, dehydrated and starving, we were found in a barn and returned home with a ransom for the finder's silence.

Over time, most accepted Willomena as the youngest child of Mother and Father, Rachael and Edward Livingston, after me the oldest, Ruth, Earl, and Hank Livingston.

When Mother died, I was free to lavish affection on Willomena, who never questioned the intensity of my devotion or the amazing physical likeness between us. Daddy died without a will. The probate of his estate did not include Willomena, since she was not his biological child and he never legally adopted her. Willomena was confused and outraged, but by this time, the secret was embedded like a tattoo. If removed, it could leave indelible scars. But if not, could the damage be worse?

Just as I was going to tell her the truth, I found a note from her. It read, "Don't try to find me." I knew the strength of her resolve and feared the worst: never seeing her again.

For months, I was inconsolable. Harold Mellbridge, home from the war, courted me with Jobian patience. We married and settled here in High Dunes. We had no children, and my one child had vanished. What happened to Willomena was a question that followed me like a dog given one scrap. All I could do was pray and respect that when she wanted to be found, she would be.

So now you have it, Pastor Cal; my failure of nerve to tell the truth when it needed telling. What you do with this is up to you, I trust you. Can God forgive me? Can I let God forgive me?

*Your friend,
Helen Mellbridge*

"God bless you, dear Helen. But what if Willomena comes to the funeral thinking she's your sister?" The familiar squeak of his kickstand and the thud of his bike on the sliding glass door announce Billy's arrival.

"Anybody here?" Billy Dixon enters through the back slider of the old cottage house the church built in the '40s just before war forced rationing. The original oak planks feel worn and soft underfoot. The finely-trimmed moldings and cornices lend a charm that sold Calline. She bribed the Confirmation class to strip, sand, and polish the front door.

"At least pretend to reflect on the John text 'I am the door'," the pastor implored her young flock.

The main floor of her little house is the size of closets in the mansions at Dunes Crossings. Alexis Grimsley lives there and leaves bilious messages on the pastor's answering machine when Calline preaches against America's affliction with "Affluenza."

"Why, Pastor Cal, I came from rags, married Richard, and now I'm rich! Is that your business, Missy?" In spite of her fragile condition, Grimsley still spits fire. In fact, she's the queen source of the most recent mounting unrest.

Billy puts his athletic arms around his pastor's shoulders. As she squeezes his elbow, she thinks how the youth are sweet and open, yet too fast to become hard and serious, like fruit ripening in reverse. "How's it going, kid?" Calline warms to see the young man on whose forehead she had sprinkled water and made the sign of the cross. It was Sorrel's wife who insisted Billy be baptized "again" when he could confirm his faith at discerning age, twelve. The couple waited until their only child was in high school to call it quits.

The divorce was his wife's idea, not Sorrel's, even though neither was happy. After the divorce, Sorrel disappeared from High Dunes for months. He locked himself into a friend's cabin in the forest of the Upper Peninsula, drank and smoked dope, and wrestled with a growing addiction and diminishing reasons to stay alive. Dixon's Construction Company, started by his grandfather, pressured him to take the helm. Always "the good son", Sorrel relented, when what he really wanted was to build boats and sail around the world. Now, like George Bailey of "It's A Wonderful Life", he felt stuck.

Elizabeth had worked at Dixon's as a clerk since she was sixteen. Sorrel noticed her years later, when she brought papers to his desk and leaned over, one breast nearly leaving its cradle three feet from his face. He blushed, she laughed, they flirted, and he asked her for coffee. Events followed naturally from there. After five years of co-habiting, renovating a house together, Sorrel's dutifulness trumped heartfelt desire to marry Elizabeth. The wedding was set for early June. Marathon Key, Florida.

Clad in down vests and wool sweaters, Billy and Calline, familiar like mother and son, sit at the porch table on the brick patio out back. Billy opens his Coke from her refrigerator and rests his feet on the arm of the rusted iron chair. Calline buttons the top button of her down vest to defend against the cold, and blows on the hot Earl Grey. The silence is easy between them. Bingo rests her finely-chiseled head on Billy's knee.

"I'm worried about Mom and Dad." Billy frowns, sad whenever the subject of his parents arises.

"Oh?" says Calline, feeling ashamed of the voyeur in her that craves the scoop on anything Sorrel.

"Yea, Dad is so busy with work and the church. Mom is on the phone with me, like constantly. I wish I had siblings to distract her. Or I wish I have gone to school out of state. Dad is obsessed with his 'marital house', he calls it. Elizabeth this, Elizabeth that. Man, she's another story. I always get this feeling there's nobody home. She's there and yet not there, if you know what I mean. Dad changes to suit her. I wanted to be here, not at Mom's, Cal. You're real; easy to talk to." The boy reaches to squeeze Calline's hand.

Calline squeezes back. "I'm honored you trust me, Billy. Really. I love you, I pray for you all the time." This was no lie, like when she said she was praying for someone when she hadn't. Not yet, anyway.

She studies the furrow in Billy's brow, his pensive look downward as he twirls a thread on his right sleeve. She sees Sorrel in the fleeting angst in the boy's eyes. She wonders who does those motherly chores for him: cooking, cleaning, sewing. *What a privilege*, she thinks, *to have Billy as a son*. Then her thoughts go to Sorrel and Elizabeth. What does Sorrel see in the wispy Elizabeth Cromwell? Why should she care? But she does and this bothers her. A lot. Bingo bolts away to the front, barking someone is here.

"Yoo-hoo, anybody here?" It's Sorrel.

Calline pushes from her chair and leans to brace her knee. "Ouch!" Nervously, she pulls her sleeves over her hands. Heat rises to her face and chest. "Sure, Sorrel, come on back!" She feigns enthusiasm, feeling faint.

Bingo wags her whole bottom half, gently nipping the hand that isn't holding black-eyed Susans. "These were on sale at Tucker Plants. I know you've been busy as heck, and thought you might enjoy these." Sorrel, clad in faded black corduroy and a plaid wool sweater with torn leather elbow patches, drops the bundle on the table. Calline's eyes meet the black, beady flower-eyes peering up. *How did he know these were my favorites? Why flowers, anyway?* "Hi son, 'just stopped to remind you of our foursome with Jim and your pal, Stone. Remember? Tomorrow, around five?" Sorrel walks behind Billy and massages his shoulders, smiling mysteriously at Calline, who blushes. *Why is he here*, she wonders. *Flowers*?

Billy raises his gangling frame abruptly, shuffles awkwardly between the two adults, hops on his bike and pedals off. "Bye, you two. Thanks, Rev., for letting me stay tonight. I'll be at the library."

"I've got chili in the crock pot. See you at around six?" Calline calls to Billy, already out of view.

"I've got to go, too, Cal. Thanks for letting Billy stay." Sorrel comes so close, Calline can smell him, like the ground after a hard rain. When did she start paying such close attention to his proportioned physique and large muscled thighs, his deep gravelly voice, broad knowledge of practical things, and his natural manly protectiveness of her? She's always known this sensible Midwestern boy as a no-frills man, no pretense, authentic. Like a brother. What changed? Why the feelings now? After all, she should inventory his gifts of the Spirit, not his attributes as a man. How could she not feel the natural pulses of her own humanity when the Creator has shown such handiwork in this man?

As Sorrel backs from the driveway, Cal visors her eyes to cut the glare. Does she see what she thinks she sees? He angles his hand so she sees the word written across his palm in heavy marker, the word "WAIT!"

"Later!" he yells, waves, and floors it out of the driveway.

CHAPTER FOUR

A SEARCH COMMITTEE has been working for weeks now to find a replacement for organist and music director, Gertrude Rudders. Calline will meet with them before the funeral for Helen Mellbridge commences. She will barely have time to freshen up, go over notes, and call Patty for last minute input on the Mellbridge daughter dilemma. Will Helen's daughter Willomena—who all these years thought she was her mother's sister—be there? This is the issue that troubles now, while Kathy Yost, music committee chairwoman, Nancy Dobbs, Clerk, and search committee chairman, Smit Rother, take seats around the library table. The pastor takes her usual seat, the large ornate oak chair, assigned to her against her wishes. God forbid should she sit somewhere else.

Without ceremony or sanctity, all-business Chairman Smit begins. "I've read all the resumes, called some references, but Peter's stands out. Way out!" Calline guesses Smit hopes to get beyond the awkwardness of Peter's sexual orientation, known to all on the committee after Calline's call to him to see if he was in the running still. He would be snatched up in a hurry. Smit, Kathy, and Calline snicker at Smit's "way out" comment. Nancy seems under the influence of a paralysis potion; her homophobia might as well be tattooed on her forehead.

Calline and Smit met a few weeks back to discuss Peter's orientation and whether or not they were opening a Pandora's Box. Would this small centrist-to-conservative congregation be ready to take this step? Frank, honest discussion came easily between the two after Smit's son's near-fatal car accident.

"I'm sorry, Smit," insisted the pastor, "but the fact that Peter would even submit his sterling credentials to little ol' us seems a miracle in itself, don't you think? All I can do is imagine what this great talent could add to our music program. I'm clueless what would compel him to pursue a job here, and I'm eager to find out. There's certainly no way we can pay him what he's worth."

"I respect your judgment, Preacher, but couldn't we get by with a little less talent and not have to deal with the gay *thang*, you call it, opening a hole to fall in as big as our beloved lake?" Calline didn't let on that she thought Smit was probably right. Smit just went with his tendency to cower when he knew the Reverend was on a mission, often blindsided by her tendency to do the just thing, if not the prudent thing.

"Maybe it's time, Smit. Maybe it's time to let justice roll down like a river, like Amos preached." In her journal that night, she scratched a reflection about the power of water to destroy, to heal, about its central place of importance in Christian life: "Baptism, the sacrament of dying and rising to new life; will the waters of justice heal us or drown us? I wonder."

At the meeting, Kathy, rarely found without a smile and two thumbs up, is eager to enter the conversation about Peter. "We'd be blessed to have him. Have you all read his CV? Outstanding!" Kathy pulls at her turtleneck to stretch it over her fat belly.

"Could we get him here for an interview? Our goal has been to have someone on the bench by Easter, Gertrude's hope, anyway." Smit Rother's military training keeps him in get-it-done-now gear. Smit looks at his watch, impatient. Then he looks at Nancy, still frozen. "Nancy? We losing you?" Smit taps his long bony fingers on the table.

"I abstain from voting on the Vanderlaan issue." Voice tight, arms akimbo, Nancy's face contorts with that *I must be the only one who reads the real Bible* look. Calline twists in her chair and glances at her watch. Surely Nancy will join the mounting protest against hiring a homosexual. After all, it was her breach of the search

ALL GOD'S CHILDREN

committee's confidentiality pact, and blabbing to Alexis Grimsley, of all people, whose fervor will mount a daunting charge, the likes of which? Just wait and see!

"Calline, you'll get Peter scheduled for the interview and get back to me?" This is a command, not a request. Before Calline can answer, Kathy and Nancy get up to stretch and leave. Helen Mellbridge's memorial starts now.

Calline and Smit walk toward the narthex. "Smit, let's meet again soon. I've got to get to Helen's service now." Before he can respond, Calline greets the four men in black jackets crested with the distinctive Riggs Funeral Service round badges etched with a black phoenix. One carries two huge arrangements of gladiolas, another, the urn containing Helen's ashes. Rachael Connors and Myrtle Dreiden, Helen's two best friends, lovingly arrange mums and yellow daisies at the base of the urn pedestal. In thirty minutes, Gertrude Rudders and choir will commence pre-service music.

Back in her office, Calline prays, "Lord, make haste to help me," and dials Patty for quick advice. Calline's thoughts drift to the day she and Patty met, fall of 1973. The first female associate dean of the school, The Reverend Dr. Joanna Baker, addressed the few women at the seminary. In tones of a woman who had scouted the territory and come back to report, she cautioned, "You women have to draw your own maps and paddle upstream, in white waters dominated by men, men who've occupied spaces you will not only share, but you will re-define, simply by being there." Dr. Baker spoke as a sister who had endured ridicule, insult, and even violence as she followed her inner compass to positions of clerical authority in church and seminary. "If you have any motive less auspicious than that it is God calling you to this work, you might want to reconsider." It was difficult before her younger sisters for Dr. Baker to conceal her exhaustion—bordering on cynicism— from swimming upstream in those white waters, so often stirred by blatant misogyny.

The night after Dr. Baker's warning message, Calline called home to tell her gravely ill mother, "I'm not sure anymore, Mom. Do you think this is the real deal for me?"

Facing imminent death, Joan Simpson abandoned pretense. "You are called. I hear it in the way you tell your stories of meeting Jesus, like Paul did. Remember the day at the lighthouse at Elizabeth Point when you felt you were not alone, and that something was beckoning you to follow? Had you been a Muslim, you might have heard Muhammed, or a Jew, then perhaps Moses or Sarah. But we raised you a Christian. The one who called you—Jesus, he's reliable, honey. Just like all the women and men before you, including Great-Grand, you will be shown the way and given everything you need for the journey." This conversation, one of the last between mother and daughter, speaks itself into the pastor's heart practically daily. Her mother's words are often Calline's only solid hold on anything.

"Come on Patty, answer!" Calline's damp palm irons her white satin stole while she squeezes the receiver between her chin and shoulder.

Before Calline puts the receiver in its cradle, Patty answers. "Hey. I haven't come up with anything yet on the Mellbridge dilemma. But shoot." She's the same Patty Calline met at seminary, same frizzy red hair and round tortoise-shell glasses, freckles, and clipped, quick speech.

"Thank goodness you're there. Helen's daughter might be here today; she could still think she's Helen's sister. Is it possible to betray the dead, Patty? What if I get this all wrong?" Calline drums her head with her pencil, taps her toes, and grips the phone receiver so hard her fingers go white. "Hurry, I've got to go."

"Whoa! Back up! You mean say things, do things to invoke the revenge of the dead? Isn't that a movie?" Patty giggles and exhales. Calline thanks God daily the nicotine habit never stuck with her beyond an occasional social smoke. She's got enough temptations.

ALL GOD'S CHILDREN

"Patty, stop. This is serious, dead serious." Calline muffles a giggle. "I've got to go, Sweetie. Pray, would you?"

"Sure, baby, sure, breathe now, you hear? God knows; you watch. Now go, kick some butt in there." The phone goes dead.

Calline massages the Chantilly silver spoon-handle cross that her great-grandmother wore.

Children who visited Helen at Dunes Meadows Nursing Facility light three candles on each side of the Advent wreath. A queue of people jams up at the guest book at the chapel entrance. Others visit quietly in the aisles beneath the steeply pitched cathedral ceiling of narrow tongue and groove oak, and eight huge support beams. The shadows of six finely-detailed cast-iron light fixtures shimmer to make it look like angels dance in the rafters.

Gertrude signals that the prelude is over; it's time for Calline to greet and lead confessions and prayers. The congregation settles somberly while Kathy Yost sings "On Eagle's Wings" for the ten-thousandth time. Still, Isaiah's words comfort and inspire.

"Lift us up, now, dear Lord, and may your giant pinions hold," Calline whispers.

The congregation is quiet and expectant like sheep settled for the night. The click of the chapel door and the entrance of three tall women who walk just like Helen break the silence. The oldest, is the very visage of Helen Mellbridge. The two younger women must be her daughters. They find their place on the fourth row on the lectern side. After the congregation sings "Abide with Me", Helen's daughter—it must be Willomena—rises. Her red silk dress reveals a tall, lean figure, a handsome woman in her late sixties. "Rev. Simpson, I'm Willomena Brainard. May I?" Willomena gestures to the center of the chancel.

"Please." *What now?* Calline sits, straightens her robe, fondles her cross and waits.

Willomena, silver hair perfectly coiffed and glistening, seems to float to the place where she turns to face the unsuspecting congregation. "I'm Willomena Livingston Brainard, biological daughter of Helen Mellbridge." Rachael Connors, Helen's best friend, cries out and weeps. "I ran away from Helen—my mother— when I was eighteen. For over fifty years, I believed she was my older sister. At deepest levels, I knew differently, but could not step over the years of separation to reconcile. Helen, uh, Mother, told me everything when Uncle Earl found me and called me to her death bed. I lost precious days, months, years, blessing and being blessed by Helen Mellbridge. Thank you for being her family, the family I chose not to be." Willomena's voice trembles.

Willomena reaches into her purse, pressing a check between her palms like a precious item folded into a book. She hands it to Calline. Calline puts the check in her robe pocket, reaches for Willomena's hand, and leads her slowly to her seat. Calline feels lighter than she has in weeks. The very person who should carry and relieve the burden of Helen's long and heavy secret has done so. This could be the last the church will hear of Willomena, but certainly, not of her money. The gift intended to bless, no doubt will bring controversy, like a beautiful pie brought to a room full of hungry children.

While Gertrude plays the postlude, the congregation files by the pastor to greet on the way to the reception in the Hall. Alexis Grimsley approaches Calline, practically shoving Rachael Connors to the floor.

Rachael cries, "Oh holy crow, that woman!" Calline looks over at Rachael and shrugs an apology for the interruption; an ambush is more like it.

The old woman appears even more vicious bent over from sitting for long spells. "The very thought of hiring a homosexual to replace Gertrude at the organ is just abominable! Abomination, Leviticus. Think, pledge, Cal, pledge walking. And the feet of Richard Kellogg Grimsley's pledge are considerable." Alexis— right in the pastor's face—snarls, huffs, and stomps away.

"Excuse me everyone; I'll be right back," Calline kindly addresses the group waiting to greet. Some snicker to see what transpires next. Calline breaks formation, catches up with Grimsley, reaches for the old woman's hand, and leads her to a corner. "The hiring of our next music director and organist is confidential. You've in as much as made an announcement, Alexis." Grimsley seems shorter than the last time the two women faced off. "Could we continue this later? I have people to greet," Calline says, bristling, but not enough to back Grimsley off.

Alexis steps an inch closer, stepping on Calline's toe. "How much would it cost to bring a person with all the credentials you say he has?" How does she even know anything about Peter? Calline suspects Nancy leaked this information. Grimsley's hands tremble; she fists them and bats the air, kicking her foot out toward the chair in the corner. She stumbles forward and barely blocks a fall. They both know money is not the issue. But Calline can't resist taking Willomena's check and waving it in Grimsley's face.

"You are taking this Vanderlaan situation too far in my book," growls the stubborn terrier of a woman. Alexis swivels on her left high heel and stomps a crooked gait to the Hall, mumbling to herself. She may be ornery and mean, but to most, the likes of Alexis Grimsley in action is a hoot. The Reverend Simpson is not so cavalier. She knows the shepherds and the shepherded, like cats, though all, are defenseless against a determined predator. This formidable foe has loosened the floor boards of four pastorates and collapsed one.

If this reverend has anything to do with it, she will see to it that those boards stay firmly intact, and that the sheep are gently led to nourishment. Standing at the coffee urn, Calline hears herself question, *Are we inhumane to expose dear Peter Vanderlaan to a controversy that he didn't cause and no one can control?* The answer, she hopes, is not as bitter as the coffee.

CHAPTER FIVE

ON HER DAYS off, Calline frequents the old hunting lodge, turned convent the Catholic Church named Mercy Center at Sheridon. Calline naps on the big couch in front of the bay window at the main building until her spiritual director, Sister Marie Therese, or M.T., as Calline calls her, wakens her and invites her into her tiny cell the nun calls her hermitage.

Sister M.T. has the gift of endowing ordinary events—everything—with sacred meaning; she can see the universe in a grain of sand like the poet wrote. When all Calline can see is the unfinished and the vexing, the sister's perceptiveness is a gleaming diamond that sends light to expose what should be expunged, and to highlight what should be displayed. Calline's visits with M.T. are her way of giving her soul a check-up. Can the Spirit's subtle movements be identified in the fray of busyness, self doubt, and longing?

The two women take their seats in the tiny hermitage. Still half-asleep, Calline yawns and rubs her eyes. M.T. says, "Sleep is sometimes how God gets a word in edgewise. It's God's best chance to bypass that busy mind of yours while I listen. Together, maybe we can catch the insights tossed from Heaven, hold them together, and see them alongside the Lord's merciful gaze." M.T. waits.

"Problem is, M.T., I can still hear the Baptist preacher hollering 'Sinners in the hands of an angry Gaawwd!' Merciful gaze? I heard all about winnowing forks, sheep to the right, goats to the left, wheat brought in, and chaff cast out. I still hear that preacher." Calline feels discouraged, the volume so high and reverberating.

M.T., soon to celebrate her Jubilee year in the order, folds her hands and twirls her thumbs. Her head tips back, her eyes roll upward. Calline believes the woman will listen forever, or until the Reverend's old tapes wear out, whichever is first. She hopes the tapes.

M.T. bows her head. It looks as though she's nodding off to sleep, but Calline knows better. Once, when she was sure the old woman was sound asleep, Calline leaned over and touched her knee. "Sister? You awake?" M.T. opened one eye and peered up at her. That eye said it all, though Calline was not sure exactly what. "What exactly is your God like today, Calline?" M.T.'s voice is barely audible.

Thinking back to her Sundays trapped in a pew next to her squiggling cousin, looking up at the corpulent preacher peering down from on high, she says, sadly, "With those winnowing fork messages, it felt like God ran a freak show. I figured I was better off being one of the doomed than not one of them at all." When she hears herself say this, she feels bereft; all alone. Then she stops. Waits. Silence. Her attention follows a buzzing fly to the huge view window that frames the Center's elaborate landscape. The rolling lawns turning from emerald green to frosted browns edge a mile of bulkhead lined with clusters of bright fall-colored mums; the horizon separates diamond-sparkled water and cloud-puffed sky. The sixty-acre property was once the private hunting lodge of a U.S. Senator, a devout Catholic, who donated the retreat to the Church. The Sisters of Mercy, a small group of aging nuns, keep the facility solvent and beautiful. *All this real estate, tax-free for the Church and rent-free for the Sisters,* reflects Calline. "What a deal!" With a grin, pointing to the window, she giggles, "Brother. Sister, if this is poverty, bring on chastity!"

From the next room, Sister Roberta calls, "Are you two all right in there?" Calline blows on the last tissue, tears and snot of holy laughter, the deep down kind that momentarily lifts Calline's spirits.

Releasing herself from a bear hug from Sister, Calline feels that old sinking sensation, one that never announces itself. Why now, when she was uplifted minutes ago, feeling the God of M.T.'s understanding salve and soften the calloused layers of her unholy misconceptions and shame? Only when she's with M.T. does she begin to let the volume of the voice of acceptance and mercy sound louder than the one of the hellfire preacher of her youth, the one of self-recrimination.

Calline knows that holding the truth at bay—for all these years—of why she limps has become as painful as facing it and gutting the wound by grieving. She has convinced herself that to begin that process would be to welcome the stranger who never leaves. All her training tells her, just as she says to others, "Only by going into and through can you get to the other side." Fear, plain and simple. Fear. If she would divulge to anyone, it would be to M.T., but so far her explanation has been simply, "war wounds," and M.T. is too polite to push. Once Sister said, "When we keep secrets and pray lies, deep peace circles like a dog who wants to lie down, but wanders off instead." In time, perhaps, M.T.'s divine therapy will heal, but when Calline is ready; just not now.

"Phone call for you, Pastor Simpson," the Mercy Center receptionist calls to Calline. *Who would try to reach me out of town on my day off?*

"It's Elizabeth, she tried to kill herself. Overdose," says Dalia, out of breath.

"Sorrel's Elizabeth? Activate the prayer chain, Dalia, and don't say a word to anyone, O.K.? Promise!" Calline grabs her knee, rubs it, and catches her breath as if some invisible back slapper landed her one. She dials Rachael Connors, the woman with the scoop on everything, everybody. She cares. "Rachael, thank goodness you're home!" Calline sits on the floor and leans against the reception desk, the phone cord stretched to its limit. The receptionist shuffles papers, leaning in for the scoop.

"Take a deep breath, Cal. This is a tough one for you, I know." How much does Rachael know? Calline has never let on to anyone about her attraction to Sorrel, hardly to herself.

"I'd like a little background on Elizabeth before I walk into that hospital room. I don't know anything about her, honestly." Stomach acid rises to Calline's throat. A reflex reaction to anxiety, she rubs her knee.

Rachael confesses, "I've never been sure about the relationship between those two. It's seemed pretty on and off. She's preoccupied with climbing the social ladder, which is maybe why she's with Sorrel. I overheard her at the club with her girlfriends say, 'Sorrel is a catch, the kind of guy you want in your trophy case.' I haven't cared for the woman, truth be told. I don't trust she really cares for Sorrel, so fine a man as he."

Calline wants to burst with indignation that so fine a man, as Rachael says, is wasted on so shallow and empty a woman as Elizabeth. Her thoughts shame her. But she can't stop. *Maybe the ties won't hold if it's nothing more than a relationship of convenience.* Calline hates herself for thinking this. But her thoughts are so often on Sorrel; less and less is her sympathy for his plan to marry this woman who clings to life, by whose bed she will pray in a matter of minutes.

"Her family moved into High Dunes when she was a teen. Her father was a chronic drinker, a bum. Way off the record, Elizabeth's mother confided in me that he repeatedly violated the two girls for years, went loco, and was sent away." Rachael's voice trails off.

Through tears, Calline, says, "I have to give the phone back to the lady at the desk here. It's about a forty minute drive to the hospital. Pray, Rachael. Just pray. And keep this to yourself and the immediate prayer team, if you don't mind." She knows she can trust Rachael not to leak, a rare and prized gift. Calline braces her knee to quell the pain of standing. She hails the receptionist and jog-limps to her red Buick Century.

Although anxious, Calline enjoys the dirt road exit from the Center, the outstretched arms of maples, their jeweled leaves, deep reds and golds, spinning one last time before release. The drive from Mercy Center to the hospital is a blur. Slowing to park in the spot reserved for clergy, she prays, "God, I offer myself to Thee to do with me as you will." Softly humming, "Softly and Tenderly Jesus is Calling", she walks deliberately to the "staff only" door of High Dunes Memorial Hospital and moves swiftly to the elevators.

Turning left off the elevator, Calline spies Sorrel at the water fountain, his blue and gold t-shirt wrinkled, his salt and pepper hair flattened on one side. As soon as he sees her, he forces a smile and ambles over. Uncharacteristically doleful and vulnerable, he leans over and burrows his face into her shoulder, taking one of her hands in his. Seeing Sorrel like this, feeling his body so close, is both scary and good.

"Sorrel, I am so sorry." What can she say? They hold hands; Calline's eyes gaze deeply into his. What's behind them, really, she wonders, where this mysterious woman, Elizabeth is concerned? Does he love her? Really? Right now, if ever, it's none of her business, yet she is his pastor. And her motives are mixed, of course they are, she admits. This confusion, this blurring of lines turns on the acid, rising again. She coughs.

"Want some tea, Cal? Earl Grey, is it? I'd like some coffee. It's god-awful in the cafeteria, but it's been my drug since Elizabeth..." He looks down and sighs. She's never seen him unshaven, but she likes this rough-edge look.

"Sure, Sorrel, whatever you need right now. I'm with you. The Lord is with us all." She squeezes Sorrel's hand, not wanting to release it. He turns to her and they look deeply into each other's eyes. If only she could read his as well as she believes he reads into her. She turns to walk away.

"Come with me, Cal, if you don't mind." Submissive, Calline turns to follow Sorrel into Elizabeth's room. It is a cell in a honeycomb where the queen bee, the head nurse, and her worker bees buzz with incessant, purposeful activity. Each cell is occupied by one gurney with a body shrouded in white. The worker bees constantly adjust lines, wires, and monitors. As often as she's exposed to hospital rooms, Calline still feels sickened. The cell smells like sour milk and sweat. A Coca Cola liquid with tiny flakes of black travels through a tube in Elizabeth's nostril. Sorrel takes Calline's hand and places it on Elizabeth's heart and then places his hand over hers. A line on a TV monitor blips and flattens, blips and flattens.

"This machine doesn't tell us the real truth of Elizabeth's heart, does it?" Calline squeezes Sorrel's hand.

"You know what happened to her?" Sorrel wipes his eyes with the back of his hand. Sorrel's dark green eyes shine in his tears. Calline looks back over her shoulder and reaches to touch his cheek, rough and blushed. An uncomfortable surge of energy comes and she takes a deep breath and gulps—inaudibly, she hopes.

"Let's ask the Healer to help Elizabeth, to bring strength and hope into this. That's all we can do now." Calline notices what seems like currents of energy flowing from above through her. Calline can feel Sorrel's breath two inches from her neck as they lean over Elizabeth and pray. His strong, warm hand curls around Calline's and squeezes lightly. His chest presses into her back. She wonders if he's aware of how close he is. Is his attention to her or his betrothed? Or both? What a ridiculous question, she chides herself.

"Reverend? It's time to change shifts. Reverend?" The nurse lightly touches the back of Calline's hand.

"Where did Sorrel go? How long have I been like this, alone with Elizabeth?" For a precious few minutes, she is free from anything but genuine hope for restoration, for Elizabeth. For the couple soon to be married.

CHAPTER SIX

IT'S AFTER MIDNIGHT. Weary and hung over after the hospital encounter with Sorrel and his fiancee, Calline takes the shortcut through The Town, not the best streets to travel after midnight. Drug dealers and meth labs have claimed many of the abandoned houses, built a century earlier by immigrants from Germany and Holland, folks drawn to a better life and the rich resources of land and water. White flight gave the Town to African Americans who moved in the forties from the South to assemble war munitions.

Waiting at a long red light, Calline thinks of how often she has protested the beliefs that keep separate the residents of The Town and High Dunes, using the descriptive moniker, Apart-Hate. Mostly, she remembers when she first moved to High Dunes, how she yearned for food like it was cooked back home in the South. Folks told her the best in town was at Miss Becky's Eatery.

"How comes you come to The Town and eat?" asked Miss Becky, surprised that a white lady would frequent her restaurant just near the line that divided. To Calline, it was a northern phenomenon that the line between the Town and High Dunes was as demarcated. Blacks and Whites where she came from had lived together—if even in the gross disparities of racism—for centuries.

"The lady who worked for us cooked the best greens and corn bread you ever tasted," Calline said, practically inhaling Miss Becky's collards.

"I feel ya. When I was a chil' and you was a chil', we was eatin' the same food but drinkin' outa different fountains," mumbled Becky while swishing her cornbread through red-eye gravy. "Not any differnt now, if you aks me. I could mix all these 'gredients up, add cement 'n stir, and you'd have the big ol' fat lie of Black-White prej'dice concrete." Miss Becky sounded bitter as her greens.

Calline used her pulpit freely to challenge the stain of America's original sin, as evident as the blood on Pilate's hands. "Are we any different here than in South Africa?"

Not long after her sermon and the strident protests of denial that followed—even threats from unknown sources—the High Dunes Spring Arts Council announced a hundred dollar plate fundraiser. "I see no problem holding a fundraiser with the theme *Gone With The Wind*," the city Arts Committee chair pronounced one night to the only black news reporter in the county. "Of course, The Town folks would be welcome, too." Realizing his slur, the chairman appeared dazed.

"Good, I'll come as the butler and my wife could be Miss Prissy," the reporter from The Town smirked. The camera jiggled and cut to commercial. "The Chicago Tribune" got wind of the reporter's work and hired him as Assistant Senior Editor.

That summer, the County Commission voted six to three to label six miles of shoreline "The White Coast." The three against votes were all people of color. Uproar put the Chamber's campaign on indefinite hold.

A man in a Valiant honks to move her off from the intersection where Calline has daydreamed through two green lights. At the same intersection sits Lou's Package Store, a popular Town teen 24/7 hangout. Calline sees the girl she met at Helen's memorial reception, Vee she thinks was her name. Like a lot of the city kids, Vee had come to scavenge for food for herself and her family. Calline remembers how Vee smelled like a kind of sweet grease, how the beaded strands of woven hair hanging on her forehead and down her back, swung like street sweepers.

"Mind if I ask your age?" Calline asked the girl.

"Thirteen. You?" Greedily, Vee stuffed muffins and grapes into her oversize coat. Calline always looked away, though others looked on with scorn. Once Alexis chided a child for touching the food with her "filthy" hands.

"Fair enough. I was born forty-one years ago. But sometimes I feel like I've been around four times that long." Calline grins.

"Forty-one times four, that's a shitty long time. I means, I feel ya about feeling old and stuff." Vee nodded her head to make her beads click.

Calline liked the kid immediately, and wondered where the girl was headed with her pockets loaded with reception foods. Probably home to feed a pack of siblings and maybe a single mother. But what is Vee doing at Lou's after midnight? Calline watches the girl strut her practiced sassy stroll like an altar call to every adolescent boy.

"Some day off," Calline whispers as she pulls to the curb, thinking she might get Vee in the car, safe. A couple of boys swagger over, clicking and hissing. One carries a boom box the size of a microwave oven. "Whatchooo doin' here? This is the hood, ain't you scared, lady?" The boy snaps his finger and three tall, wiry teenagers appear from nowhere, each jeering to see if the white lady will cower.

Nervous, as she wants to get the hell out of there, Calline points. "Is that girl over there, Vee?"

"Yeah, she hot! Hey, Vee, there's a lady here wants to see you." They laugh and high-five. One takes a long swig from a brown bag. With a mother's anxiety, Calline wants to get the girl in the car, lock the doors, and scram.

Vee saunters over, her white large teeth flashing like strobes around shiny plum lips. "Oh, itshoo, Preacher." She offers one of her who-gives-a-crap laughs and waves as if to say, *Go on, woman, whatchoo think you're doin' in this part of the world. Helping?*

"I don't know, Vee. It's pretty late. I saw you and stopped. Want a ride?" Nervous and exhausted, Calline is now sorry she stopped.

"Hey, Rev. Thanks." Trying to decide if she wants to be little, or grown-up boy bait, Vee pulls out a cigarette from her silver-studded ersatz Gucci and lights one. "Want a smoke?" She examines her nails and looks down at her feet, then drops the cigarette and digs into it with her toe. "I guess you can give me a ride." Once the girl is belted in, Calline floors it.

In a soft, surrendered voice, Vee directs Calline to her house. For most of the ride, she sleeps, her head bobbing like a rear view mirror ornament.

"I think this is your house, Vee." Calline touches her knee.

Vee opens the door. A voice screams loud enough to reach kids playing miles away. "Where the hell you been? Get your fat ass in here!" Vee's mother, Calline assumes.

Calline drives away for home, wondering what Vee's life is like and what her future holds. Somehow, the pastor is going to have a part in it. "I already do," she sighs, turning onto Main, headed straight and quick for 476 Oak Place.

CHAPTER SEVEN

"I'VE GOT TO call Peter Vanderlaan who's our consideration for organist and music director, but the darned phone weighs about a thousand pounds," Calline confesses to Patty. "I promised the search committee I'd do this sooner than later."

"Your fingers did the dialing and you got me instead." Patty laughs. "From what you tell me about Peter, it seems you two might work well as a team. Sounds like he's not as, well you know how musicians can be. Not as . . . ."

"Temperamental?"

"Yes, that," Patty says, "Of course we all know you are as predictable as High Dune's weather." Calline laughs, not because Patty sees her in her defects, but because she sees her and still loves her.

"You know how pastors and musicians cohabit?" Calline giggles, welcoming some comic relief.

"How?" asks Patty, inhaling.

"Like divas under a dimming spotlight. He has a boyfriend. Randy Campbell."

"The gay thang, it's a bear." Patty sighs.

"This is West Michigan, not Berkeley." Calline feels the downdraft of thinking this could be the most divisive issue yet to bring to her small congregation. "Plus, now there's all the hoopla about A.I.D.S. to inflame the homophobes about the 'gay lifestyle' and how God is punishing them. I don't know, I . . ." Calline chews her cuticle. Patty waits for her friend to abandon her doubt. "There are no other applicants who come close to matching his qualifications, and on a good day, I have absolutely no qualms about hiring whom I know would do a great job, and whom I already like, and I don't even know the guy," Calline says with growing conviction.

"Then get off this phone and get on that phone and call the man, while you've got the gumption. Now go." Patty hangs up.

As she dials Peter, Calline knows the next conversation could hurl the church onto the most challenging course in its history, most certainly in hers as pastor.

"Peter, is that you? It's Pastor Calline Simpson, High Dunes, Michigan." Music plays in the background and a dog barks.

"Oh, hi Rev. Simpson. Hold on, let me turn down the music." Peter's easy, spontaneous style is one thing that attracts her to this man. "Honey, could you get on the other line? It's the church in Michigan. If you don't mind, I'm asking Randy to listen in."

"No, of course not." *A little out of the ordinary, but why not,* she thinks.

"Hi Pastor Calline, this is Randy; nice to meet you." His voice smiles, contralto and sweet.

"Peter, the committee voted to have you interview. Would you be open to that? We'd pay all your expenses, of course." Calline twirls her cowlick.

"Gosh, I'd be honored . . . could Randy and I discuss this and I'll get back to you?" They both sound enthused.

"Fine, Peter. I'll look forward to your call. God bless." What can the Pastor say? He's the fish. And everyone's barely in the boat. Calline hangs up and hears the door slam. It's Dalia.

"Cal, I'm back. Brought you some baklava Mom made. Want some?" Dalia hands her a pastry and skips to the phone.

"It's for you. Ever heard of a Bev Tinkers?"

"No. But hand her over. And if Peter Vanderlaan calls, interrupt me." The baklava goes down like a drug.

"Bev, this is Calline Simpson, how might I help you?" She's still got Peter on her mind and an appointment to maybe cut and color her hair like Patty's.

"Thanks for taking my call, Pastor Simpson. I'm calling about Vee Morgan, the ninth grader who says you know her? She put your name as a reference."

"Ms. Tinkers? I'm sorry, I'm lost. What application? To what?"

"I represent the Braves Scholarship. We fund underprivileged children who show promise in music. If we take them, we pay for lessons, camp, even continuing education if they are exceptional. Vee Morgan's orchestra instructor has submitted her name with you as a recommendation. You know Vee, of course?"

"Yes, absolutely, great kid." Calline had met Vee twice, once at the funeral reception and then for the rescue at the liquor store. "She has a real gift on that violin." What possesses her to lie other than this might be the one thing that liberates Vee from early promiscuity, where the signs are so evident. Her self-esteem could benefit. "Bev, really, I have a sense about this kid. I think this is just the thing . . ." Even if Vee flops, no harm in getting at least a start at something that could potentially change her entire life direction. Get her out of the hood. *If prevarication is ever justified, now is the time*, she reasons.

"Great," chirps Bev Tinkers. "I'll count on you, then." Click.

"It's Peter Vanderlaan," yells Dalia.

"Peter, hi, thanks for getting back so soon."

"No problem, Pastor Calline. We'd both like to come to High Dunes so Randy can scout jobs." He says this like a "yes" is a slam dunk. Dribbling, shooting and near-missing is more how Calline sees this whole process, as she pencils in possible dates for their visit. Nothing's going to happen until after Christmas, but something will happen, Calline is sure. She sings, with thinning hope, *"He's coming, he's coming the Light of the world. Dear Jesus, come soon."*

CHAPTER EIGHT

ON RARE OCCASION, Calline lets her well-behaved Bingo accompany her to church. It's cold, dark, and windy out, a haunted-feeling time to walk from Oak Street to church, but Calline does, just to stretch and to let Bingo run. After being cooped up all day, she's wild with Boxer enthusiasm, sprinting and spinning. Bingo emerges from a leafless bush with a flattened, dirty tennis ball. It pooches out her flues, slobbery and bubbly, with leaves stuck like colorful sticky notes. Clownish, she leaps and twirls, begging Calline to take and throw the slimy ball she grips tightly with locked jaws, her posture the downward dog, her tail stub wagging wildly.

"Bingo, you nut, let go!" Calline welcomes the comic relief Bingo readily provides. Then she wonders how the funny dog can be all joy, and the leaves so easy to let go when tonight's Governance agenda could bring anything but joy or surrender to God's will instead of egos way off leash. Calline clears her throat. The acid is bad now; her knee aches to the marrow. Tonight's choices will have enormous repercussions. Will they pursue Peter's candidacy? Will Willomena's check bring more hassle than harmony? Sorrel, of course, will be there. Calline gulps, prays, takes a deep breath.

"Can I take with me boxer joy? Letting go like the leaves?" She whistles to Bingo and snaps her fingers, "Here, girl, come." A cold draft sucks itself into the foyer where Calline meets others removing coats, hats, and scarves. Sorrel, Moderator Thomas Dreiden, and music committee chairwoman Kathy Yost follow the pastor to the library.

After polite greetings and weather talk, folks take their places around the old library table that smells like pencil erasers and wax. Suspended students from the only schoolhouse in High Dunes, over a hundred years ago, carved indelibly their resentments and profanities as if to prove kids were gross then, too. As Clerk Nancy Dobbs and her husband Gunther left for Florida for her mother's funeral, Kathy agrees to take minutes. Sorrel, cute as ever, wears a baseball cap with the church colors, gold and brown, inscribed with "High Hopes." He and Calline catch glances, sending her heart from its cradle. She hopes she and Sorrel can speak briefly of Elizabeth's status. *But just that, dear God. An update, nothing more.*

J.B. Johnson, Treasurer, is his usual erect self. Intensely introverted and bearing a grudge against the pastor, he avoids all contact with her except to issue a pay check, via Dalia. Pastor Calline and other like-minded picketed J.B.'s bank for its redlining lending practices in The Town. Resolute, J.B. argued, "Cal, High Dunes Family Bank has been an anchor of this community for over a century. And what would you and the church do without me? What on earth are you thinking?" In moved the news reporter as J.B., harried, scowled at his pastor.

"J.B., I'm not against your bank, or you," argued Calline, "but refusing to lend to residents of The Town only diminishes property values and insults the pride and respectability of the countless who are responsible. Drug pushers are overrunning the neighborhood like maggots on a carcass. Homeowners would care about safety and what their yards looked like."

Introspective, off somewhere, the proper Swede, J.B., searched for a comeback. "Pastor Cal, I respect you. Sometimes, though, you go too far with this Jesus and Justice thing."

"I know, J.B., the conservatives have trouble with the 'J' word, Justice. The liberals shirk the 'J' word, Jesus. But, to me, 'J walking' means both 'J's' walking hand-in-hand, all the while avoiding oncoming traffic—the traffic of denial, greed, and fear."

The writer from "The High Dunes Journal" moved in closer. "Got that?" Calline said to the reporter, feeling smug. She knew she was right.

"Yep, you'll be quoted in tonight's 'Journal'." The reporter snapped a picture of the pastor and J.B. shaking hands. Even if red-lining is soon abandoned as a banking practice and three hundred renters are now homeowners stuffing the bank's coffers, J.B.'s grudge holds like Bingo on her favorite toy.

"We've got a lot on the agenda tonight. Can we settle? Cal, the honors?" asks Moderator Thomas, stalwart leader, and calming force in the storm-tossed waters currently stressing the balance of the church. Calline knows he's God's pick for these days. For a man so small in stature, Thomas is a giant. Preacher on Laity Sundays, his messages reveal a tender heart for the Lord, the Word, and a strong grasp of the world and its waywardness. A lawyer by trade, he is good at hearing and mediating disparate viewpoints. Thomas Dreiden's patience, wisdom, and restraint are a balm. All that this man embodies is, she thinks, God's way of assuring her that for such a time as this she is not alone.

"Let's sing our Advent tune," says Calline, clearing her throat, setting the beginning note too low for the women, too high for the men. She lights the same seasonal purple candle brought from the corner table in her office.

Thomas opens with, "We may not get to everything tonight..."

"We'd better. No one is stepping up to teach in January. And I'm delivering any day now," Chair of Christian Education, Lilly Smith, interrupts. She pooches way out, as big as Mary might have been, so close to Christmas.

"And we keep shelving the telephone issue," this from Tendal Harris, senior trustee, who wants the church to purchase a high tech phone system from his company, at cost. He and Margaret would pledge the difference.

"O.K. everyone, if we don't let some things slide, we'll be here to greet Lilly's baby. And Mary and Joseph's. We have the matter of the check from Helen's daughter, Willomena. "And..." Thomas stalls and shuffles papers, "... Peter Vanderlaan." Papers flutter, chairs shift, throats clear.

"Why don't we start with the check from Mrs. Brainard?" The easy one first, and a few sighs of relief. "Cal?" Thomas looks at Calline.

"As everyone knows, Helen's daughter, Willomena Brainard, showed up at Helen's, uh, her mother's service with a check right there on the spot. I gave it to Tendal to give to J.B. to put in a C.D. on the Q.T." Laughter relieves the pressure of waiting to see who's going to get his or her agenda met first and foremost.

"We have got to replace that old antiquated hand dial thing," Tendal complains again.

"And our nursery equipment is nasty," Lilly intones, massaging her belly.

"How are we going to pay the new music director, if he or she ever comes?" Kathy waves her papers in J.B.'s direction.

"Hold on now, wait. We've not even gotten to the figures yet. Just hold your horses, now." Thomas waves an imaginary wand; all settle momentarily. He looks at Calline.

The pastor drums the table. "The amount of the check is sixty-thousand dollars."

Kathy claps. Tendal waves his arms, and J.B. jolts upright, stiff as a board, rubs his hands together, and licks his lips. Thomas registers each reaction, poker-faced. Sorrel grins bigger than a crescent moon, thumbs up, then high-fives Thomas.

"Sixty grand, that's a ton of dough," says Thomas, reaching for what to say next. "It's not so much the amount that's at issue here, as how we go about managing and distributing it." Wisdom comes, but doesn't stay.

"Save it for a rainy day," shouts Kathy over Tendal over Lilly.

"Whoa, back up, now," says the level-headed Thomas, laughing. "I suggest we bow our heads and listen for a bit. We can't climb on each other trying to get our agenda to the top, leaving someone crushed holding theirs at the bottom, now can we? There's a better way." Wisdom is back.

Silence fills the room. The candle flickers; shadows dance on the wall. Bingo's front legs bicycle. *Woof-woofs* inflate and deflate her bubbly flues. In her silent dreaming along with the others, Calline reviews the day's events. Alexis Grimsley was in the building today to help Dalia stamp envelopes. Overcome by a strange sensation to check her office—for what, she's not sure—Calline tip-toes from the library. Bingo gets up, shakes herself and follows.

"Be right back," she whispers to Thomas.

Not sure why, she slowly turns the knob on the door to her office, enters, and scans every surface. *Oh, dear God, this can't be.* She leans on her desk for balance. Her journal is gone! She never brings her most private jottings from the anointed cradle next to her reading chair at home, but she wanted some of its entries for Advent and Christmas sermons. Her thoughts flash on the contents of this particular journal, one in a long series of over twenty. The journal's pages, tear-streaked, cuss-marked, reveal the most intimate details of the pastor's life, including, could it be? Including her struggle with her attraction to Sorrel Dixon! Did she mention him by name? She honestly can't remember.

Instantly, her thoughts go to Grimsley. Alexis's self-assigned importance and prerogative give her unusual freedom of access, even when church by-laws forbid. People just look the other way. *She was in the building, I was out most of the day,* realizes Calline. *Who else could it be?* Bingo follows her nose to the foyer, then pushes open the door, aided by the wind that lifts a small crumpled handkerchief onto the top of a potted mum. Bingo snaps at it, but Calline leans to get it, grabbing hard at her knee. Maybe it belongs to the journal thief. She pockets the thing, disgusted, and goes to the library.

Intense discussion carries on about the disposition of the sixty-thousand. Thomas keeps order more like a coachman driving eight runaway horses. Calline gestures to him. "Thomas, I am so sorry for this. I have to go to the hospital to pray with someone and . . ." Vagueness is justified, but *I must be desperate to lie like this.*

"Go, Cal. We'll be fine." Thomas waves his invisible wand and takes his handkerchief from his pocket.

"Let's talk tomorrow. Call me?" Calline and Thomas have worked together enough not to need words to express that the pastor's departure is necessary. But over a missing journal? This is a first. This is a crisis, not in a parishioner's life, but in the pastor's.

"First thing." Thomas hollers, "whoa there now" as Calline scurries into the cold night. A leaf, reflecting a beam from a floodlight, spins and floats from a branch that overhangs the entrance. *That's me: Spinning, falling, going to hit.* She watches the leaf until it lands. Bingo nips Calline's hand as if to assure herself that her person is going to make it. Calline's leg hurts like the dickens, its ache pulling her thoughts back, way back. It's not as bad now as then, but it's pretty awful. Right now, someone is feasting on her most private possession, her no-holds-barred private revelations.

CHAPTER NINE

CALLINE BURROWS INTO the leather chair with a pillow under her feet, and wraps a plaid wool shawl around her shoulders. A flame flickers and dies and rises again. A call to Patty, even if it's almost midnight, implies desperation. "Come on girlfriend, answer! I need you. Now!" Patty answers on the fifth ring.

"O.K. I hear you. You don't have to say a word." Patty breaths in, makes a sucking sound, then exhales.

"Damn, P, get over the cigarettes." Calline's voice is tight and edgy, familiar signs of overload. "Got a minute? I know it's late. But . . ." Calline coughs, a prelude to tears and quiet sobbing. Patty knows Calline seldom cries. No sirens, bells, or whistles are needed to alert that her dearest friend is in crisis.

"Direct ministrations are needed," says Patty with tenderness only she can offer her friend. "And fast. I can be on the ferry at dawn and in High Dunes by one tomorrow if all goes by schedule. I can cancel one class, no problemo. Don't argue with me, you hear?" Patty's insistence feels to Calline like two strong hands fastening ripping seams, preventing her life force from gushing out. Patty would have made a fine minister, she thinks, but it was not to be. Patty took a call right out of seminary as first female associate pastor in a large New England congregation. In the mid-seventies, this fiery woman—all 4' 10" of her—was not going to put up with a senior minister boss twice her size and weight, who daily ordered, "Get my coffee and make it strong and dark, like my women." The final straw was, "But for the independent will of the congregation, you would not be here, girly, except to mind the children. Maybe."

Patty's Irish temperament, inherited from her mother, flared. "But for the fact you are an arrogant, misogynist, son of a bitch, boyo, I would never agree to continue here beyond the end of this month. Consider this my resignation, creep!" Such outbursts did not bode well for the Christian ministry; Patty went for her true heart's passion, teaching at university level. Patty Fritz knew the beast, Church, and could serve as a realistic guide and able confidante for her best friend.

"God, I love you, Fritz. Meet me at Curley's Diner. You remember it's downtown? When does the ferry dock?"

"Noon," says Patty, yawning. "I'll see you at 1:00."

"Thanks, I love you. Did I say that already?" Calline yawns, feeling better, but still terrified, even though her best friend is stepping in to help carry the load. "Thank you, God." She yawns, stretches, and collapses onto her bed, too tired to pull up the covers.

But for Curley's Diner on Main Street—once the center of commerce and social intercourse—few would frequent the original center of High Dunes. Businesses moved to the new mall, but Curley stayed. It was Van Reuters who built buildings to last: the library, hospital, school, and an asylum for the deaf converted to the city's municipal center. Constructed in large gray stones with ornately crafted rich oak interiors, they all bear the name of and memorialize founder Evan Van Reuters.

Calline finds her usual table next to the front window--- the one where she and Sorrel sat--- and scans the menu, nervously tapping the table and checking her watch.

"What can I getcha, miss?" The waitress seems to appear from nowhere. It is quarter after one. Did Patty say one? Calline knows she'll order the usual, corn and potato chowder, fresh garlic bread, and a large Coke. She hopes more than she would like to admit that Patty will walk up to that door right on time, and not a second later. That's how desperate she feels for the anchoring of her best friend.

"I haven't seen you here. You new?" Calline smiles at the waitress, a lean woman whose belly pooches under her pink and lace uniform apron. Calline looks at her watch again. "I could use some hot lemon twist and two pieces of dry rye toast to start, easy on the stomach." From the corner of her eye, she spies Patty. A hard wind forces the diminutive woman to strain to open the door.

"Hey girlfriend. Get me one of those big mugs of hot chocolate with whipped cream. Be right back." Patty hangs her ankle length wool coat on a hook in the entrance and finds her way to the ladies' room. Calline, off in thought, sips her tea. As anxious as she feels, the sight of Patty is always a salve, always a source of hope. "Thank you," she whispers when Patty approaches, red-cheeked, curly hair hat-flattened. She pulls her chair to the diner table, close enough so the two women's knees touch, as if literal physical contact is required to anchor the pastor through this squall.

"You look pale, Cal." Patty reaches for her friend's hands and presses them between hers and blows. "And your hands are freezing."

"My mother always lauded my toughness, but this time I feel like a scrawny wet kitten left in the cold. Things are piling up, Patty. I'm getting too old for this, dear God."

Patty orders two small orders of curly fries and a large Fresca.

"When I get into a fix, I start kicking myself. I need you to remind me I'm not in charge here, that there's a bigger plan, and I just have to trust and ease up on myself." Calline exhales as if she's held her breath since the last time she laid eyes on her best friend.

"O.K. You're not in charge here. There's a bigger plan and you should ease up on yourself." Patty smiles and reaches in her purse for a cigarette.

"My journal disappeared. Last night, when Governance was meeting I got a message—you know how I do—to go to my office.

So, I did. And my journal was gone. Grimsley was in the building that day. She acts like she owns the place. She's deeply suspicious of me on a good day, and downright hostile on all others. Right now she's reading every confession, conquest, and musing, straight from the horse's-ass mouth. My journal takes the crap I'm too ashamed to give, even to God, Patty." Calline cradles her head in her hands. The room spins and she feels she might throw up.

"Bless her Lord, bless her," the waitress, a short red-head, whispers, all ears, as she places a mug in front of Patty.

"This is awful, Cal." Patty turns her head to blow smoke away from the table. Seldom has she seen Calline so not able to take the bull by the horns and wrestle it down. Calline knows her friend well enough to sense Patty's concern.

"It's the not knowing for sure that drives me insane. On top of that stress, we're going ahead with the process of maybe hiring a very out gay man to take Gertrude's place at the organ." Calline hugs her chest and shivers.

"Not like gays have never occupied organ benches, Cal. What's the big deal, really? This is the late eighties," Patty baits.

"Good point. The man is a genius with a both-ends-to-the-middle repertoire to help attract the young people and keep the old timers paying their pledges. He can play five instruments and sings like Pavarotti." For an instant, Calline sounds uplifted and hopeful. "He has a partner, Randy, who will come with him as 'husband'. Their words."

The women both try to repress giggles. "Mr. and Mr. Peter Vanderlaan. Or is it Mr. and Mr. Randy Campbell? Look at us cracking jokes. Who am I to expose these dear men to the likes of some of our good Christian folks?" Cal finger-quotes 'Christian.' "To the downright homophobic, these guys will be toast. Have you ever met an educable homophobe, so Biblically reasoned, with a stance against homosexuality absolute, unalterable? 'Sexual orientation is a choice' they opine, like anyone would choose to be a social pariah."

Patty takes an audible gulp of her hot chocolate and snuffs her cigarette, then offers her usual thoughtful input on things church. "You and I are beneficiaries of the radical witness of justice and inclusion. We, as women, could be ordained and will serve in the church openly and without a whole lot of rebuff. But gays? When, how, where, do they win the struggle? To the closet for those folks!"

"Really Patty, what do you believe is God's way in this matter? If we take the Bible seriously, which we do in the United Church, would we ever go so far to use it as a weapon to deny a freedom, instead of as a liberating word from God who, yes, judges? But who created us all in his/her image?" Calline sips her tea, pensive.

"A theology of love and justice can't rightly condemn a child of God for being who he or she is," Patty intones. "Jesus sure was silent on the topic."

"The shame, the bullying, the abuse drives gay kids every day to drugs, bridges' edges, gunpoint. I'm sorry, Patty, but if we don't speak out, take tangible action to show our solidarity, and to speak our mind, the misguided and murderous will set the agenda." At this moment, something clicks inside her. Calline knows that after hearing her conviction, she will proudly pursue the gifted Peter Vanderlaan for director and organist, if not without fear, at least with right theology, in her opinion.

"Pull up a chair, why don't you? Join us," Patty offers to the waitress who has hovered during the entire conversation. They all laugh, and the kind young woman does just that. "Rachael, is that your name? Don't you think if God could think up the ostrich, the avocado seed, and monkeys, why couldn't homosexuals be flung from the firmament as well?

"Sure, why not," says the innocent Rachael. "God said, after making everything, that it was good. God doesn't make junk, my pastor says." Rachael seems proud of herself for offering such depth to an important subject.

Patty leans over the table and holds Calline's gaze. "Here's your chance, Cal, to confront prejudice and exclusion, right here in High Dunes. I saw you at seminary when you rallied the youth at the New Haven church to sign petitions for nuclear disarmament. You were, you *are* a leader! I believe in you. And I know God does. Isn't it the prophet's job to afflict the comfortable, to comfort the afflicted? Our own William Coffin's words." Patty takes her friend's hands in hers.

"Speak truth to power, all those slogans that have become so deeply ingrained in us both," Calline offers, rubbing her forehead to relax her tensioned brow.

"It wasn't long ago when we women vied for equality among the fraternal order of the ordained. We rocked the foundations. Now you're daring me to rock mine, huh?" Calline exhales.

"Jesus just went for the prize, straight through the inferno. The vision was so compelling you'd think He didn't even feel the heat. It's unfathomable, the intensity of it all. But the prize . . ." Calline looks at the floor, pensive, sounding sad. She turns to face Patty, pressing all four of their hands into her chest. Rachael joins the huddle and bows her head, oblivious to her boss's perturbed stares.

"Pray for Grimsley, huh?" Calline whispers, feeling defeated and powerless.

"And Peter and Randy!" whispers the waitress, looking coy.

"Don't forget yourself, Cal," says Patty. "For the guts to walk that lonesome valley. He did it. He did it afraid. Zip up good in your rhino skin. Keep your heart and belly soft; your mind razor sharp."

Rachael trembles, "Amen, praise Jesus. Oh Lord, help her, please Lord, thank you, Jesus." The waitress gently touches Calline's shoulder.

"You'll keep an eye on this girl for me, won't you?" Patty insists of Rachael.

"I'll lift her up at Reviving Fires this Sunday, you can count on that!"

Patty hands Rachael a five dollar bill. The two old friends walk arm-in-arm to the door. Calline trips at the threshold and nearly falls, holding firm to Patty's hand, as they face the bitter wind that slams the door shut behind.

CHAPTER TEN

SETTLED AT HOME, Bingo begging for treats, Calline reflects about the gracious demonstration of love and loyalty of her friend. She writes in her journal, "Had the three Wise Men been women, Patty Fritz, Sister M.T., and Miss Becky would have visited the manger, and would have brought diapers. M.T.'s spiritual guidance, Miss Becky's warmth, wisdom, and good food, and now Patty's generous gift of an impromptu visit . . . . They (and John 1) remind me that as hard as right now is, nothing will extinguish the Light." Calline sighs and closes her eyes, her soul filled with a first hint of Christmas spirit.

Now might be a good time to open some cards that cascade from the green and red woven basket her mother placed every year on the same table at Christmas. To nestle herself into her overstuffed chair in front of a fire with a hot cup of Java, hugging those cards to her chest—not a bad idea. To savor the memories of old friends and families announcing their Christmas greetings would do her heart good. "Just no trivia, no tragedy, please God." Calline ceremoniously lays the big rectangular basket on the ottoman in front of the chair that Bingo occupies. "Off, girl." Bingo yawns, stretches, and spills her lazy body onto the floor.

Christmas cards always bring some surprise; certainly these will, too. She sniffs each of the four envelopes that have no return address. One smells like hairspray, one like magazines, one like candle wax. The fourth smells like gardenia. The nose has the best memory of all. Calline sits up straight. "I know that smell! It smells like Grimsley! Bingo, here, girl. Let's see if you can remember how to play detective sniff." Bingo sits up and yawns, then plops down again. Calline takes the four envelopes and lays them on the edge of the carpet, about four feet from the chair. She goes to the closet and reaches into the pocket of the coat she was wearing the night her journal disappeared. She returns with a box of stale saltine crackers, Bingo's favorites, and the kerchief. The dog sits erect, eyes intent on the box, saliva dripping from her jowls. "O.K., Bingo. Sniff this." She puts the handkerchief to the dog's nose, walks to the envelopes, snaps and points. Bingo goes straight to the cracker box and whines. "No envelope, no cracker. Go get, Bingo!" Snap, snap. She waves the hanky. "Go get, Bingo. You can do this, girl." Bingo sniffs the envelopes and stops at the one that matches the scent of the tiny wadded up cloth. She nuzzles it and pushes it toward Calline, then stops and stares at the cracker box. "O.K., Bingo. Good girl." Calline gives the dog a cracker and takes the envelope. "Smells like the kerchief to me. You too, huh, girl? Let's open it." Calline feels dread as she rips the edge of the envelope and pulls the contents from within.

 The card, square and simple, red and green on white, reads: *"I will publish the contents of your journal to the congregation if you hire Peter Vanderlaan."* The note is typed and unsigned. Calline is sure the faint scent of gardenia is the olfactory signature of Alexis Grimsley. Calline coughs, heaves the card to the floor, and rises from her chair. Although she overdid it at Curley's, Calline's first thought of comfort and ease is food. Add the soothing features of the one who fixes it and serves it with love, Miss Becky's Diner is the place. She spits on the fire, and says without emotion, "Off to Becky's, Bingo. Let's get out of here. I need to see Becky."

 She drives recklessly around corners to get there, Bingo panting and lurching in the back seat. Parked in two spots, she gets out, slams the door, and marches into the little corner restaurant at Whipple and Corning. Becky stands intently at the stove and stirs something that smells sweet and bitter; she looks up, her eyes always knowing.

"Got any greens left from lunch, Miss Becky?" Bingo finds the one place Becky lets her be, and she'd better stay or else.

"L'od it's you. You don' be by, this time o' day, less the Devil's on you. From the way you walks in, looks like he be." This woman is like a blind person who sees everything. She reads the lines on a person's face like Braille and knows just what's gotten into them. She shines like she's been plugged into a socket that gets its juice from Heaven. And Calline is certain the woman cooks the best turnip greens on earth.

"You have no idea." The pastor's darkness pales next to Miss Becky's brightness. The short, stout woman stops stirring and crosses her arms over her chest. No one wants to mess with her mad. Her olive and sometimes-brown eyes are soulful and deep. *What can she see?* Calline wonders. Becky channels.

"Well, you ain't gonna whoop the Devil drinkin' buttermilk and eatin' co'nbread, and bein' no crybaby. You gonna whoop him by prayer, the Devil-beatin' kin' of prayer. Hell, yo' the reverent; don' you know?" Becky rolls her eyes, as if disgusted at the pastor's wasting of good anointed prayer, like the powerful ones of her great-great-great grandmothers and fathers, the ones passed on to her. How they drummed and called to Jesus in feverish pitch, praying he would soon come to split the skies and bring them to glory land, free from the master's whips and chains.

Becky dries her hands on the stained cotton apron. Calline chews, feeling little. "Could the Devil have a name like Grimsley?" Calline runs a slice of cornbread through gravy, tilts her head back, and stuffs the morsel in her mouth, waiting for Miss Becky to let go.

"That lady you say stol' yo book? Why, hell yea. The Devil does his prancin' and masqueradin' anywhere someone'll let him in. He like that snake in Eden. He slips 'n slides like that ol' biddy. Right up yo' ass!" Becky guffaws, so hard the flour on her rolling board flies up and lands on Calline's sleeve.

"Actually, Becky, she's, oh well, she's right ON my ass!" Calline looks down, not sure what to do with such a strong metaphor.

"There's one thing, Reverent, you can do. Only one." Becky sips from a long wooden spoon.

"What? I've got the waitress at Curley's praying at Revival Fires. That's a lot of power there."

"Zactly! When I get Bro' Tom and Sistah Sheila goin' at Greater Harvest, watch out, ol' Devil. Now back to you, Miss Priss." She drills holes into her subject with piercing dark eyes.

Calline isn't sure she's ready for Becky's seeing now. She knows it's coming, and when it comes, it comes hard.

Miss Becky stabs the pastor with what she knows: "They be some ol' Devil on you, you know. I practic'ly smell him. He's been eatin' on you fo' a long long time. He be the worse kin'. He suck you dry like a tick on a coon dog. He suckin' on you now, if you aks me. He in that limp of yourn." Miss Becky knows she's cut into some hard flesh that protects the pastor, but robs her of the truth she needs to heal and be set free. Becky touches Calline's cheek, leaving a stripe of flour. "Yo' gots to forgive yo'sef, cuz you know HE do."

The searing truth, like a surgeon's cut into flesh, cuts into her. Tears stream from Calline's eyes and pool where Becky's palm touches her cheek. Both are silent for what seems to Calline like God's time. No time. She cries and sniffs and cries and sniffs some more. Becky hands her a clean old rag. "Here, take this, blow and cry. Bleed all that Devil-makin' goo out. Now go on outa here and don't be long comin' back. You hear?" Calline leans her head into Becky's shoulder and holds it there for a long second, then slowly limps to her car to ease on home.

CHAPTER ELEVEN

DURING THE DINNER hour, the office is quiet, no popping, spinning, or flushing from Dalia. The phones are silent, and no one wants a piece of her. The words for Sunday's message manifest in and out of Calline's consciousness, as the flame of the melting purple candle dances in the corner. Feeling burnt down as well with too much worry, on top of the added duties of Christmas, she raises a prayer for a helpful message to offer the congregation. Who isn't stunned by life and living? Isn't it the human condition to be overcome with grief, worry, and desire . . . and to still muster the courage to reach for something, anything to soften the blow? "We must," the preacher writes, "look in the direction of something enduring and real, a truth that can't be bought, possessed, displayed like a badge of self-serving honor. We must look to the place we would think of last, or perhaps never in this lifetime. We must look within, the place where the baby is born and grows us up."

"O.K., that's a start," she says to no one, when the door hinge squeaks, announcing a visitor. She thought she'd locked the front door.

"Rev. Cal, you in there?" Oh, for a moment to not be interrupted. Thus spake the inn keepers the night the couple looked for a place to bear the child. Of course there was room; there just was no time, no interest, no space that could be shared. The child of the Universe can be born in a pile of dung and piss-filled straw. And here, at her very door, stands a beggar. It's Vee.

"Vee, dear, come in." Calline rises to greet her, concerned by the girl's appearance. Vee looks like she has not slept or changed clothes in days. Her hair flies loosely over her shoulders, an indignity to someone who takes such pride in braids and beads. The top buttons of her blouse have popped off and her breasts bulge from a bra long outgrown. A faint yellow film covers her top teeth. Even her odor is stronger than usual, a thick greasy smell mixed with underarm odor. "Rev, I gotta talk to somebody." Her usual tough veneer threatens to crack.

Calline rises from her desk chair to direct the girl to the chair her guests, as she calls them, always take. A pop cools on the window sill. Vee grabs the root beer, pops the lid, and hauls ravenously on the opening. It's after six, dark, and snowing out. *Why isn't Vee home with her family having dinner about now?*

"Vee, are you O.K.? What's going on?" Calline sits knee-to-knee with the girl.

She looks worn out, unusually sad. "Well, I got the Braves thing, the scholarship!" Vee pulls a folded, wrinkled paper from her rear pocket and hands it to Calline, who remembers her conversation with Bev Tinkers. In brown calligraphy, it says, "Awarded to Vee Morgan, The Braves Foundation Scholarship for Music." The certificate is embossed by a gold seal in the upper right hand corner and signed by a woman whose family money makes music enrichment possible for hundreds of youth like Vee.

"That's fantastic, Vee. Summer music camp, a violin you can buy, not just rent, and private lessons if you need." Calline's mind races to imagine all the ways this could be Vee's ticket from her oppressive world of horny boys, crazy relatives, and zero expectations. For a fleeting moment, Calline sees the girl unshackled, her chin to instrument, bow flying, in a renowned symphony hall performing the music of masters, joy in her face. Free.

"I'm going to have a baby." Vee looks at Calline sheepishly, wondering if this white lady will understand. Does Vee expect Calline to burst at the seams with joy? She's thirteen, for God's sake. Calline's face reddens, her skin goes hot; she doesn't know if she's saying it or thinking it.

I'd almost rather have my journal stolen by Alexis Grimsley. I'd rather have the church divide over hiring Peter Vanderlaan. Vee wants me to be thrilled? She's going to bring a child into this stupid world unprepared, under resourced, and unaware of the burden and responsibility of child rearing. And she has no clue what she will sacrifice to do this: the chance to be a child herself, the scholarship . . . . Dear God! What now?

"Why Vee, why?" Calline says, watching the girl look down, more forlorn than when she arrived.

"I'll have a party and get presents? I'll get a check," she says, having learned a baby is a necessity for security. Vee stares, seeming disappointed that the pastor isn't popping champagne over this. The truth the girl can't name is the drive just to be loved, to be held in the esteem of her peers who crave something, anyone, adoring them, depending upon them. Neediness: this is what silences the sirens that warn she's steering her life and the life of an innocent into a ditch that may be too deep to ever climb out.

"I could help you end the pregnancy." It's already out when Calline realizes what a horrid thing to say. A fetus's heart is beating. In Vee's culture, it's normal to bear a child at her age. Her mother did and her mother. Vee looks like a six-year old just told there isn't a Santa Claus.

"Well, I thought you'd like to know. I want you to dunk her." Vee grins again, hand over mouth.

"It's called baptism, and how do you know it's a girl, Vee?" To continue the conversation like it's all really happening—which it is—indulges the truth of the matter; Calline hates this.

"We did the ring thing. You know, if it goes right and left, it's a girl, and if it goes up and down, it's a boy. It went right and left. Her name will be Shantira." Vee puts her hands on her belly and belches and laughs. Her breath smells like a mix of cigarettes and wine cooler.

"Welp, better be going. Thanks, Rev. I wanted you to be one of the first to know. I like you. And, hey, thanks for helping me get the Braves thing. It'll be hard to find time to play with the baby and all, but I won't be showing that much to go to camp in June." She's serious. Then it occurs to Calline that God's child interrupts to turn the whole world upside down, so who is she to complain about this inconvenient piece of news?

"Want a ride home, Vee? I have my car today." Calline reaches for the girl's hand and squeezes it gently.

"Sure." She bounces to her feet, hands on belly, and tosses the can into the wastebasket. "Two points."

Vee is poorly clad for this weather, but doesn't seem fazed. Calline raises her coat collar and stomps her feet to get warm. They rub their hands and blow fog while the engine sputters to warm. The car slips and slides out of the parking lot. Vee sits quietly, not saying a word, as if being driven home by this lady of the church is as natural an occurrence as getting pregnant at thirteen.

They pass a house with a crèche in its front yard. A hand reaches up from the tiny cradle. In light of these latest events, Calline thinks of her sermon. Yes, she thinks as she ponders what Vee is going to do with a baby, *what on earth is God's Baby going to do with us?*

"We're waiting, we're waiting, for Jesus is coming, He's coming, the Light of the world. Dear Jesus, come soon," sings Calline under her breath.

"I like that, can you sing it again?" Vee draws a heart on the window, fogged with ice. Meanwhile, Calline's thoughts go to Sorrel. She goes right by the rehab hospital where Elizabeth heals, her future, their future, on hold. Perhaps she'll drop in to say hello. Sorrel might be there. That old heart tug is back, and she welcomes it because it's warm and makes her feel alive.

CHAPTER TWELVE

THE SNOW FALLS in huge clumps, powdering the evergreens that line the porte cochere of Tall Grasses Rehab Center. A middle-aged man in uniform stands at the entrance smoking a cigarette. Calline parks undercover by the curb; he nods and waves her over. It's after visiting hours and it's quiet. Elizabeth may be sleeping already.

"Evenin' ma'am," says R. B. Jamison, R.N., the name on his badge.

"Evening, R.B., mind showing me to Ms. Cromwell's room?" Calline feels ashamed this is her first time to see Elizabeth after her transfer from the hospital.

"Surely, miss. You family? Cuz visiting hours ended an hour ago." He just states the facts while taking a last haul on his cigarette.

"I know it's after hours, but I'm her pastor. Could you take me to her, R.B.?" Calline looks at him with kind, tired eyes.

"Why, sure Reverend, I saw her in the snack room just a second ago. Follow me." He tosses his butt into the hedges and pushes through the giant doors, holding one for Calline. Sorrel might be there and she wonders if she's up for intensified emotions beyond what seeing Elizabeth might bring.

"If you'll go straight down that hallway, the first opening on your right is the snack area. You should see her there. If not, her room is just beyond that door, on the right, number sixty-two. Good luck." He turns and walks away, humming and snapping his fingers.

"Thanks," Calline says, heading to meet with the woman who has done little but evade contact with anyone associated with the church, and with the world, for that matter.

"Elizabeth?" An emaciated figure sits in a Queen Anne chair that swamps her. Her feet rest on a coffee table. Her thinning hair is longer than when Calline last saw her. Streaked blonde, it streams over her shoulders, almost to where once-full breasts were. She wears a bright pink fleece bathrobe and slippers to match.

Calline conceals shock at how thin and colorless Elizabeth looks. Her eyes look as if they would pop out were she were given a light back pat. If eyes are the window of the soul, then these are the eyes of a child who wondered off from home years ago and is still missing. Not sure how in-touch she is, Calline whispers, "Elizabeth, it's Calline Simpson from church." The woman looks delirious and stunned. She looks down and squeezes a tissue in her hand. Her other hand sweeps back across her head and remains there. She begins to rock as if to sooth herself.

"Yes, Cal, I know you. It's just that I . . . I . . ." It sounds like she's holding back a torrent of emotion. "Please, do pull up a chair. It's been awhile." She looks up at Calline with big brown eyes that look detached from their sockets, swimming in a pool of water. She dabs her eyes with the tissue and twists it again in her lap with both hands. Her fingers seem unusually long, narrow, wrinkled, and very pale. Her hands tremble.

Calline pulls a chair close enough so that if the two women wanted to touch hands, they could. Seeing her like this brings the pastor's heart to her throat. She knows that before her sits a victim of the most heinous crime. How could a father repeatedly molest his own children? Calline's chest tightens with indignation.

"You seem hot. It is a bit warm in here." Elizabeth reaches to touch Calline's knees.

"You're consoling me and I came to bring comfort to you, Elizabeth. Are you up for talking a bit? Or just a prayer? I won't stay long." Calline suddenly feels tired and worn, unable to erase the ordeal of Elizabeth's life from her thoughts; really, it's the thought she could be—rather, is—Elizabeth's betrayer too.

"Thank you for your kindness, Reverend Cal. Today has been a good day. I don't know if I will get out of here and return to a normal life, whatever normal is. A dial on the washer, I suppose." Elizabeth's sense of humor surprises Calline. The frail woman in front of her is a mystery, a woman alienated from herself, who enchants like a fairy in a mystical wood, but who cannot offer any real substance. Calline listens. "What *does* make life make sense? Whatever it is I've done up til now, it hasn't worked. I need to throw out those so-called living—or is it just existing—instructions and find new ones. That's what I'm focused on right now. I can't handle more than that. I feel ashamed of so many things in my life. Now, the burden on my heart is dear sweet Sorrel. You know how he is."

Discomfort rises as heat around the pastor's neckline. Elizabeth, fragile as a newborn, confiding her affection for the man who takes up spaces deep in her own heart, can't be happening. Calline can't help but wonder how devoted Elizabeth could ever be to any one person, or family, when her illness is so raw and apparent. Pools of tears gather in Elizabeth's eyes, then let go like an opened faucet. Is she crying for herself or for Sorrel? Both, perhaps?

"Do you want to live?" A daring question of someone Calline hardly knows.

"I'm not sure. I'm so overwhelmed by the past and the harm done, I lose my focus, my desire. I just want the pain to stop without recourse of, well, you know." They both know she means pills. She looks down at her cuticles, red from gnawing, and brings them to her mouth to chew. Calline gets a box of tissue while Elizabeth sobs into her bathrobe sleeve. Her pain is a river. The levies of her grief must break or she will, and Calline suspects Elizabeth doesn't have many breaks left.

"I'll just hand you tissues, Elizabeth. Don't worry about me. Do what you need. Let it rip." Elizabeth sobs, taking tissue and blowing, sobbing, taking tissue and blowing. Her agony is so loud, the nurse comes to ask if they are alright.

"We're fine Mr. Jamison, just fine. Thank you. I'll let you know if we need anything." Calline is aggravated when nurses intrude with "there-theres" to settle their discomfort with feelings, the very steam that needs release lest the pot explode. While Elizabeth weeps, Calline thinks of Jesus digging his hands into the mud, spitting into the dirt and rubbing it into the eyes of the blind beggar. *Isn't this one way God scoops the gunk from our souls?* she thinks.

Elizabeth sighs deeply and blows her nose. For now, she seems to have finished. "Maybe this is our prayer, Cal. Do you think?" She laughs, like something happened as a surprising, wonderful gift.

"Inhaling and exhaling deeply feels good. Have I been holding my breath all this time?" Her skin has reclaimed its pink and even shines a bit. Her eyes seem to have moved back into her head, appearing more peaceful, less terrified and lost. She looks girl-like.

"You said you wanted to discover a new way to live. Maybe just breathing is a good place to begin." They laugh while Calline gets up to leave. They embrace and hold, Calline worrying she could crush Elizabeth, all skin and bones. Elizabeth wants to cling. Calline blesses her with her hand on the patient's head, a benediction of God's blessing her and keeping her.

Elizabeth follows Calline into the hallway and turns right, while Calline turns left to go to her car. A car's headlights brighten the snow beyond the porte cochere, then go dark. A car door slams and a familiar figure enters the foyer. It's Sorrel. Calline feels her throat tighten. She plasters a fake smile on a face that has just mirrored so much pain.

"Cal, great of you to come by. I'm on my way to the Pub for some pop and pool, to relax. Thought I'd check on the wife first." Sorrel seems distracted, fidgety. If she were in her right mind, she'd press his precious hand between her two palms, give a pastoral blessing, and get the hell out of there.

Instead, she says, "May I join you?"

"Great idea. Go ahead and I'll meet you there. I won't be long." Sorrel turns to walk away and waves back over his head. Her gaze back at him lingers.

Oh Lord, here I go again. Acting before thinking, Calline chides while her car warms. On the way to the Pub she hears, *Your best thinking isn't even close to intelligent or wise. It could be a disaster to be seen at the Pub with Sorrel whose fiancée is so ill.* At the Pub, full of community college kids and cigarette smoke, she finds a phone and calls back to the Rehab Center. Nurse Jamison catches Sorrel just leaving.

"Sorrel, look, I realize that I am bone-tired, it's late, and I would rather bring a fresher self to our visit. Rain check?" Calline twirls her cowlick.

"Not to worry. I wanted to thank you for seeing Elizabeth. I don't know what you said or did, but she looked fresher than I've seen her in a long time. I don't know, Cal. I was hoping to see you tonight. I need to talk. I'm confused about Elizabeth, who she really is; who I am in this relationship. I feel I'm doing the right thing by standing by her; I love her. But she gives me a look with eyes that seem not to see any real part of me. I've been busy as hell, trying to get time with Billy when he's home, and working on the house. I remembered I was the highest bidder at the mission fair for the Cunard Line Bermuda trip out of New York, New Years' week. Elizabeth said if she felt up to it, she'd go with me and Billy. Oh God, here I go, on and on." Sorrel sighs. "Later, I hope. I mean, if you have time and all." He hangs up.

It won't be she who lets on that she accepted an irresistible deal from the same travel agent who donated to the mission fair: a week at the Resort at Church Bay, Bermuda. New Year's week.

CHAPTER THIRTEEN

BEFORE HER GOODNIGHT prayers, Calline scolds herself for even the thought of meeting up with Sorrel at the Pub. "Thank God I made it home safely to bed. Alone," she says to Bingo, who begs with her scratch-me-now whine. In a minute both are sound asleep.

"I'm coming," she calls to Bingo scratching at the door to go out. The coffee maker beeps and another headache tightens around her brow. Stress? Never mind, it's time to dig out from under a heavy down comforter and stand at the glass door in long johns, fleece vest, and wool slippers while Bingo nips at the cold white powder, then tears for the door to get warm. The snow that obscured her vision coming home last night has spread a glistening white blanket over everything that doesn't move. Its beauty and freshness brings Calline's thoughts to the youth church lock-in. The kids were asked to list their crimson sins. Reading from Isaiah, the Lord promises to make those crimson sins white as snow. What began as an insufferable downer for the youth ended in a snowball fight, a few bloody noses and bruises. The parents unable to associate church with raucous hilarity and fun withdrew their kids, and those who stayed became fast fans of the reverend and youth lock-ins.

Bingo's scratches at the door bring her thoughts to Sister M.T.'s invitation: imagine Jesus standing out there with Bingo, looking in. There is no door handle on his side, only on hers; Jesus politely waits for when, without suspicion or condition, she will say, "Yes, come in, sit for a while." Now would be a good time to say, "Come in," she reasons, feeling a surprising warmth enter her body. "Now, Lord, visit and prevail in this day, whatever it brings," she prays.

When did the message on her phone come in? It's from the moderator, Thomas Dreiden. "Cal, I've called a special meeting of Governance. I got something in the mail yesterday. Alexis Grimsley's up to no good." Thomas, rarely ruffled, sounds worried. "I've asked folks to come to my house. We can be private here. Myrtle has volunteered to put out finger foods and drinks. Sorry for the short notice, but we may be too soon on the defensive if we don't act quickly. Noon today. We have a quorum."

Oh great. She was hoping to have the day for finishing touches on her sermon. Anxious and unsure of what will come of this, she dresses slowly in casual corduroys and a pink angora Christmas cardigan Patty gave her. The sweater is tighter than last year. Irritating. More irritating is the thought of Alexis Grimsley on a rampage.

Thomas lives only a few blocks away. *How exhilarating to step into the freeze, even if on a cold march into Grimsley's latest trap,* she imagines. Calline assures Bingo she won't be long—a lie—locks the door, and watches the poor dog's head appear and disappear at the pane window. Bingo's mournful calls follow her along the plowed walkways by which houses glisten with lights still burning from the night before. Dogs bounce hilariously on the backs of sofas at the windows, such fierce protectors of their territories. Calline dreads seeing the two Griffons who own Thomas and Myrtle. On a recent visit, one took her left ankle in his mouth while the other sat up on his haunches and yapped. Freedom from their grip came only when their caretakers stopped admiring how cute this all was.

She crosses over Sheridan and Westbrook and slips up the slope to the big ranch house at the highest elevation in the Glensdale subdivision. The house is a lovely stained split level that once sheltered the eight Dreiden children, their parents, and their parents. Church folks park wherever they can, by embankments plowed high by plow trucks that have worked since before dawn. Frozen walls of shoveled snow edge the path to the Dreiden's front door. A giant wreath, replete with small gourds, red berries, and sprays of dark eucalyptus decorate the heavy oak French door. Calline feels too frozen inside and out to pray much more than an idle "help." Yet she feels the most unusual sensation, one of a warm covering around her shoulders. She thinks she hears, "*You are under my protection.*"

"Cal, come over here." It's Sorrel who slams his car door and bounds across one of the snow-packed ledges to catch up to her. He reaches his hand for hers and their eyes meet. He wraps his big arms around her shoulder and draws her to him. Is Sorrel Dixon the warm covering? Calline glances at the others to see if they detect the electricity she feels from his brazen and forward show of attention.

Back from Florida, Missions Committee chairman, Gunther Dobbs and wife Nancy—ready to abdicate her position as Clerk over the music director issue—kick off their boots in the foyer. Coming from a family funeral, Nancy looks wan. Gunther is youthful for his age. Tall, slim and fast-moving, he rubs his whiskers and crams his wool cap into his back pocket. "Hi, Rev.. You ready for this?" Gunther boxes his hands in the air, ready for a fight.

"Hi Gunther," Calline says warmly. "I'm not sure exactly what we're meeting about. I have a hunch, though. Let's hope for the best!" Calline wonders how he and Nancy, married almost fifty years, settle their differences, of late, about possibly calling a gay married man.

J.B. Johnson arrives gripping a brown bag, no doubt full of fresh-baked goods from his wife's gourmet kitchen. He pushes to get into the house, ignoring Calline. Turned inward and private, he ignores everyone. Although she's been ordered to bed rest, Lilly Smith for Christian Education can't not be in the middle of things. After greeting and handling boots and overshoes, everyone files into the house.

Myrtle hollers at the two dogs, "Back off, boys; to your rooms, now!" The dogs slink away, confused by the onslaught of ankles entering their domain.

"Welcome, all. Let me take your coats. Hello J.B., Sorrel, Cal. Hope things went O.K. in Florida, Gunther and Nance." Thomas warmly touches Nancy's shoulder and offers to take her coat first. She touches his hand and smiles at him, looking frail but happy to see her old friend from college. Gossip has it the two had a serious fling in college and almost married. "We have a few stragglers: Tendal, for Trustees and Kathy for Music. Let's go ahead and have refreshments and devotions." The natural and gentle take charge of Thomas wins people's confidence and reminds the pastor again how relieved she is for his leadership.

"Dad wanted me to be a pastor," he confided once to Calline, "but I wanted lots of kids. You know how they like to eat and buy stuff."

After everyone settles, Thomas lights the family Advent candle, the rose-colored one, for Joy. It burns with the other two purple ones, in a circle of evergreen and berries with one more unlit purple. The large white candle at the center will burn Christmas morning. A stone fireplace big enough to heat a mansion lobby dwarfs a stack of logs that smoke intensely.

But for the lack of a blaze in the fireplace, Myrtle Dreiden's living room would rival any House Beautiful holiday scene. Rubbing her shoulders, Calline rises from her seat and gestures to the others to stand and sing: "It only takes a spark to get a fire going . . . that's how it is with God's love once you've experienced it . . ." As they enter the last verse of the familiar camp song, the smallest log perched at the very top of the pyre ignites into flames. Soon, a blazing fire vacuums out the cold. People clap as if the burning bush itself has ignited in the desert.

Thomas prays strong petitions for help with the task at hand, and then moves quickly to stop a burning log from tumbling from its cradle onto the carpet. Removing an empty pipe from his mouth, he clears his throat, nervously straightens his vest, and glances at his watch, as if to suggest this whole ordeal can't be over fast enough. Everyone is quiet, as if mystery has robbed them of any word that could say it right. Myrtle goes to the door to welcome Tendal and Kathy, who quickly find their seats.

CHAPTER FOURTEEN

"I'D LIKE TO watch the game tonight, and I'm sure you all have lives beyond church," says Thomas, his voice blank and inscrutable. He removes papers from a faded calf leather briefcase and passes them around.

"This is a letter I received yesterday from a very disgruntled bunch of folks. The Petition, signed by, well, you can see for yourself." Thomas grows quiet and waits while all eyes rivet. Eyes are popping, except for J.B.'s. He looks down, an expression that might emulate Judas' that night in the Upper Room, before he ran off to rat on Jesus.

Twenty-nine signatures, one-third of the lettered members, line up under a paragraph that reads, *"The below signed members of High Dunes First United Congregational Church, on the grounds that the Bible is God's holy and infallible Word, and referencing the texts Genesis 19:1-29; Judges 19:1-30, Leviticus 18:1-30; 20:1-27; 1 Corinthians 6:9-17; 1 Timothy 1:3-13; Jude 1-25, and Romans 1, will not endorse or support the hiring of any staff person of a deviant sexual preference. Based on obedience to God's Word, and principles of Godly stewardship of the morals of the next generation, if such an action is taken, the herein signed will withdraw membership, effective immediately. God does not lie (Titus 1.2)."*

Not a surprise to anyone, Alexis Grimsley's signature takes top and center, followed by her husband Richard's. All are quiet, calm after a sudden, unexpected invasion, but then everyone blurts out at once. Thomas interrupts, "Everyone quiet now, you'll get your turn. Could we go around the room starting with you, Sorrel? This obviously is a charged issue for all of us. We need to take turns speaking and hearing each one out. We can do this. Do we need another prayer?" Heads nod. "Let's hold hands," Thomas says after a pause. "We need help, Lord. We need help knowing what to say, how to respond. Thank you. Amen." Everyone seems anointed by calm, for the moment.

Sorrel, now in the spotlight, examines his nails and looks sad. "Well, guys, so much for High Hopes for High Dunes." Kathy, always giddy, laughs, then blushes. "That's okay, Kath. A little levity never hurts. As stewardship chair, naturally I see the dollar signs. Everyone on this list, if you total their pledges from last year, supports at least eighty-five per cent of the budget. If they pull freight, we'll be out of business by spring."

J.B. Johnson, whose distinctive signature is fifth on the Petition, drums his fingers on his knee, avoiding eye contact. "I guess I'll get this over with. I don't know why I even came today. And I don't know why I signed this thing. It's not like me not to take a stand, nor to speak my convictions. But on this gay business, I feel like I have one foot on the dock and the other on the boat pulling out. It's too late to go back and too dangerous to leap on board for some wild ride into who knows where." He shakes the paper and looks pale. "Bonnie and I married in this church and baptized our children here. Up until now, we've been happy and satisfied with things." J.B. plays the piano on both knees now. This many words out of J.B. Johnson in one breath is a phenomenon.

"Kathy, you're popping at the seams. Want to speak?" asks Thomas.

Her knees poke through holes in stretch pants covered to the knees by heavy wool red knee-highs that match her sweater. No one ever accused her of high fashion. Comfort, yes. Kathy's devotion to the music ministry of the church is unexcelled. Intelligent and earnest, she is a gifted musician, and zealous to have the likes of Peter Vanderlaan on the organ bench and directing the choir. "Because I'm so intent on having Peter and Randy here for a first interview, I knew the Bible attack was coming. I've been doing some reading up. The texts quoted in the Petition are called the clobber texts. Scholars show all the times in history where the Bible has been used to condone all forms of prejudice and exclusion against women, people of color, and now homosexuals. I just don't get it. It disturbs me how the Holy Word is used to harm God's own children." Kathy huffs. Gunther, Thomas, Calline, and Lilly affirm with a nod. Nancy grunts, sitting as stiff as a starched sheet.

Lilly jumps in boldly. "Did you guys notice the part in the Petition that refers to homosexuality as 'deviant sexual preference'? Since when was being gay a preference, anyway? Who would choose to be bullied and condemned to hell?" She giggles nervously, looking to Kathy, who gives her signature "you go girl!" grin.

"I don't like this whole issue one bit," pipes in Nancy Dobbs, a bold pronouncement from the passive-aggressive church clerk. "Gunther's boss's daughter came out and it nearly destroyed her mother. Over time, they got used to the idea and really love both girls. I'll concede that truth." Nancy grimaces, then grins in spite of herself, like she's sniffed something that doesn't smell so bad after all.

Tendal scratches his bald spot and nods his head in that I-don't-know fashion of his. Words aren't his forte, but he's not one to bite his tongue when matters of such gravity call for everyone's input. His great- grandparents were among the eleven founders of the church. "I have to say something or great gramps and grandma will visit at my bedside from the grave about their church splitting over the likes of queers—excuse me, but this is the word I grew up with. I had a friend I hung out with before we started looking at girls. Ted. We were inseparable. When we were in ninth grade, I caught him dressed in his mama's cocktail dress and putting on makeup in the mirror. Back then, as now I guess, bullying queers was fair game. When a bunch of kids started beating him pretty bad I just stood back . . . and watched." Tendal wipes his eyes on his sleeve, sniffling. "Ted's folks left town when he was in twelfth grade, to protect him, I suspect. I learned at a high school reunion that he died of A.I.D.S. I can't make it up to Ted, but I s'pose I can do something now." Tendal's commitment to support Peter's candidacy seems sealed.

Thomas glances at his watch and waves the Petition. "Anybody else have a burning desire?" He doesn't wait, wishing things will wrap up soon. "We haven't heard from you, Cal. What's your sense about where we should go with this?" He clears his throat and glances over at his wife, who dutifully straightens like a flight attendant just before landing.

Calline remembers her sister, who had gotten herself pregnant out of wedlock. "So Mary, what are you going to do now?" Calline had asked her. Her sister was clueless.

"I believe the next best step is to call this meeting to a close, go home, and hold a vigil of prayer through Christmas. Thomas, would you ask Alexis if she and the petitioners would halt the offense like they did on Christmas Eve during the war."

"But picked up weapons again," pipes Smit, a highly decorated WWII veteran.

Thomas brushes his hands as if having rid himself of some odious thing. Kathy hauls her large frame from the sofa and stretches. Gunther rises to help Nancy, grimacing from stiffness, and J.B. swivels in his chair, quietly excusing himself to the restroom. Tendal follows J.B.. Lilly and Sorrel exchange niceties while Sorrel takes his cap from Myrtle, then helps Lilly untangle her huge belly from her cardigan. Nancy collects dishes, and Calline sits and watches, mulling over these recent events: shocking, telling, terrifying.

"Perhaps we should say a closing prayer before we skedaddle. Truce or no truce, we might find ourselves huddled again and I want to be as armed by the Spirit as possible for what lies ahead," says Calline. Except for J.B., who waves and is out the door, all are quiet while Kathy sets the pitch. "I'm waiting, I'm waiting, for

Jesus is coming. He's coming, he's coming the Light of the World. I'm lighting a candle to greet him, Dear Jesus come soon!"

While pulling on his rubber and leather boots, Sorrel seems to announce to the whole group, "Cal, how 'bout going with me to catch the last run of 'The Christmas Carol?'"

Oh great! Ears are burning twice as hot to know what I'll say as what the direction of the church will be. Will they judge me if I answer "yes"? But what if I say "no?" The good thing is, they know Sorrel as a man of honor and integrity. But what do they know of me? Exceedingly more than I care to imagine.

From years of Saturdays spent for Sundays, the pastor's response is habitual. "Sorrel, a rain check? I've got to prepare for tomorrow. Thanks, though." She's relieved that her response was so even, betraying her true feelings of fear and desire.

"Cal, it's the matinee. And it's such a great story. Might give you ammo for your sermon." Sorrel is casual and easy; the fact that he's selling her on the idea in front of a seemingly supportive audience removes all hint of the illicit.

"He's right, Cal. Go and enjoy yourself." This from Kathy and her chorus, all pressing hats, gloves, and scarves into place to face the cold.

"Sure, Sorrel, why not?" In jest, he offers her his arm. Surely it's the cold that lights up her cheeks Christmas red.

CHAPTER FIFTEEN

SPEEDING OFF IN Sorrel's Durango, slip-sliding from the Dreiden's driveway, was not Calline's plan for the afternoon. But something inside her feels like a bird taking flight, wings spread and soaring on a breeze so fresh and strong that she wants to scream, laugh, or both.

"I haven't heard that kind of laugh out of you ever, Calline." The surprising Sorrel Dixon blows on his hands while his gloves warm on the dashboard where the heater blows full strength.

"The meeting went much better than I had hoped," Calline offers, trying to keep things formal, in the church line of business. "What do you think?"

Sorrel gears down to turn into the Citgo, fishtailing on black ice. "Let me do this first, I'll get back to you." He parks, hops out with the ease of a gazelle, pumps gas, goes inside, and returns with two cups of steaming hot chocolate. His gait is clipped; he is always a little bent over, like his feet can't keep up with what's on his mind to get done next.

"Hot chocolate?" He hands one to Calline. As she takes the cup, warm on her palm, she remembers Sorrel's confession to her of his drinking history. Not of coffee and hot chocolate, but of hard liquor. He tells everyone he's been sober for years, until his next move makes her think maybe he's slipped. Sorrel pulls from the fueling station to idle in a spot where the sun pours in. He turns to put his hand on Calline's shoulder.

"Now Cal, I have a bit of a surprise and I want you to take a deep breath before you flip at my suggestion." Their eyes lock. She can't look away and her throat tightens. His eyes are more intense than she's ever seen. *What can this dear man possibly have on his mind?*

"I've been so shell-shocked these past weeks, Sorrel; if you don't mind, bring it on gently." Calline warms her hands on the cup and waits, wondering what the creative and spontaneous Sorrel has up his sleeve now.

"We're going to get your journal back. It's at the Grimsleys' and we're going to play a little game of seize the booty."

Calline sits up in shock, hot drink spilling onto her sweater. She gasps and grabs the napkin to dab at the spilled cocoa. "How the hell—heck—did you even know about the journal?" She is shocked.

"It's the church, Cal. Swiss cheese, leak city." He shrugs.

"How bad a leak?" she moans. "How many people know about this?"

"Well, like any leak, the hole starts out small, then . . ."

"You can stop there. I don't want to know. Oh, dear God." She spits on her finger and dabs the spot again, harder and harder, like Lady Macbeth. The chocolate stain sets in, the sweater ruined.

"I don't think Grimsley has leaked the contents of your journal, if that's what has your britches in a twist." Sorrel sounds almost too assured.

"How could you possibly know that?" Calline feels like throwing up.

"I think she's holding it to trump with," says Sorrel, tapping the wheel with his index finger.

Calline's mind races. *How on earth did it come to this?* "You're right. She blessed me with a season's greeting threat to publish the thing if we hire Peter. Oh, Dear Jesus, help us!"

It must be the caffeine, nerves, tiredness, but suddenly this all seems so ludicrous that Calline laughs uncontrollably. The pastor and her illicit lover are planning to break into the mansion of two prominent High Dunes citizens and biggest givers at the church.

Suddenly, her bladder rebels and at the moment, holding her crotch is the only hope of holding it in. When she returns from a near-miss to the bathroom, Calline settles, turns to Sorrel and says, "Let's do it, Sorrel. Why limit your gifts to fundraising? And mine to preaching?" He reaches over to hug her. She pushes him off, feeling drunk with confusion and adrenaline.

Sorrel throws it into gear, backs and turns, and heads straight for the lake. "Wheeee, high hopes for High Dunes, here we come," he squeals, like guys do before the game, like they do when they're in need of a big hit of adrenaline.

"Bonnie and Clyde were pretty-looking people . . ." Calline invites, to Sorrel's reply,

"Reach for the sky, sweet-talking Clyde would holler as Bonnie loaded dollars . . ."

Sorrel reaches for her hand and says, "Here's my plan. I was just over at their place for a party. I was in the kitchen when Alexis asked Richard where he'd hidden the house key. She wanted to let the cleaning woman in while they were away seeing grand kids. I heard Richard say it was hidden under the ceramic toad next to the mailbox. God forgive me, but I paid attention, thinking this day might come. Hey, the cost and joy of discipleship." Sorrel pokes at Calline's ribs and laughs. Calline feels terrified.

"What about security, Sorrel? I bet the place is armed like Fort Knox. The Grimselys have probably ten million dollars' worth of valuables. Did you see that Dali they brought from Florida?"

"I'm thinking Mission Impossible, baby. I think I can remember how to disengage an alarm and set it back. I hope so, anyway." He grins wryly.

"Sorrel, I've never prayed in a situation like this. Do we start by asking forgiveness or for help for a just cause?" Calline feels an inexplicable weight descend.

Dunes Crossing, originally a 250 acre farm, subdivides into ten estate lots. The entrance was supposed to be gated, but the Board decided against, hoping to manage the impression they weren't elitist, which of course they were. Sorrel swings through the towering brick-turreted entrance and heads for the pond where people feed the ducks and sit for solitude. For the first time since she's known the man, Calline's rose-colored glasses for Sorrel turn to a shade of real. He's serious, and she believes for the time being, she actually will go along with his wild-hellion plan to recover her journal.

"I'm going to park down by the duck pond and we'll walk from there. You still with me? You're shivering, Cal." He reaches to squeeze her freezing hand to calm her, but never mind, the man is on a mission; the only way forward now is, well, forward. He reaches back and pulls a fanny pack from under the passenger seat and belts it over his wool pants. His puffy ski jacket conceals the load.

"I'm with you, Sorrel, and I'm petrified." Calline inhales deeply for courage, then jokes, "O.K., Max, let's get going before Ninety-nine backs out." *An apt allusion to the bumbling private-I's of television's "Get Smart" comedy*, thinks Calline.

The house, an English manor-style mansion, sits atop an incline, back from the road at least two hundred yards. It casts a huge shadow across the sparkling white blanket that covers everything and makes walking difficult. Their four tracks leave conspicuous evidence of their intrusion. Old walnut trees stand like infantry along the long entrance drive. The estate lots are large enough to ensure privacy. Never mind, Calline imagines every tree, shrub, and post, bugged with a device that reads, registers, and reports their every move. Any second, sirens will scream. Helicopters will hover with bright lights and ominous weapons aimed to fire. They'll be lifted away, questioned, tried, and put away for life. Forgotten.

"Look Ninety-nine, I'm going in. You can stand back and wait, but you're here because you know what we're looking for. Are you in or out? No time to equivocate now." Sorrel sounds official, like another side of his personality reveals itself and claims him to accomplish this single task: retrieving the stolen journal.

Calline whines, holding her crotch. "Sorrel, really. This is not Maxwell Smart's goofy make believe." It more than bothers her that Sorrel, and admittedly she also, can seem so giddy while breaking into the home of prominent church members, respected community leaders, while committing a crime. Alexis may be the pastor's nightmare, but Calline, at this most unpredictable time, can acknowledge that the woman has contributed considerably to good. Maybe it's the lingering loose screw of the never-fully-recovered alcoholic that drives Sorrel now. Maybe it's her feeling of unmanageability and desperation to have her private confessions in her possession, not in Grimsley's, that keeps her in this game. Or maybe it's that she's letting her "no" to Sorrel lose its grip. Torn between the fear of possible repercussions and the drive to retrieve her journal, assuming that it's here, brings acid to her throat and a shooting pain in her lower back. She smiles, "And some had gifts of teaching, of preaching, of helps, of healing. But stealing? My Lord!" Calline reaches for Sorrel's hand to guide and to anchor.

"I think I see where the key might be. I'll get it and meet you at the opening at the hedge that borders the left wing. See that gate there? Right there. Now get going." Sorrel points to the meeting place and moves like a seasoned agent, his athleticism and daily workouts paying handsomely. He kicks the ground through a mound of snow and crusted ice and leans over, surfacing with the key. Calline finds a small gate in the fence that surrounds the snow-covered patio and waits, needing desperately to relieve herself.

"This way," says Sorrel once they're inside the fence. "See that double-glass sliding door? Let's go in there." Sorrel arranges the contents of his fanny pack in his hands so that critical seconds can be put to use dismantling the alarm. Calline shakes, and her heart races. Sorrel jabs the key in the doorknob. It fits. When the lock clicks, the door slides. An ominous beeping sound gives warning, like the clicking before a bomb goes off. He waves Calline to move quickly.

Sorrel goes straight to work, moving like a dentist in the mouth of a yawning alligator. Calline, shaking, watches him dismantle the box. "I've gotta kill this thing, then we've got to haul tail." Sorrel's hands and fingers work furiously. Tiny beads of sweat break on his forehead. "Damn, they've changed the colors. What do these mean?" Sorrel squints at the quagmire of lines and squares and dots. "Cripe, I can't see the darned map." He quickly grabs at his fanny pack and pulls out a pen that shines a light. "Better. Now I think I can make sense of this. Get a move on, Dixon," He chides himself, as cruel as any drill sergeant.

Calline holds her crotch. Sorrel grins at her and bends his head in the direction of the bathroom. "I got the thing. Off. Let's go hunting." Sorrel walks to Calline and ushers her ahead like he did from her yard not long ago.

"Let's go peeing, if you don't mind." The bathroom is the size of Calline's living room. She reminds herself why, in this very moment, she compromises her ethics and her pride: her journal. While she relieves herself, she searches the vanity drawers and a reading rack by the toilet. Nothing.

"In here, Cal." The library is large enough to spend a day in search. Calline joins Sorrel there. She scans the room, fastidiously appointed with designer fabrics, smooth wide-board floors, and cathedral ceiling. The adrenaline flowing in her body brings a clarity and certainty of movement of which she never believed she was capable. She likes this rare confidence she feels, the feeling that she's invincible. Like a teenager.

"Sorrel, I'll take the desk and reading areas, you cover the book shelves. The journal is narrower and smaller than a typical hardcover book. It is bright red with red binding with 'CPS Journal #23' scripted in magic marker on the spine."

Sorrel climbs the ladder and shines his pen across sections and rows of book spines. The ladder spires to the highest shelves stocked with memorabilia, plants, and countless sterling frames with family photos. While Sorrel climbs and searches, Calline rifles through stacks of papers on an enormous dark cherry desk. She tries to ignore the contents, until a financial report catches her eye. The numbers are too staggering to ignore. A seven figure bottom line beginning with a three draws her in. But what really grabs her attention is the church pledge card right next to the statement. It is blank. Her stomach roils again while her hands reach into each desk drawer, patting and shuffling stacks of papers and office supplies. No journal. Across the room, two overstuffed reading chairs upholstered in deep blues and tans flank a gate-legged table surrounded by baskets of newspapers, writing pads, and books.

"Sorrel, this has got to be the place!" she says while she presses into each basket, shuffling their contents. Still, no journal. Calline gets quiet. She waits and cocks one ear as if listening for the whistle of the wind.

"Sorrel, master bedroom. Where's the bedroom?"

"Up the stairs, turn right immediately. First French door." He looks down from perilously high on the ladder. Calline dashes to the stairwell. A light beams through the windows in the captain's perch three stories above. Calline thinks of the old South, the ladies ascending and descending wide, spiraling staircases, gowns and petticoats swishing, pale hands and innocent spirits yet untouched by the agony of war. In spite of the pain in her leg, Calline skips a step at a time until her leg grabs and slows her. Finally at the top, her knee gives out. She trips and barely blocks a face-on fall with her hands.

Straight ahead, the French door, the width of four doors and higher than her ceiling at home, beckons. Through the glass, she sees the king-sized bed tailored in plush piles of oriental silk and rayon of rich golds, reds, and browns. The bed holds prominence in the room, the size of her whole house, she figures. She pushes herself off the floor and tests the door handle. The door opens. The giant bed and the piles of pillows and reading and writing material draw her in. "Sorrel," she calls, "there must be at least twenty pillows and shams at the head of the bed. You should see the piles of papers, books, writing materials, magazines. Someone spends a lot of time in bed." Then she spies it: a red binding poking out between two decks of cards and a newspaper.

"Sorrel, I see it!" she screams. She dives for the journal, as if catching a runaway kitten. Calline lies across the Grimsley nuptial bed, crying and laughing. Her feelings resemble something of a mother-child reunion after a painful separation. Sorrel comes in quietly and slides onto the bed. He cups her into his belly and pulls her body to him. The two look like castaways adrift at sea on a tiny raft. She feels his breath on her neck, warm and rapid, and suppresses a powerful urge to moan with desire. She shimmies closer, if she can, into the cavity of his chest and belly. Somewhere from outside herself she hears, "Don't let me go, Sorrel. Please hold tight."

CHAPTER SIXTEEN

"OUR FINGERPRINTS ARE all over the Grimsley's house. Will Richard and Alexis find out? Who will show at church, and who won't, since the Petition? Will Thomas get to Grimsley to demand a Christmas truce before she leaves for the holidays? How do I look at the folks at church? Innocent, baby lamb eyes? Downcast? Blank?" The pastor lifts these prayers to the Lord.

How about my eyes? Eyes of love?

Calline feels her cheeks warm with embarrassment. "Of course." Vee Morgan's family missed the Christmas drawing at Citizens for Neighbor Concerns. Clothes, toys, and food will be collected for her family. Sorrel's son, Billy Dixon wants Calline to meet his new girlfriend, Martha, and has asked to lead the youth group preparing and performing a live crèche. Tendal and Margaret Harris left a dramatic message that their special-needs daughter, Connie, wants to marry David Somers, whom she met at college. He's fifteen years her junior and has his own set of emotional and behavioral complications.

"The sooner the better," the desperate Margaret intoned. *Pregnant?* Calline wonders.

All this on her mind, on her to-do list, and the pastor will be in the pulpit in an hour. Quickly, Calline dresses, coifs, eats, and feeds Bingo while ruminating on Zechariah prophesying the Savior's purpose: *"To give light to those who sit in darkness, and in the shadow of death to guide our feet into the way of peace."*

"Guide us into the way of peace," she whispers as she locks the door. She limps the shortcut through the neighbor's frozen mums, topped with snow. *Whipped cream,* she thinks, as she hurries to the parking lot of the church.

Up ahead, Billy and a handful of the youth, accompanied by Sorrel, assemble a ramshackle straw shed with flimsy two-by-fours and bamboo. Two tall fake palms lean against the side of the building.

Sorrel directs. "Billy, bring the manger and let's put it right here. And that straw bale can be opened and spread. Martha, if you don't mind, there's a closet in the back of the bride's room that has costumes. When you get a minute, maybe you could take charge of that department."

"Hey guys. Billy mentioned this is a *live* crèche?" Sorrel asks, not sure if the Svensons will show after last year's debacle with his goats running off.

"Mr. and Mrs. Svenson said we could use their burro and two sheep," says Billy, full of the enthusiasm he inherited from his father.

"A pig, too, if we can stand the smell," says his new love interest, Martha.

"Mr. McAlister over in Alva said we could have some goats and rabbits if we need. We'll use the Torn Jesus again. That sorry looking thing," says Billy, laughing.

"Anyone want to tell that story?" Calline calls out, remembering the drama of the Christmas pageant eleven years ago. "It would explain to newcomers why the torn-up doll is so sacred."

"I guess I will, since I was in the middle of the action," pipes Billy, loaded up with straw. He faces Martha in the telling. "All Rebecca Harris and I had to do as Mary and Joseph was to stand and look at the manger. Tommy Druthers just had to stand there and look angelic. But he lost it, and grabbed Jesus from the manger. He pulled one of its eyes until it popped from Jesus's head. I grabbed one of Jesus's legs. Tommy and I got in a tug-o-war for the doll. Jesus was ripped bad. 'I want the baby Jesus!' Tommy yelled." Billy scatters straw around the stall floor as he wraps up his story. "Tommy's mother screamed from her pew. 'He talked! He talked. Tommy talked! It's a miracle!' Tommy hadn't talked for months. Tommy's mother never misses praying at the crèche since that day."

Calline's attention turns to the parking lot, the best gauge of Sunday's attendance. Except for the seasonal absentees, it seems there will be a full house. The truce must be on. Calline enters the building feeling confident, in charge, and hopeful. She feels a light touch on her shoulder.

"Rev. Cal, I want you to meet Martha. Martha Heckman." Billy perspires from his hard work. Next to him stands a beautiful rail-thin blonde with dark aqua eyes. Her smile exposes perfectly straight white teeth, a genuine freshness that endears Calline immediately. They are a beautiful pair, both soon to graduate and launch lives of their own. *Together?* She wonders.

"Martha, if you are Billy's friend . . . ." Calline takes her hands and presses them to her chest. She and Martha walk to the narthex while Billy does something he's done since he was little. He gets the pastor's guitar, puts the strap over his shoulder, and grooves like a rock star. While Calline adjusts her robe, Martha admires the silver spoon cross and helps arrange it neatly at center front, between the satin-silk extensions of the purple stole.

"Be sweet to my boy, Martha. Need I tell you? It's just that . . ."

"Say no more. I understand your bond. I'll . . ." The girl beams broadly.

"Say no more," Calline interrupts. The women hug. Billy hands the pastor her guitar. She quietly plucks the six strings to check the tuning. "Martha, would you like to light the candles on the Advent wreath?" Calline, swelled with a mother's love, smiles.

"I'd be honored. Three candles today?" Martha gingerly takes the taper and turns to Billy, who lights the small waxed wick at the end of the taper. Martha adjusts it so that a healthy flame will withstand the journey down center isle to the wreath.

Calline and the tiny choir follow Martha, leading the congregation in "I'm waiting, I'm waiting for Jesus is coming, He's coming He's coming the Light of the world. I'm lighting a candle to greet him, dear Jesus come soon."

Calline turns to greet the congregation. Many unfamiliar faces smile from the pews, the C & E (Christmas and Easter) attendees, and friends and family of regulars represent a strong contingent. Petitioners and petitioned, for the time being, sit peacefully together, like the peaceful kingdom Isaiah foretold, lions and lambs lying together. Vee sits next to the father of her child. The pastor is all too aware of the Grimsleys' absence. Even Calline's keen imagination cannot fathom the nature of her next encounter with Alexis.

A stranger, a straggly looking man with silver dreadlocks, a handlebar mustache, very tall and rail thin, enters and sits in the back pew. Smit Rother, greeter for the day, welcomes him warmly and hands him a bulletin. The stranger sits and scans the congregation with a rugged smile. He seems to zero in on Calline with eyes like stars. They are so bright and full of pure love. Calline feels the hairs bristle on her neck. She can't take her eyes off his incandescent eyes. *Eyes of love*, she thinks, and smiles back to the stranger, thanking him for the reminder.

Worship goes seamlessly. Greetings and well wishes go routinely. Calline finds her way to the Hall when Tendal Harris's wife, Margaret, approaches.

"Cal, I know it's a bad time, but Connie is coming home tomorrow and we have to set something up." Calline thinks, *it's never a good time, Margaret, but through eyes of love, I can see you are a wreck.* Tendal stands behind his wife of forty-one years with his hands on her shoulders as if she'll float off like a Bozo blimp in a parade. Most of the parishioners put on their winter gear to leave. The pastor and frenzied mother stand in the corner of the Hall, private enough for now.

"I'm disturbed, very disturbed. Connie met this man, David Somers, at college and now they are convinced, beyond all reasoning to the contrary, they should get married. She's fifteen years his senior and he might as well have been let out of a zoo!" Margaret takes a lipstick-smudged handkerchief from her purse and wipes a tear.

Tendal joins them for support. "You know our Connie, Cal. You've seen her operate." Tendal clears his throat, a clear sign of distress.

Calline remembers the youth group when Pizza Palace messed up their order, how Connie heaved pizza against the wall and stormed out. The stain never came out.

"Well, multiply what you've seen by a thousand and that's the way she is a lot of the time. You know the story." The narrative about her child is one Margaret and Tendal repeat as a litany of regret, of grief, really. "None of her foster families could handle her. Naïvely, we were sure we could give her what she needed, extra care for seizures, attention deficit, and of course, attachment disorder. She's been a bundle of complications the whole damned time, frankly. Now she wants to get married and if we don't support her she'll—no telling what she'll do." Tendal sounds surrendered.

"It's hard to admit, but we're afraid of her!" says Margaret, crying and blowing.

Tendal and Margaret turn to face each other and hold hands. It seems that the gift of Connie is the couple's solidarity, if even as hostages to their thirty-seven-year old adopted daughter.

"What do you want me to do?" Calline asks, sympathetic, touching Margaret on the hand clenching tissue.

"Talk some sense into her, Cal. If anyone can, you can. She likes you. When we try to tell her anything, she goes berserk." Margaret exhales hard again and looks at Tendal.

"You're objecting to the marriage? Why, may I ask?" Calline is thinking that having a stable partnership might be just what the girl needs.

"Babies! They'll have babies and Connie is about as prepared to be a mother as any five-year old with ADHD, seizures, and attachment deficit." *Sounds just like a lot of parents out there having babies every day,* Calline thinks.

The pastor sees the panic in both their faces and genuinely wants to calm them. For the dear Harrises sake, she will meet with Connie and David at their convenience. "How's about tomorrow afternoon sometime? I'll be here." Calline reaches to take Margaret's hand to squeeze.

"Thanks, Cal. We'll send her over." *Why not David, too?* The pastor wonders. Momentarily, the Harrises seem calmer, convinced their pastor has special powers to manage the entirely unmanageable. *Best secret going about this mantle I wear,* she thinks more than once.

Calline spies an opening to leave, with high anticipation of a walk at the lake, when Vee and her friend approach. "Vee, hi, and who's this with you today? Welcome." The tall young man can't be older than sixteen. Calline glances at Vee's belly, then laughs to see her pockets stuffed with coffee hour goodies. "For the family?" Calline smiles at Vee, who squints mischievously, then points one thumb to the tall boy standing beside her.

"This Roscoe, the baby's daddy." Inside of him is a baby boy, who is lost and afraid and wonders how he landed so fast in this big wad of flesh he's in, man enough to produce a baby. All he does is look at the floor, hands jammed in his pockets, and kicks his shoes, leaving a big scuff mark. Annoyed, a flash of raw judgment hits Calline hard, because a baby will depend on the likes of them. Anger shoots up in her along with the acid.

"You guys want to go get a burger? I'm hungry. My treat. Ya'll come with me and I'll drop you off where you tell me." Maybe the pastor can get something out of the boy, see if there's a hint of father-potential.

Settled at a booth at Curley's, Calline hopes to get a word out of either of them. Roscoe chews and stares out the window. She sees a straggly group of teenagers waving before he does.

"You know those guys?" Calline asks Vee. Silent, Roscoe looks to the group and drags his gangling body up. His denims slide halfway down his boxer-clad buttocks.

He says, "Be back," and goes to join the kids, high-fiving, reaching deep in his pocket. He pulls out a wad of cash and hands it to one of the other kids, who slaps something into Roscoe's palm. That hand pushes deeply into his other pocket. Roscoe looks over to see if Vee and Calline watch.

"The father of your baby, Vee—does he use?" Calline snaps.

"Yep, he do." She chews, expressionless.

She might as well have asked the kid if he drinks milk. She spits fire. "Let's go, Vee. I'll give you a ride home. Roscoe can stay with his friends. It looks like he's taking care of some serious adult business."

"But Cal, he with me," she pleads, babyish, sure the boy has got the prayer of a snowball next to a hot furnace of getting a ride with the minister. Roscoe disappears with the pack, not looking back. Vee sleeps all the way to her house. Calline wants to scream that an innocent child will be born into this mess.

She thinks she hears, *"So? I was born into yours."*

CHAPTER SEVENTEEN

AFTER ALL THAT'S transpired in one weekend, the Reverend Calline Simpson actually feels relieved to know: It's all a mess.

Speaking of messes, Dalia hollers, "The bride, Connie Harris, for you." Dalia seems frantic to get caught up on her petite-point. The Christmas Day service is on the pastor's mind, but evidently not on the secretary's. Calline raises a quick prayer. "Patience, Lord."

"Con, hey girl. Glad to have you back lakeside." It's the strange and the marginal that pull the pastor's heart strings; Connie Harris's strangeness, though, brings pure wonderment. "Whoa, slow down. Can you speak a little more slowly, Connie?" It sounds like the young woman has marbles in her mouth. Medications, perhaps.

"I'm getting married. Can you do the service?" Anyone who knows Connie knows that short of bringing on a terrorist maneuver, there will be no brooking interference on this one.

"Are we meeting at 2:00? Just you and me? Your mom said so." Calline looks at her watch and taps her foot, impatient.

"No, David and I are coming over right now. See you in fifteen." Click.

Enter bride and groom. Their entrance is a siege. "Whoa, you two! Can you wait?" Dalia steps between them and the pastor's office, but is pushed away like a clerk in a bank robbery.

Connie is short and stout, butch hair, very long fake eye lashes, wide flat nose, skinny lips, her hygiene scores low. She plops on the couch in the narthex and pats the cushion next to her for David to sit. "This is him, David. Say hi honey!" She throws one leg over her other knee, one knee popping through in over-sized army fatigues. Her top is an open blue denim shirt stamped on the back, "Boss Hog." Her bosoms bounce loose when she pulls David with a force that earns respect. He giggles and scratches his chin, unshaved. His greased hair flattens to his head. His cotton Oxford shirt is opened four buttons down and appears to have been slept in. Neither of them comes with coats, and both are in shoes with no socks. If Connie is thirty-seven and David is fifteen years her junior, who would know? They both look shaken up in a bag of lint, grease, hair. *Two ragamuffins on a mission,* Calline thinks, trying not to laugh at the sight of them.

Rather than squeeze themselves into Calline's tiny office, and to give the pastor an exit passage should she need one, they settle in the waiting area outside Dalia's office. It is doubtful that anyone will enter to interrupt. Certainly, Dalia will listen on. What's new?

"Well, you two. Your mom told me your plans. Tell me yourselves."

"Mom and Dad are pissed as crud, Cal, and nothing is going to stop us," says the defiant-as-always bride.

"Runaway trains are my specialty, Con," says Calline, winking. Connie finds the image of herself as a runaway train hilarious. She slaps her knee and leans to kiss David square-on. "We've already found a place to live not far from the lake, up over the skating rink."

David, shorter than she, and almost as wide as he is tall, drops his torn loafers and tucks his bare feet under his knees. His grin betrays two missing bottom teeth, something on the cover of *Mad Magazine.* He smells of cigarettes, and she a cross between an unkempt pet and Walgreens perfume.

"Okay, kids, what recommends you to this marriage? I have to ask, you know. It's my job." Calline is genuinely curious.

"Easy. We met in class three months ago. David thought I was cute, didn't you, baby? And I thought he was cute. And we held hands on our first date and then we did more stuff on the next date."

"And more," adds David. Uproarious laughter and frantic hand clapping and bouncing on the sofa ensue.

And then comes a baby in the baby carriage, thinks Calline.

David is beet red embarrassed. Connie rubs his stubbly cheeks with her hand with enough friction to start a fire. David winces and slaps her away.

"Well, you two. If you are determined, then when did you have in mind to tie the knot?"

"New Year's Eve, right at the turn of midnight," more laughing and bouncing.

"*This* year?" Calline chokes on her saliva and coughs to clear it. She was not prepared for this.

"Yep," they chime in unison.

"I don't know, y'all. That's a strange hour and it wouldn't please a lot of people to come to a wedding at . . ." David stands and then Connie. They gaze down like two combat soldiers holding Calline at house arrest.

She holds up her hands. "Whoa! Look guys, if your folks are a little skeptical of you two tying the knot, midnight might make it even harder for them to accept your plan. Would you think something a little less dramatic would help them decide in your favor?"

At that suggestion, Connie does what has worked for most of her life. She collapses to the floor and flutters her feet in the air. "I want to get married at midnight!"

David flops on top of her and holds her wrists to the ground. "Connie, stop that now, baby. You hear me? This is not the time or the place. Rev. Cal is trying to help us." Connie raises her knee and jams it hard into David's groin. He caves, rolls off of her, holding his crotch, groaning in agony.

Calline looks at her watch and yawns. "Connie, David, it's time to get up now. Let's talk again about the date, and we have some meetings to do before I'll tie your knot. Could be a slip knot the way things are going. Lord knows." She conceals a grin.

Connie, confused that her tantrum didn't work, sweeps her hand through her hair and sniffles and throws her head back, her dignity thoroughly intact. She reaches a hand to David, hauling them both from the floor.

"Rev. Cal, do you think I should marry her? She's a real ball buster, but I love her. I'll be safe with her in dark alleys, that's for sure." He slaps his rear, takes Connie's hand, and out the door they go, laughing.

"What the heck was that?" Calline prays.

"My children," she thinks she hears from off somewhere.

"Mother of the bride on the line," Dalia says, popping gum.

"Margaret! Just saw the kids." Calline wonders what the beleaguered mother of the bride has to offer. Margaret Harris is almost always pissed. Calline doodles Christmas trees and tiny elves, punctuating the mother's tirade with an occasional "uh, huh," but overall, she can't engage with the tempest of a parent who can't let go of her child. She may be petulant, she may be a mess, she may be all those things, but….

"It must be awful to have to stand by and watch your children make choices you don't agree with, Margaret. I know this sounds patronizing, but Connie is thirty-seven and David is uhhh, what?"

"Twenty-two, for God's sake. A baby!" Margaret huffs and blows.

"Margaret, did they tell you about the midnight mass?"

"You didn't agree, I hope! Midnight, for God's sake. I told them I'd lay off of them about getting married if they'd be considerate enough to have the thing at a reasonable hour."

Calline's fingers cross. "And?"

"They accepted seven p.m., last day of the year. Can you be there?" Margaret sounds resigned.

"Or be square." Calline's relief is palpable. "Are you coming to the crèche tonight? Might bring some peace to pray to the Torn Jesus, to just stand by and ponder the miracle of the season and all.

Dress warmly, it's supposed to dip into the teens again, with light lake affect and a hefty breeze." Calline feels real love welling for Margaret. What a sacrifice she and Tendal have made for Connie, giving their all and having not much but pizza thrown back at them. Grace is not tit for tat. Life is unfair.

"Connie and David said they'd help with the crèche. Tendal will be one of the kings." Margaret blows her nose.

"And you, what will you be?" Calline teases, knowing Margaret Harris is as much live crèche material as Connie and David are compliant.

"I'll be pissed off." Margaret, caricaturing herself, is in itself no small miracle.

CHAPTER EIGHTEEN

BINGO BEGS TO go with Calline, not aware the bitter cold would kill her.

"Sorry girl, you've been banned from the crèche." Calline laughs at the Boxer's every antic in her vast repertoire to change her person's mind. She rubs the whining dog's belly while she puts on a third layer of underclothing to bear the brunt of the wind chill factor, predicted below zero. "You had to go and bite a piglet and I had to pay vet fees, write a letter of apology, and promise this would never happen again." Calline remembers that Farmer Mcnell never came back with his pigs, but he did come one year with an old horse that kicked one of the youth. "No more dealing with Farmer from hell," folks liked to say.

Calline is sad to leave Bingo alone, and swears soon she'll get her best walking friend out for a very long romp at the lake. The walk to the church is blustery and slippery as soft flakes of snow accumulate. As she approaches the tiny ramshackle crèche lean-to, Calline spies what looks like a very frantic Easter egg hunt. Kids dash from one place to another, knocking on doors, shaking bushes, opening car doors and slamming them.

What on earth is going on? Calline wonders. Animals offload from trailers, people queue and rub hands and exhale like smoke stacks. Floodlights send bright beams directly to the manger. Everything seems to be in good order. The weather is cooperating enough, so what's the problem?

"Hey guys, it's Cal! Cal, come quick!'" It's Billy. Calline steps into a run, limping. Four youth run to her.

"Cal, the Torn Jesus is gone! We've searched for almost an hour. What should we do?" Billy, always the responsible one, is frantic. The star of the project under his supervision is gone, flat disappeared.

"The Torn Jesus is gone!" Rita, the woman who believes the Jesus doll performed a miracle on her son Tommy, weeps.

Tommy, over six feet tall, wraps his arms around her. "Mom, we'll find the Torn Jesus. Relax." When has she not embarrassed him?

Calline, at a loss, looks up; big snowflakes land in her nostril. "You got any ideas?"

An immediate and strong impression from somewhere says, "Melinda Suarez."

"Does anyone know a Melinda Suarez, I think I heard?"

"I do!" shouts a little girl—Roseanne—new to the neighborhood, a curiosity seeker at the crèche.

"Well, out with it," commands Calline, smiling at the girl.

All eyes are on Roeseanne, tiny, maybe seven; her family immigrated recently from Mexico. "Melinda Suarez. She had three babies in October. She lives down the street from us." She hops on her toes and pulls her cap down for warmth. The youth gather, quiet now, as if for a collective think-it-through. Then, as if struck by Heaven's inspiration, Billy shouts, "Melinda could bring live babies to the crèche until we find the Torn Jesus!" Everyone thumbs-up and high-fives.

"Three Jesuses! What potential for tomorrow's message," Calline roars with laughter. Great excitement stirs at the idea that now the manger will be occupied by not one, but three babies. Real live babies.

"Well, never say never. Maybe she'd be game. It's mighty cold, though. Who'd like to try to find Melinda?" Calline asks.

"There she is right now!" Roseanne points off to the distance. Melinda's image sharpens as she approaches; her eyes wide and smiling. Her dark wool cape swells in the wind. Somewhere under the mound of blankets, the stars of the hour sleep.

"Word gets around. I heard you needed some babies!" Melinda's smile is as bright as the moon. Not much older than the youth, the mother has that daring of the young to do something as crazy as donate her infants to the manger of a living crèche on a bitterly cold winter night.

"Melinda, would you do this for us? If we can make it totally safe and warm for the babies. Would you?" Calline is cautious. She doesn't know the girl, but by quick impressions, she seems game, sensible, and not about to put her brood in harm's way.

"I'd be honored, Reverend. To put my babies into service for the Lord in this way, to think that my babies, all three, would be my Lord Jesus. It will bring them good luck all their lives." Melinda swells with pride as she pulls back layers of blankets. Three little squiggling dolls bundled in fleece and wool, two pinks and one blue, dark beady eyes, peer up from their stroller pods. Each sucks on a pacifier and seems impervious to the cold.

"We could work them in shifts. Melinda. It'd probably be best for you to be Mary so you can watch your babies and they can see you," Calline takes charge.

Melinda goo-ga-gas over the babies, Juan, Juanita, and Juananna.

How to keep the babies warm is the question on everyone's mind when Sorrel pipes in, "A heating pad. We can plug in a heating pad and put it underneath them. The outdoor heater behind the crèche and the bright lights are throwing some good warmth. Ya'll agree?" Sorrel hustles to get the heating pad from the first aid cabinet.

Sorrel disappears and comes back with all the supplies needed to make a nest as comfy as any newborn could need in this god-awful cold. While Sorrel runs the extension cord to the building, Melinda lifts one of the girls from the stroller, bundling her like a tiny papoose, and lays her gently into the manger. The baby peers up from the cradle, blows a bubble, then lets out a scream to beat the band. In a nanosecond, Melinda has the other girl spun in her cocoon and placed in the cradle. Both girls bump heads and coo, then cut loose with haunting complaint. Melinda goes for little Juan, who pipes full-lunged, spins him in fleece and wool, then wedges him between the two howling girls.

"That's enough Jesuses for one night, no?" says Melinda crooning melodically in her native Spanish. Without removing her winter covers, she slips into the one-size-fits-all Mary-muslin sheet and veil covering her head and draped across her shoulders and down her back. She kneels and adjusts blankets and hats.

Melinda-Mary's gaze, moonlit smile, dark hair, skin, and eyes transcend. But for now, all eyes and devotion are riveted on the three Jesuses: all three sleep, their tiny faces aglow from heat and light.

"Silent night, holy night," the bystanders sing as neighbors and church members trickle by to admire the triumvirate of saviors.

By eleven on Christmas Eve, the goats have chewed the center post of the ramshackle stable almost in half; the roof beam splinters. The shepherds have broken rank, crafted a stockpile of snowballs, and are at war. A snowball thumps the rump of Svenson's burro who jack-ass kicks, barely missing the back of Melinda's head. Thank God she is leaning into the babies, who have had it, too. Melinda strips her costume, scoops up the screaming poop-smelling babies, and places them at cosmic speed into their stroller pods, covering them with layers of wool.

"Bye everyone, Merry Christmas!" Melinda hollers over her shoulder as she pushes like a tractor through snow two inches deeper. A snowball splats between her shoulders and she shakes it off, pushing valiantly through zero visibility.

"Thanks, Melinda, Juan, Juanita, and Juananna. Merry Christmas and God bless you!" hollers Calline.

ALL GOD'S CHILDREN

Calline spots the man who sat at the back of the church last Sunday. He leans his lanky body against the street lamp, arms and legs akimbo. A long canvas green coat with an ankle-length scissor-cut hem keeps him warm. The lamp light casts a glow over his silver dreadlocks and mustache, where giant snowflakes settle. Seeing him again throws Calline off balance, but Christmas hospitality edges out her fear. She waves him over. He nods and twinkles, "Reckon I will."

"You new around here?" Calline reaches a gloved hand to shake his. He smiles down at her, not saying a word. Up close, she sees the hurt and pain in his eyes; they still shine like when she first laid eyes on him.

"Just passing through, ma'am. Just passing through." His hand covers a smile, and then takes her hand in his. Wordless, a friendship forms between strangers.

"Hot chocolate, cider, and pastries in the Hall if anyone wants," Myrtle Dreiden hollers to the scattered crowds. Calline is relieved to walk toward the building to get warm. She turns to the man and invites him in. Kids slip and slide hurling snowballs, banging into the door the wind catches and swings open, then slams back shut.

Calline invites animal handlers, the McAlisters and Svensons, to come and get warm. "Thanks," says Mr. Svenson. "We gotta get these critters loaded." The burro follows Mrs. Svenson's sugar lumps. Mr. and Mrs. McAlister play push-me-pull-me with their adolescent pig who moves only for lack of good grip on the ice.

An ample deposit of excrement delivers a strong odor into the wind. Children make crude jokes. David and Billy offer to muck the area clean and move the remains of the little shelter to the burn bin out back.

Calline, Tendal, and Sorrel are the last to leave the building cleaned and ready for Christmas morning worship, just hours away. They are satisfied that this year's crèche was a triple success.

Still, though, the fact remains: the Torn Jesus is missing. Many came to pray to the doll, believing it to have healing properties.

"I am wondering if it's that man with the dreadlocks. Did anyone talk to the guy? He seems harmless enough, if not elusive," Tendal says, holding Calline's left elbow while Sorrel takes her right. Calline swells with love for the strength and faithfulness of these two, even if Tendal is tipsy and Sorrel intoxicates her.

"There's always one in the crowd," slurs Tendal who veers off to his car, wiping his mouth on his sleeve. "I hope he's not some stalker up to no good. We'd better keep our eyes open, it's a screw-ass world out there," he mumbles, swatting the air.

"Yesserreeee, screw-ass world all around," heralds Sorrel, laughing at the tipsy Tendal. He waves his wide hands to the sin-filled world, his voice echoing down the street, punch drunk from double-duties of the past weeks.

"All at once, now!" invites Tendal, slipping on the ice.

"Screw-ass world!" the three call in unison, as if they are the only ones exempt.

Tendal hollers some nonsense from his car window as he fishtails from the parking lot. Sorrel holds Calline's arm more firmly to balance them both.

"S'pose I need a lift home if you don't mind, Rev. I forgot Billy took the Durango," he says, cozying close for warmth.

Calline moves as close into him as she can. Hers is a Christmas kind of warm and jittery. They walk arm-in-arm down an empty snow-powdered street lit by lamps decked with giant bells and bright bows. It dawns on Calline that Sorrel is one of the few souls she trusts to the bottom of her snow boots. "Holy infant so tender and mild," she hums with a peace she hasn't felt in months.

"Sleep in heavenly peace, sleep in heavenly peace," the two sing.

Heavenly peace, Calline mumbles. "We could use some down here," she says, squeezing Sorrel's hand and looking up to the sky, God's dandruff floating to the ground.

CHAPTER NINETEEN

CALLINE DOESN'T GET between the sheets and under her favorite comforter, threadbare and lumpy, until well into morning. She did drive Sorrel to his house, but not before stopping at the Citgo, the only store open, for a hot toddy resembling eggnog without the liquor. The two sat in the running car, reminiscing about the journal capture at the Grimsley's.

In spite of her high spirits, serious remorse fills her when she thinks of the ridiculous charade, even if what was rightfully hers, her journal, was restored. "I still can't believe we did that, Sorrel. Maybe I should check myself into some insane asylum, turn myself in to the cops, something to adequately atone for my crimes." His glance is doubtful. "No really! I'm serious." She slaps at his shoulder.

"Now, Cal. Don't go on so." He leans in to peck her cheek. She pushes him away, laughing, feeling an electric current in her privates.

"You are practically married, Sorrel. I'm getting you home where you belong." In no time, Calline parks her Buick in his driveway, her arms crossed across her chest, both for warmth and for boundaries.

"Merry Christmas, Calline," Sorrel says, seeming sad, tired, not sure of anything. She's never seen him so vulnerable since the hospital. An impulse overtakes her. She leans toward him. "You look like you could use a hug."

"Or two, or three," Sorel says, happy to oblige.

Calline reaches her hands to cover his and locks her eyes to his gaze. Their stare is of two people exquisitely unsure of a future forbidden, yet absolutely certain all at once.

"Good night, Sorrel. Big day tomorrow." The Reverend backs out, looking over her shoulder to watch this dear lost man find his way to the door while she opens the door to her heart a little wider to let him in.

Her alarm startles her only three hours after she's fallen asleep. The early dawn of Christmas morning energizes her. A quick dark coffee and a croissant, warm casual attire, a silent prayer by the fire, and the pastor is on her way back to where, just hours earlier, the crèche mystified its visitors. She hopes the wind shifts before the service. The odor of manure is still strong. Clothed in layers, heavy socks, and snow boots she walks the familiar worn path to the church.

Jiggling the stubborn church door lock, she wonders the fate of the Torn Jesus. Where could it have gotten to? Melinda's babies were a perfect solution, ample fodder for the message today, but still . . . who? Where? The deep freeze has stiffened the lock. Not without a heaving and pull, heaving and pull again, the door swings open, knocking her down on her good knee to stop a fall. Aggravated, she pulls herself up. Oddly, a blast of warm air streams from the open door, when she was sure Tendal and Sorrel, compulsive about saving energy, had lowered the thermostat as low as it could go without freezing pipes. She hangs her coat and exchanges snow boots for her black pumps. Even stranger, the doors to the sanctuary are closed and through the spaces stream light. Cautious, a little frightened, Calline opens the doors.

"Holy Mother of Mary, Joseph, Jesus! Everything's been moved!" Agape, she examines every detail of what's never been like this before. At the center of the chancel sits the crèche manger, the baby there. The hands of the Torn Jesus lift to the ceiling. Rigged from the ones used for the crèche, the spotlight shines directly onto the crib. Twenty pots of fresh poinsettias, purchased to raise funds for the Children's Society, have been removed from the chancel steps and rearranged with a decorator's touch, to offset the manger at the center. The greens and bows on the Advent wreath look freshened. The Christ candle rises higher among the circle of evergreen. The candle stand is also in the center of the room, along with the manger and flowers. The a capella voices of a medieval choir sing from four old speakers long abandoned for ruined by the youth group. A faint scent of pine and cherry fills the room. The multi-sensory beauty, the surprise of it all, moves her so deeply, she kneels and bows like a Muslim praying,

"Behold, I bring tidings of great joy, for unto you this day is born a Savior who is Christ the Lord," she hears inside or out? She's not sure.

"You did this, Cal? It's stunning? I didn't know you had this touch." It's Kathy, who has come early to practice the piano. So caught up in her spell, Calline doesn't hear Kathy.

Calline lifts her head, her cheeks wet from crying. "No, it was all like this when I got here; I have no idea who." For a moment, the pastor is unabashed to weep. She can't not.

Kathy walks the center isle back and forth, agape. "Who put that smell in here? These voices? Renaissance. Absolutely gorgeous. Haunting!" As nonplussed as Calline, she exclaims, "The Torn Jesus is back. Who's responsible?"

Calline gets up and irons her pants with her hands. "I have no idea, but, hey, Kath, it's Christmas; anything can happen on Christmas." The women embrace. The show must go on, mystery or no. Kathy goes to the piano. Calline robes and stands near the wreath while the worshipers arrive.

Lilly Smith's two ragamuffins rush straight to the manger and kneel, calling out, "It's the Torn Jesus, Mommy! Come see!" Lilly and Calline exchange a quizzical glance and a shrug.

Nancy and Gunther Dobbs linger in the narthex next to their son visiting from out of town. His two children dash to the manger. Myrtle and Thomas approach the Dobbses to share Christmas tidings. The Dreiden's granddaughter, Rebecca, joins the other children. Rachael Connors, looking her age—over eighty—enters, leaning on her son George's arm. Calline struggles to conceal her dislike of the man, especially since he signed the Petition. Yet on Christmas, she can offer a warm smile to George and hug Rachael. She is shocked at how much weight her elder mentor has lost.

"Rachael, you all right? Merry Christmas!" Calline has missed her talks with her beloved support, and friend.

"Cal, I've missed you. We need to talk. Lots has happened since we spoke of Elizabeth." To Calline, Rachael is usually such a bright light, recently dimmed by some trouble, some tribulation.

Tendal and Margaret light the white window candles planted in sprays of holly and red berries. They join the bride and groom, Connie and David, in the second pew on the lectern side. Rita and Tommy Druthers enter. Rita sees the children kneeling and chortling in the chancel and goes to investigate. She pushes herself into the crowd of little ones, calling out, "Torn Jesus, Torn Jesus, you're back. Thank you, you are back. I knew you'd come back." Rita falls to her knees and embraces the children beside her like a hen pressing chicks beneath her wings. Tommy blushes and goes to the pew where he and his mother always sit. The children bicker over who will hold the baby. Rita chides them saying, "Now children, miracles happen when we pray to the Torn Jesus. We must be reverent."

Rebecca Dreiden, five, pipes in, "But I thought Cal was the reverent."

The unexpected arrangement causes a stir, both of amazement and awe, and of outright rebellion. "How dare they change the arrangements! It's never been this way! Some complain bitterly. On Christmas Day, the place never smells like cherry, or feels so warm, or has the candle at the center of the sanctuary. A capella Renaissance carols are foreign to a congregation that prefers early American carols, Bach, and the red hymnal.

When the voices from the speaker fade, and the congregation settles, Kathy begins a familiar medley of carols. She looks to the pastor and shrugs as if to say, "Oh well, here we go, ready or not." Calline smiles, thinking to herself how refreshing "off-script" can be. Wonder grips the soul; hers, anyway. For the many who are devoted to ritual more than meaning, that anything changes is pure sacrilege. She reaches for little Rebecca's hand and leads her with the lighted taper to the Christ candle, a large white cylinder rising higher than ever before from the circle of evergreen and berries.

"I can do it by myself," Rebecca complains with a jerk, almost losing the flame. With steady hand and careful eye, Rebecca, not over four feet, holds the sputtering flame to the wick of the Christ candle. The wick ignites. Kathy comes in with a rousing rendition of "Oh Come All Ye Faithful." It's as if the whole world is biting its tongue because it must.

"Emmanuel, God is with us," the pastor, feeling full and alive with such good news, announces. For this brief moment, she forgets that half the members may walk in a matter of days, the budget will collapse, and she herself may be history.

Even before the first hymn is finished, she imagines the killjoys strategizing how to catch and prosecute the S.O.B. who stole the doll, took the manger, broke into the building, upped the thermostat, moved the Advent wreath and Christ candle, rearranged the plants, resurrected the speakers, and added the foreign tunes. Calline dreads hearing once again the ancient, worn out chant, devoid of meaning or truth: "but it's not how we've always done it."

George Connors is the first naysayer to push his way to the pastor in the greeting line. "Did it not occur to you to ask the children to go back to their seats during the service? They were a disturbance, and others complained, too." *When has George not been miffed?* thinks Calline, as she bites her tongue. *This is the time, perhaps, Jesus meant not to waste pearls on swine,* she thinks.

Rachael, more frail than Calline has ever seen her, pushes her son to the side. "Let's talk soon, Cal. I need you right now."

Pulling at her robe, Lilly Smith's little girls, bright and tiny, cry, "We prayed to The Torn Jesus, that he'd bring us a little brother. Will he, Reverend Cal? Do you think he'll answer our prayer?" The girls look up as to an oracle.

Calline blesses their heads and swoops to lift them, each in one arm, their red velvet dresses flowing, their faces peach-pink, and their eyes as full of wonder as unscathed newborns. "Let's wish the baby a happy birthday, girls."

"Happy Birthday, Jesus," they call in unison.

"Infect me with enthusiasm for life, trust in the unseen, belief in all that is beautiful and good. Won't you? This is my prayer this day, dear Lord," the pastor tears-up as she hugs the girls, secretly wishing they were hers, and moves to share Christmas goodies with her flock.

CHAPTER TWENTY

AT THE COAT rack, people wrap in thick overcoats, hats, and scarves to leave. Thomas approaches, seeming particularly joyous. "Cal, wasn't this morning amazing? We couldn't have staged that if we'd tried. On a less uplifting note, another meeting at our house should happen soon. Grimsley is spinning her web as we speak."

"I agree, Thomas, about soon. I'm doing the Harris and Connors wedding on New Year's Eve, then off to Bermuda for seven days. Of course, you know that. I just like hearing myself say it." Calline giggles, then shrugs to think her church seems on a mission to kill the Light, so irrepressible in the sanctuary this morning.

"A break for you will do your soul good, I hope," says Thomas, supportive and caring. "Perhaps you'll return all revved up, good to go."

"Nice pun, Thomas; I'm thinking a lot these days of crystal waters, soft sands and warmth, lots of sun. But don't think I'm not thinking about what Alexis has up her sleeve. I'm dreading it." Calline frowns.

Terrifically out of character, Thomas turns toward the pastor and gazes at her eye-to-eye, throws his arms wide and beckons a hug. Never inclined to hug any parishioner except Sorrel, she finds it easy to return the gesture, swelling with love and gratitude for this man capable of wonder, compassion, justice, and patience. *How will he navigate the weeks ahead?* she wonders. How will they all?

"Merry Christmas, Thomas, and thanks for everything. God be with thee and us."

"In more ways than one," he laughs, alluding to the three Jesuses mentioned in her sermon. She helps him into his tweed vest and navy coat. He grabs his old Scottish wool cap, stuffs it on his head, and trots to meet Myrtle. Calline watches him reach for her hand, as if without her flesh on his at least once a day, life itself would lose its charge.

As Calline pulls on her hat and wraps her scarf, Sorrel and Billy approach. Sorrel's cheerfulness seems out of place given Elizabeth's sorry state. "You seem chipper this bright day, Sorrel," says Calline, warmth rising in her spirit.

"What about the scene in there today, Rev? Who do you think went to the trouble to do all that? I'm wondering if it wasn't that stranger, that tall guy with the dreadlocks." Sorrel kicks ice from the stoop and puts his arm around Billy's shoulder for an anchor from slipping. Calline hauls on the door to lock it.

"Whoever did it, I think it was a God set-up, to show us skeptical mortals once again that mystery and surprise can come any time, any place. The point seems to be whether we can receive what God brings, the way God wants to bring it. Profound, huh?" Calline plays with her scarf. "I'd just as soon revel in it a bit before trying to solve the whodunits. You know the skeptics and doubters are already on the case. Killjoys." She puts her arm in Billy's and the three walk toward the parking lot.

"You said that in your sermon, about accepting God's actions, being open to God's timing and stuff," says Billy. "It takes me a while to get what you say sometimes, but after the Torn Jesus disappearing and all the stuff in the sanctuary today, I'm guessing God is in charge pretty much, and kinda likes to keep us off balance some." Billy kicks a hardened clump of dirty snow and puts his arm around Sorrel. "Huh, Dad?" Poignant and deep is the affection between the two men. Sorrel looks over at Calline flanking Billy, and winks.

"I think you're receiving some good stuff this Christmas, Billy. Romance, too? I love your girl. She's awfully sweet." Calline squeezes his hand.

Huddled together at the Durango. Sorrel offers, "Well, we're off to see Elizabeth. Merry Christmas. How about a group hug?" The three move in together and press cold, pink cheeks. A surge of precious affection overcomes her, but as abruptly the sensation of a boxer's winning punch right into her solar plexus, overtakes. That people depart from the church accompanied by a loved-one is not unusual, but at Christmas while she stands watching the two most special men in her life, besides her Dad, drive away and leave her standing there in the parking lot, alone? "Oh my, this hurts," she whispers and turns for home, hunching into a sub-zero wind chill.

Although the tradition of visiting the Cemetery for Indigents on Christmas Day ceased to be, Calline continued the trek to the cemetery on her own. Adorning the simple grave stones with poinsettias satisfies a need to reach out to those whom Jesus was the first and last to include. She is drawn by the eerie silence of the stark surroundings and the solitude it invites, by her sermons about the folks buried there ("Everyone buried at the Cemetery for Indigents was important to someone at some time. Ignoble endings through bad choices or bad luck do not define them. The only ending with God is a good one. John and Jane Doe just gave up.")

Dressed in her dad's navy wool trousers over long johns, three layers on top, a thick scarf and cable-knit cap, Calline loads two poinsettias and a wool-coated Bingo into her car. The Buick's engine coughs and sputters in protest. The sun is finicky; the thermometer hovers at ten. Except for an occasional quick-stop gas station, stores are closed. Calline eases the car around corners and down streets littered with the morning's superfluity. She drives slowly by the land that abuts the cemetery, land held in perpetuity for High Dunes' first people, the Little River Band of the Algonquin. "Don't you think, Bingo, that God has a special unit in heaven that collects the prayers of the elders still here, who drum, and whoop, and call?" Bingo's jowls slosh spit on the window.

"Who are the savages today?" She recalls her sermon on "Native Remembrance Sunday." A lot of church folks didn't like her mixing politics and religion, but who else would turn the tables in the temple, awaken the slumbering giant of indifference, speak truth to power, if not the church and her prophets?

The tiny wooden post and a faded hand-painted sign that reads "Burial Place" pokes from a sumac bush and is evident only to those who know to look. Naked shrubs and a dilapidated wooden split-rail fence border the field that, in its dimensions, could have been a football field. In the middle stands a huge, bare old maple, which two months ago was as adorned in its leaves as Scarlet O'Hara in a crimson ball gown. Snow covers the burial markers, simple red bricks, but Calline knows they line up in rows with no indicators that a person lay beneath.

A small melted spot at the maple's base allows Calline to kneel and bend forward to place her poinsettias, wilted from the cold. In her imagination, the flower adorns the grave of a woman whose life held promise. But life's ups and mostly downs caused pain so hard, she numbed with drugs and alcohol. One night, she leaned against a building at a Salvation Army doorway, finished her fifth, went to sleep, and froze. The medical examiner tagged her toe "Jane Doe #7". Two volunteers from St. James Catholic Church threw dirt on the pine box purchased by tax payers, and prayed for Jane's soul to transcend Purgatory.

Calline, emerging from her reverie wonders if she should be alarmed to see Bingo's back hairs up. Here she is, out in the boonies with a mush for a dog, while a stranger approaches. Bingo leans against Calline and wags her whole bottom half. She plants all fours, and growls an intense *don't come closer* to none other than the man with the dreadlocks and the incandescent starry eyes. If this man were truly dangerous, Calline wonders, would Bingo, the sweetest canine on earth, be of any use in the defense department?

"It's okay, pup. I'm harmless, I promise." The man reaches to the dog with a soft open hand and she sniffs it, her behind tucked in. Up this close, in the light of day, he is much taller than Calline realized, and he's skinny and older. Deep wrinkles and stubs of beard, a saloon mustache twirled and waxed, dreadlocks twisted from beneath an old wool cap, tell her he's lived hard, but has learned. His chapped lips cover rotting teeth that disappoint an otherwise fabulous smile. He's wearing the same scissor-hemmed long coat. It's worn, but neat and clean. Rough brogans and worn wool socks, Calline hopes, keep his feet warm and dry. His gait is slow and labored, and he depends on a stick he picked up along some wooded trail.

"You're not a serial killer, I hope." A bizarre question of someone she knows nothing about, but who seems as harmless as Santa, and truly loving.

"The only serial killing I've done is of love and joy, and if I do any more murder, I hope it will be of my own sorry attitude." He rubs his chin, spits, leans into his stick, and watches Calline and the dog. as if waiting for the wisdom of the world.

"Girl, I think I'm probably safe, you can relax," Calline assures her guardian. This could be a mistake, but Bingo relaxes and sniffs at the man's pockets. He hands her a morsel of chewed jerky.

"You and I seem to have the same destinations of the past twenty-four hours." Calline grins, leaning against the tree trunk, arms akimbo, as casual as if standing at a bus stop.

He grins and won't move his eyes from hers, putting her off-balance.

"What brings you to the cemetary?" She is genuinely curious.

"I was always told I was a Nobody, and I bought that story about myself. To keep the story alive I did everything that had me headed to this place, until I decided to change. I got rid of the dead wood, lost the people who weren't helping. I asked the Almighty to teach me how to be Somebody, how to do things His way." He spits out a dark liquid. "I come back here to be reminded of where I could end up any day if I don't resist the slide of complacency and laziness." He leans over and spits a dark wad into the snow.

"His way, you said. God's way? Which is?" Calline is fully engaged to hear from this man, a man who once was lost and now seems found.

"I like surprising folks. I like to help them see there's something beyond their own limited projections, beyond ego, beyond the two dimensions most of us think are reality, when they're not. There really is something out there. Ever heard of quantum physics? Don't get me going." He laughs and pulls up a wad from deep inside his throat, and spits on the poinsettia. Gross, but Calline is too captivated by morning's mysteries to care.

"Was that your quantum physics in our sanctuary this morning?" Calline asks, gently chiding, sure it was he who stole the doll and reset the sanctuary. "How did you get in, get the doll? Tell me. I'm all ears." She shifts from foot-to-foot for warmth, her hands dug deep into the pockets of her coat. Bingo nips at the man's hand.

"Your door lock is an amateur's dream. You left the manger outside and I was in the building that one Sunday, you remember. I watched a couple of kids go into a room, then one came out with the Jesus doll, saw me, got scared and handed the doll to me and ran. I figured a helluva surprise was in the making. Did you like it?" He grins, big black holes where teeth should be, and rubs bony, scarred palms on his tattered coat.

Calline kicks her boots on the ground to keep her toes from numbing. "I have to say, you put a real twist on our season, which has been twisted in a pretty good knot already." She laughs, letting the tensions of the day roll off.

"To me," says the gentle man, "the surprises in life force us to trust God bringing whatever God wants to bring in God's time, a kind of cosmic peek-a-boo, wouldn't you say? But you have to be willing to trust and wait and hell, nobody likes to wait for a damned thing. Just the human condition, you reckon?" He rubs his hands together and scratches his chin.

Calline rubs her hands for heat and stretches up on her toes. "I don't know you from Adam, but it feels like you have come at a good time. That was some show in there. Our church is going through some tough stuff right now. I'm not sure if we needed that or didn't? I just know I did." Suddenly she feels vulnerable and shy feeling driven into by his mysterious blinkless gaze.

"Our little secret," he winks and smiles. He turns to walk away, Bingo following, her slobbery jowls pushing against his pocket.

"Hey, what's your name, anyway?" Calline imagines that if she follows him, he'll vanish into thin air.

He calls back, "Wonder-full Counselor." He knocks his tattered cap on its side, waves it in the air, spits, and hollers, laughing, "Y'all go on home. Enough surprises for one day." His entire countenance is alchemy.

CHAPTER TWENTY-ONE

FANTICIES OF HER behind burrowed into pink, warm coral sand on an island far away in five days and counting, the mystery and wonder of Christmas Eve and Day, the man called Wonder-full Counselor, and the encounter with Sorrel when she dropped him home on Christmas Eve—these thoughts make her heart sing.

"Ahh, Bermuda. But hell first," she murmurs, as she slips into her white wool trousers, boots, cap and gloves, and situates Bingo with her toys and bowl of fresh water. The second emergency meeting at the Dreiden's will commence in thirty minutes. *What havoc can Alexis Grimsley and her troops bring? How will we respond?* Calline's anxiety rises.

The critical nature of the meeting draws all but J.B. whose absence is due to an ill family member. *An excuse, most likely*, thinks Calline. He can't be proud to have been one of the signers of the Petition. Chairman Smit will be there for the Search Committee. The very pregnant Lilly Smith, defying orders to bed rest, can't wait to get her ears burning; that's probably why she's come. Gunther for missions comes without Nancy, for whom the kitchen has become too hot. Kathy, Sorrel, and Tendal are as reliable as clouds in November. Myrtle passes out macadamia cookies and pours hot Lipton. Thomas is fidgety, evidence that he's more eager than at the last meeting to get this over and done with. To him, it's just plain un-Christian to hold a meeting like this so close to Christmas.

"The honors, Cal?" Thomas invites Calline to open with prayer. She notices feeling jittery and tired, as inspired and as inspiring as cold, under cooked grits.

"Contemplatives tell us that willingness to consent in silence and trust to God's action within, is all we need to do. God will do the rest. So, I invite us to just be silent."

"You mean do nothing?" Kathy asks, always digging for deeper understanding. Calline nods assent and smiles. Kathy shrugs her shoulders and surrenders to the process.

"Okay, get comfortable, close your eyes, and pick a word; stay with that word and return to it when you feel distracted. I'll time us for five minutes—a long time when you're not used to silence, but I think this time will do us good," Calline gently encourages the skeptical group. She fears this was a bad idea. Sitting still for long is not in these folks' spiritual toolbox. But after coughing and giggling from Gunther and Thomas, calm descends, and the five minutes go quickly. Calline feels strangely refreshed and the group appears to have relaxed a bit.

Thomas puts his tea cup aside and takes charge. "Well, we are now at part two of the issue of the Petition. After a talk with Peter Vanderlaan, Cal said we should go ahead with our intention to interview and possibly call Peter; we should not let the threat interfere with how we feel the Spirit leading us to act. So here we are and I thank you all for coming."

Everyone agrees in theory. The facts are daunting. If Sorrel is correct, eighty percent of the budget walking would effectively end church.

"We do have the gift from Helen's daughter. Perhaps that money could keep the lights on, pay Cal and Dalia until we can figure something else," says Sorrel. "Pledges are not even half what they were this time last year, according to J.B."

"We can't let those meanies control the church. What a crummy way to deal." This from Lilly who folds her hands on her full-orbed belly and belches unreservedly. "I'll make sure the children have their Sunday school, lights or no lights, pastor or no pastor. We will need heat, though." Lilly belches again. "Excuse."

"God's frozen people," blurts Sorrel. "We can't have that!" He grins at Calline who can't conceal her amusement even during such a grim exchange.

Smit, who speaks only in tones of authority, pipes in, "Plain and simple, we've been hijacked. Never negotiate with the bastards. I play bridge with J.B., and not long ago, played a round of golf with Richard. And what's with Rachael's son, George?" Smit is beet-red from this effusive outpouring.

"If we use Willomena Brainard's gift, then how do we pay Peter?" Kathy asks.

Since J.B. is absent to explain treasury details, Sorrel takes a stab. "Several of our members have made bequests to the music program. There's probably enough to pay Peter and use the sixty grand to cover membership and pledge shortfalls until we can rebuild."

Thomas looks impatiently at his watch and offers, "If we have a consensus to move ahead, then the next step would be to let the petitioners know we have no intention of backing away. Calline? You haven't said anything." He fidgets hoping she doesn't get long-winded.

"Is there any chance for some gesture of reconciliation? I think we have to sit down and reason with one another, try listening." Calline knows her words are more obligatory than heartfelt. At least they're biblically consistent.

"Just what format do you suggest, Cal?" Thomas sounds incredulous.

"Something like the shouting match we had when we were renovating the chapel?" says Sorrel, rubbing his head. "We almost split over that, you all surely remember."

"Something like that," Calline says, deflated by the gap between the vision of Shalom and incorrigible human nature.

Suddenly, the two griffons bark insanely at the front door. Myrtle gets up to look through the peephole and gasps, "Oh my God, it's Richard Grimsley, J.B., and George. How'd they know we were here?" As if she'd practiced the drill a thousand times she locks the doors and pulls the curtains and shades. By some instinctive prompting, everyone pulls chairs in closer.

"Pray? I have no idea what we should do," Thomas says, pulling on his socks.

"Call 9-1-1?" giggles Kathy.

"Hide?" Lilly joins in the feigned mirth.

"We've got to think of something, quick. They're not going to stand out there in the cold, knowing we're in here meeting about what to do with them," Calline says lamely. "You got any ideas?" She looks to heaven.

"Let them in."

An insistent knock follows the doorbell chimes. The dogs are crazy now.

"We could turn the dogs loose on them," says Smit.

"We could all just leave out the back door; Myrtle could let them in and feed them her killer cookies," says Kathy, who hacks out an anxious giggle.

"Sugar does loosen stiff necks," says Myrtle returning to the door to peek.

"I believe we're supposed to let them in," Calline says in a broken whisper.

All heads nod, but no one has a clue what to do once George, Richard, and J.B. are in.

"Myrtle, honey, open the door." Thomas rises to bring three chairs from the dining room. He places them in a straight row facing off with their chairs, as in conventional warfare.

Two sharp knocks and the knob clicks. Silent, Myrtle opens the door. J.B., Richard, and George, also silent, march in formation behind Thomas to their row of chairs. Everyone seated, battle lines are drawn. Now what?

The toilet flushes. "My water broke. Call Tommy. I think we're going to have a baby! Now!" screams Lilly.

CHAPTER TWENTY-TWO

SORREL CALLS CALLINE shortly after he arrives home from the Dreidens'. "What were J.B., Richard, and George up to, anyway, Cal?"

"Honestly, I'm not sure, Sorrel. But I do sense some funky divine intervention. We seem to be receiving a generous supply lately." Calline giggles, as if all a person can do when God intervenes in such unexpected and creative ways is laugh.

"Smit sure stepped up to the plate with a confidence I've never seen." Sorrel laughs.

Myrtle and Thomas half-carried, half-walked Lilly to Smit's Bronco. They laid her in the cargo area where she could stretch out and breathe. "I want Kathy to come with," she moaned to the gawking onlookers. Kathy climbed in and positioned herself awkwardly among hunting equipment and dog blankets, taking Lilly's hand and blowing on her belly. Why, no one quite understood, but Lilly didn't seem to mind. Smit placed a red lamp atop his vehicle, backed out gently, and then floored it, fishtailing such that everyone thought his tires would never gain traction.

Lilly, with her knees up, blew like a locomotive climbing as each contraction came closer. "Not too soon, Lord," Lilly prayed, then screamed, "Oh God, no, not now, please!" Lilly was situated in Delivery no more than thirty minutes when Contesta Lolita Smith entered the world gooey, red, and smooshed. The two older sisters seemed to have forgotten their wish for a boy. Each ecstatically took turns holding and kissing their newest family member.

"It occurs to me Sorrel, maybe this baby came to save, too," said Calline. "She bought us some time. When those three men walked into the Dreidens' living room, I thought I'd, well you know, I'd . . ." Calline giggles, stifling an expletive.

"Should I fill in the blank?" Sorrel laughs, his fertile imagination running a million miles an hour.

"Spare us, dear. Spare us. For now, I just need to burrow into some serious sleep."

"By yourself?" Sorrel teases.

"No. With the dog. Good night, Sor." Oh God, to have some neutral place in her heart for this man, especially now that Elizabeth is getting better. Elizabeth divulged on the phone to Calline that she was hopeful she would be back to her old self, confessing she wasn't sure who that was, but she intended to find out. All Calline knows is that Sorrel and Elizabeth's trip will coincide with hers by two days. It will require power from beyond to enjoy solitude and sun on the same island without obsessing. Calline is fairly certain Sorrel doesn't know her vacation plans. They've been too busy with crisis management and Christmas to speak of island vacations.

Seven hours of comatose sleep later, Calline grabs the phone receiver before her head is off the pillow, eyes stuck shut with sleep. "Lord, it's freezing in this house! Hello, sorry?"

"Cal, hate to call so early, but Rachael Connors went by ambulance last night to the ER and Nancy Dobbs just called to say they moved her to room 2332. There's a message from Vee Morgan for you to call. She sounds not too hot, but not as bad as the bride and groom who fought their message into the phone, and . . . ."

"Dalia, is that you? Did I just hear that Rachael is in the ER?" Calline sits up and picks the crust from her eyes. Goosebumps rise on her arms from the cold. Bingo whines to go out.

Dalia repeats all three messages. In uncharacteristic, but welcome expediency she says, "Your trip. Anything you need from me?"

This may be the last time Calline has Dalia's full attention to the details of her Bermuda vacation. "Folks know you're the person to contact. But short of some catastrophe, and I mean something really bad, I'm as good as gone, got it? Only you and Dad know how to find me if absolutely necessary. Got it? Please don't pork Bingo up on treats. Her heart, remember? Promise?" Calline shivers and holds her crotch, while Bingo's whining and scratching at the door intensifies.

"Promise. I'm doing a few things to help Pastor Vanderplast for Sunday, then I'm out to return gifts and get candles for the wedding. Anything you need?"

"No, sweetie. Hey, thanks for all you're doing during this busy time. Talk later. Bless you, D. Bye." Dalia can be cooperative and thoughtful. Calline is grateful Reverend V. can fill in the Sunday after Christmas so she can concentrate on Connie's and David's wedding. This knot has a few extra loops to it. Weddings with extra loops aren't in textbooks, certainly not this one.

I've got to see Rachael, Calline thinks, while waiting at the door for Bingo. She knows Sorrel, Elizabeth, and Billy are right now en route to Bermuda, the Petition is still circulating, and money has dried up. Her prayers this morning are brief and perfunctory, as she tries in vain to get warm and to find the number for Benny's Heat & Air. Hot anything tastes good and Bingo looks pathetic, like there's no way she'll keep her bare belly warm in a house whose insides almost match the outside.

"You can come with." Calline says to Bingo, as the dog spins and stares dead on at the front door. In no time, Calline, dressed in dark wool slacks, a cowl cable sweater and angora scarf, takes off on foot. The day is young, the sun hidden; the freeze numbs the tip of her nose and fingers.

But for the draft that ripples the curtains, her office is warmer than home. The church trustees, via Tendal Harris's recent memo, have asked that Bingo not bring her odors to the church office, but today has to be an exception. Poor dog would freeze in her own living room. Calline answers the phone after the first ring.

"Yea? David, stop it, damn it! Hello?" It's Connie.

"Connie, Rev. Cal, here." *Now what? These two are killing me!*

"Oh, hi Rev; David and I are fighting so I think the wedding's off. David needs a proctologist, not a wife; he's being such an asshole."

"Give me that phone, bitch. Give it here, now!" Something falls and breaks. "Rev. Cal. This is David . . . . back off Harris, before you're dog food. Cal, I don't think I can handle her. She's a bitch on wheels. You touch me again, I'll . . ." David's voice fades.

Connie utters something in the background, a muffled sound, like David has her in a mug grip.

Calline rubs her forehead, feeling tight and intolerant of the characteristic buffoonery of Connie and David. "Hey, you two. Now stop! Connie, please put the phone on microphone and both of you sit down. Or I'll hang up now and there won't be any wedding." To her surprise, the receiver goes silent.

"Do you want to talk now, or should you come to my office where Bingo and I can supervise? I've trained Bingo to put on a mean ankle lock. If you want to go that route then come on over, we'll talk. Peacefully." Frankly, she hopes they stay put.

"I'm allergic to dogs and a dog almost bit off David's wee-wee. Sure glad it didn't!" Connie laughs. David laughs. Feels like a thaw.

"Our parents are all fighting, Cal. All four said they might not even come to the wedding. We're having it no matter what," growls the determined bride.

"New Year's Eve, seven? We still have to tie up some details. We'll just have to hope your parents can act grown up and get along long enough for you two to say 'I do'."

"What if I say 'I don't'?" quips David.

"Ass! Then I'll say, 'I won't either!'" Connie snarles. Vicious.

"Hey, now you guys, nerves get real tight before a wedding. You don't want your parents' nerves going haywire, so you'll have to white-knuckle good behavior to calm them. If you two calm down, they'll follow your example." How come the pastor doubts?

"Hey, didn't think of that. Kissy-huggy, honey." Connie teases David who makes some kind of weird barking sound.

"Remember, I need you two and your parents in the sanctuary right after worship. Rehearsal." More giggling and click. Calline looks at the receiver and wonders what all that was? In walks Vee.

"Darling, I was just going to figure out how to find you. I got your message. Sit." She spins her desk chair to meet the eyes of a very forlorn young woman. And if a dark face can look pale, Vee's is a ghost.

"Cal, I don't feel so good." Much too thinly dressed for the weather, Vee looks horrid. She still isn't showing. Calline puts her hand on the girl's forehead.

"Child, you are hotter'n Hades. Dalia, we need your car. I have to get Vee to the hospital!"

CHAPTER TWENTY-THREE

WHILE SITTING IN the waiting room Vee dozes. Delirious, "Rev., my baby? They savin' my baby? I feel so hot. And then I feel cold." In spite of her fear, Calline finds inner reserves to comfort the frightened girl.

"I think I know why they call these places emergency rooms, Rev. You sit here so long 'til you almost die, then you have your emergency," says Vee, miserable.

Finally, an attendant comes with a wheelchair that transports Vee to a gurney in cubicle 4 in the High Dunes Hospital Emergency Room. A doctor steps in, puts his hand on Vee's forehead while he speaks fast doctor gibberish to an intern.

"You're not family, Reverend Simpson, but given your relationship with Miss Morgan, can you be ready to stand by the family if need be?" Calline's anxiety spikes. *Stand by if need be?* "A fever like Miss Morgan's—we think it's from something she ate—is a danger to mother and baby. She's out of the woods, but the jury's still out on the baby's safety." He takes his pen and makes notes on a clipboard. "We've notified Mrs. Morgan." The doctor gently shakes Vee's shoulder, shines a light in her eyes, presses around her belly, and orders her to open her mouth. He asks her a few questions, mostly which he answers before she can speak. He jots more notes, and gives an order to a nurse, then leaves.

"They will do all they can, honey. Shhh now, take a sip of water." Calline hands her a cup with a straw. A nurse lays a cool cloth on her forehead. "We'll just have to wait and see and pray. While you sleep, I'll slip up to the second floor to see Mrs. Connors. Is that O.K. with you?" Never mind, Vee is in la-la land.

"Rachael? It's Cal, dear." She whispers loudly at the threshold of Room 244, beyond a sleeping patient in bed 1, to the bed by the window where Rachael rests. The woman lifts her head and smiles brightly. She radiates, in fact. Calline has seen how, often, before people cross over to the next life, they become unusually animated. Is Rachael being prepared to make the transition?

Calline pulls a chair to the side of Rachael's bed and takes her warm, flaccid hand. It is pale, skeletal, and bruised. Bags overhead drip clear solutions into tubes attached to the needles that pierce her other bruised hand.

"I was sipping my morning coffee, reading the paper, then got up and felt like a black veil had been dropped over half my face. My brain went haywire with confusion and fear. George came with mail and saw me go down. He called 9-1-1 and here I am. Stroke, they tell me." Her words slur. "I spoke with mother yesterday." Her mother has been dead for forty years. Rachael's deep gray eyes smile between layered, drooping lids. Calline thinks she can almost see a glint of her soul, eternal within the flesh that seems transparent and stretched over twiggy bones and swollen, gnarled joints.

"I feel Jesus standing close by these days. He always has, I just feel Him more. It's sweet, really. This old tin can I'm in, rattling, loosening, and rusting, but inside the container I feel the me that's always been rising to meet heaven's gaze; it is quite beautiful."

"What a beautiful vision, sweet lady." The affection between the two women is strong and deep. Just being together, no words required, fills them both with the luster of deep friendship. "Our Vee—you met her a few times, scavenging in the Hall for food—is in the ER right now," Cal whispers. Rachael smiles weakly and nods. Her compassion for the children in the neighborhood will carry beyond her death. Calline knows Rachael will leave a sizable portion of her estate to Children's Haven, a layover before foster placement for children rescued from abusive homes. "Vee's baby might be in trouble. Help me pray, would you?" Rachael shuts her eyes and squeezes the pastor's hand and prays in soft, lilting tones. She calls it her talk-to-Jesus voice. Calline feels the same spirit raising the hairs on her arms, like when she and Sorrel prayed at Elizabeth's bedside.

Rachael's grip loosens; a small bubble forms at the corner of her mouth when she exhales. Her breathing would hardly flicker a flame. Calline places the woman's hand by her side and pulls the blanket up to her chin. A kiss on her forehead seals the visit. "Thank you for all you've shown me. Thank you. Sleep sweetly, dear friend." Calline tip-toes from the room, down the hallway, to the hospital parking lot.

Snow mixed with sleet, coming down in wind-driven sheets, makes the drive home a chore. The slowed trip gives Calline time to think about Vee, a child herself, nurturing an unborn infant whose life may be in the balance, while Rachael prepares to leave her earth's journey. A blinking rear light in front startles her from her thoughts of the circle of life, turning, Reality holding it all in exquisite, delicate balance.

She cannot strip herself from her formal clothes and get herself covered in her worn flannels and lamb's wool slippers soon enough. A bowl of Dalia's mother's special clam chowder—just like her family made for generations in New England—tastes exquisite. She feeds Bingo, builds a fire, and indulges her favorite reprieve: talking to Patty.

Patty is on break from her professorship at a small liberal arts college in Chicago, where she has been tenured for ten years. After her short stint in the church in New England, a small Midwestern college approached her to teach philosophy and religion as adjunct. Soon she met and fell in love with Patrick, Professor of English, married, and was blissful for two years until she saw Patrick in a restaurant, ogling a student. She forgave him, sought counseling for the couple and for herself, and got pregnant. She was sure the marriage had turned a corner. A miscarriage in first trimester, and a strange woman's voice on their answering machine that said, "Patrick, honey, please call as soon as you can, I'm desperate," convinced her that God had written new orders for her life. Patty returned to single life, relieved, if not bruised and disappointed.

"Hey, woman. Merry Christmas, again," Calline says, delicately sipping soup from a hot spoon. "Tell me of you, your Christmas, family, and all." Getting her friend, who was trained from childhood to keep secrets, to open up is an ongoing challenge.

"Mom and Dad insist on having the annual New Year's get-together at the Club, when I wish we could just be together at the estate, just us: mom, dad, kids, and grand kids. Not the whole crazy bunch. The place is so tainted, yet it symbolizes for me, oddly, the stability I felt before I knew the truth about Dad's sordid history."

One summer, Calline visited Patty at her grandfather's estate home on Lake Michigan on the Illinois side. The mansion was built by Patty's great-grandfather whose ties to the mob were legendary. Only to her best friend, to whom she trusts her life, does Patty share her experience of being her father's daughter; half Italian, traceable to a small village at the tip of Italy's boot. From a very young age, Patty knew that her life was different than that of her schoolmates. Insulated by old country ways, both Italian and Irish, Patty created for herself an imaginary life, one she promised for herself as soon as she could escape the adult world surrounding her of secrets, lies, and subterfuge. Yes, and violence, too. She knew that for the rest of her life, demons of the evil underground in which her grandfather and father operated, as veiled as it all was, would follow her. The day she walked away from the family compound to lay claim to her dreams was the day she knew she would, at the deepest levels, never feel safe again. A target as big as a neon spot might as well be painted across her back. Only Calline knew that her dear friend, Patty Fritz, was formerly Patricia Callahan Frizzola. And that she was under constant protection by thugs whose job it was, literally, to cover her back.

"Your life is much more colorful, dear. I'll give you ten seconds for the six o'clock news beat, and then I want the scoop, baby. The scoop," says Patty, goading, happy to speak no more of herself.

Calline isn't sure where to start, so much has unfolded in such a tightly-compressed time. "Sorrel's in Bermuda, and I'm going after the wedding. I think I told you about the David and Connie knot, fit to be tied, those nuts, but lovable in their own outrageous way. Couldn't have planned Bermuda any better," Calline says, like she's sucking on a lemon.

"Does he know you'll be there?" Patty gets to the meat of matters. Calline loves and hates this about her friend, yet is happy to press on. What other human being will bear her burdens, look on with both objectivity and truth, pray for her, laugh, cry, and sacrifice time and money to make a live appearance? Friendship: God's apology for just about everything and everyone.

"Geeze, Patty. Yes and no. I haven't said a word, but how could he not know? Dalia works the switchboard. Need I say more? It's like if he and I acknowledged we'd be on a romantic island with no duties pressing, God would evaporate us, poof! Not like we don't already deserve some form of smiting, mind you." A long pause and a sigh on Calline's end; an exhale from the other. "He's so, well so—everything: sweet, attentive, handsome, smart, and funny. Sorrel's inventory I've mentioned a thousand times. My blood rushes when I'm with him, and I love beach walks and moon sets as much as the next unoriginal romantic, and what more beautiful place than Bermuda, and with him next to me? A condemning voice in my head practically yells, 'don't go there' and of course, I don't." She pauses. "Fantasies only, allowed."

"Far out, I've no doubt. Care to divulge? Or would I be shocked?" Patty exhales and feigns a big sigh.

"It's been so long since my desires were off-leash with a man. I just don't have anywhere to go with this, so I tell my heart to shut down and it only beats harder and more persistently. Geeze, Patty, what do I do with this?" Calline sinks into her chair, hugs her knees and watches the cinders glow. Like her love and lust for Sorrel, without something to feed the cinders, they eventually die out. She expects this will be her fate with Sorrel.

Patty's reluctance had not fanned the fire, when she said in another conversation, "I don't know, Cal. I'm with you, because I love you. I hear how perfect Sorrel is in so many ways. On the other hand, I fear for you in this, because I know how strict the injunctions are. The Code, and all that, you know. Never mind that he's practically married." Best to change the subject, Patty figures, resigned like her friend that the Sorrel fantasy should stay just that. "Heck, I don't go back to school until mid-January. Maybe I can fly over and join you for a couple of days? We haven't played Backgammon in ages. I'll bring my board and cards, too," Patty says in her rally-for-my-friend tone.

"Having you there would be a perfect distraction from obsessing about Sorrel and Elizabeth. Yes, do come, dear girl!" Talking to Patty does her soul good. She offers thanksgiving, pulls the comforter over herself and Bingo, and forgets everything until the radio says it's after nine. Worship begins in two hours.

The Sunday after Christmas is what folks call play-hooky-Sunday. Few children are present, and only two clusters of adults take their pews: a mix of the regulars and the Somers-Harris wedding party.

As soon as Calline enters the building—ruffled from the hurry to be there and look official—she can't avoid Alexis at the coat rack. Others crowd around to hang coats and hats. Richard hangs Alexis's fur-collared long black coat, looks over at the pastor, then whispers something to his wife. Alexis straightens quickly and glares at Calline. Their first contact since the house break-in, it gives Calline the creeps to see her now. What can either of them say? Do?

"Alexis, Richard, Merry Christmas. Welcome back," Calline says mechanically, her mind racing to the break-in at Dunes Crossing. She's been with a man on their bed, searched the private contents of desk and vanity drawers in their home, pried into Richard's bank statement. But could that be more criminal an act than stealing and reading personal intellectual property? Just returning to High Dunes two days ago, surely Grimsley must wonder where the journal went. But what can she say? "Somebody stole the journal I stole"?

Smit Rother, on search committee business, reaches over Calline to hang his coat. Within earshot of the Grimsleys, Smit says, "Can we set up an interview with our candidate as soon as you get back, Cal?"

Tipping her head in the direction of the Grimsleys, Calline fires Smit a look of intense warning. She reaches for his hand and guides him to the side. Alexis must be firing energy beams from behind. It feels like her back is on fire. Alexis must know, or strongly suspect, the journal was confiscated by none other than the Reverend Calline Simpson, spiritual leader of the church Alexis's great grandfather-in-law founded. "Sorry, Smit, but those two were the last I wanted in on this conversation." The harshness in her voice takes both by surprise.

"Sure, Cal. I understand," says Smit, eager to have plans for the interview with Peter sewn up. "Cal, I still don't know what the three men had in mind when they came to the Dreidens' when Lilly's water broke. Never mind, I want to get on with it. Kathy said she'd call Peter this week." Smit, intense and driven, waits for a response.

All Calline can say is, "Smit, you drive one heck of a delivery truck." They both laugh. "When and if we call Peter, the exodus of members who signed the Petition—and their money—will begin." Calline whispers sadly to Smit, who has the irritating habit of saluting to her whenever he feels insecure.

"It already has. The budget is a disaster. Sorrel and I talked on the phone this morning. J.B. and I will manage what money there is to keep us out of the dark and cold, and you and Dalia out of the red. Prudent reserve, earmarked for emergencies and pledges to the wider church, will take the hit. Let's hope it don't rain and the creek don't rise." Smit turns to wave at Thomas and Myrtle.

Calline is grateful to have the likes of Smit, Thomas, Sorrel, and others at the helm, which selfishly means guilt-free sunbathing and a rested body and soul to face the next rounds of confrontations. She recalls the conversations at the recent meeting with area clergy. Except for Pastor Hildreth's Revival Fires, a church spun from a movie theater, most were declining in members and dollars. First Methodist's Rev. Kindel said, "By necessity and by Spirit's compelling, the ministry will be returned to its rightful place: to a true priesthood of all believers." Like dinosaurs just before the comet, though, no clergy person in the room cheered.

Calline finds her way to a seat next to a couple who visited Christmas morning. Gertrude winds down the prelude, signaling Reverend Vanderplast to begin with warm greeting and a spontaneous opening prayer. For Calline, his message is poignant. "If you pay attention, you'll notice the italics and bolds of Christmas are really the ordinary high points of every day. Look closely, dig. Each day holds the potential of the gift of the birth we celebrate once a year, a gift that offers itself every day: Love." Calline reviews the punctuations of Advent and Christmas: the lost-then-found Torn Jesus, the visit of the stranger with the crystal eyes—God's eyes, and the stranger's message: there's so much more than meets the eye, and not the least, the triplets signifying to her God's abundant offering of Godself to all creation.

She thinks, *how easy to shy away, to give up, to fear that if we scratch the surface only bad things await, instead of expecting love, hoping for love, the never ending longing of each soul.* She hums the words to the Bette Midler song that repeats on the radio: "In the winter far beneath the bitter snow, lies the seed that with the sun's love, in the spring, becomes the rose."

Prayers go up for Rachael and Vee, family and friends, neighbors and countries torn and downtrodden by poverty and violence. Special blessings are offered to Connie and David for their nuptials, then announcements about food collections, a potluck next Sunday, and a special meeting of the music committee in two days. Good wishes extend to the pastor for vacation renewal. Love for her people rises in the pastor's heart. As if given an elixir, a Godly affection neutralizes her anxiety, her skepticism, her doubts, and she feels ready to face what lies ahead.

The blessing and benediction send folks to warm drinks and stale Christmas cookies. In ten minutes, Calline will face a jittery wedding party. She stuffs two rum balls in her pocket and quickly washes down some flat ginger ale punch.

"David, you creep, those shoes are gross." Unfortunately, the bride is her pissy self; Calline seriously doubts that Connie will get a grip for the wedding.

"Honey, David will wear the patent leathers we ordered with the tux, remember?" Margaret deals reason like a Vegas card shark.

"Now if everyone would follow me, we can begin." Calline talks softly and evenly, a voice a mother uses as not to wake the baby—a very colicky baby.

Things go calmly until Connie mentions her choice for the prelude, "You're So Vain" by Carly Simon.

"Our policy," Gertrude insists with as much control as she can muster, "is for classical, sacred only. This is . . ."

"O.K., everyone, let's take formation." Calline interrupts Gertrude, who has no idea of the consequences of inciting Connie's wrath. "I'll discuss this with you later," Calline says, aiming one of her 'please let this one go or there will be hell to pay' looks.

"Fight'em Red and Blue, Kill'em Red and Blue," David sings, sending Gertrude into a complete tizzy. He wants the recessional to be his school's fight song.

"Not to be! This is beyond the pale. You'll have to get another organist. I'm sorry." Gertrude covers her eyes and bows her head into her knees.

"O.K., we'll settle for Carol King's 'Will You Still Love Me?'" What possesses Connie to concede is anyone's guess. David attempts a struggle but instead, covers his groin, grins, and says, "O.K. I'll give up the fight song." Things seem to be proceeding quite smoothly.

"Ugh, March is not coming too soon," Gertrude sighs and waves the party on, as if shooing flies. Calline confirms that Mrs. Somers has the rings that she will hand to David's best man, Carl, who will hand them to the pastor, who will hand them to the bride and groom. A quick run through before the actual event should be enough preparation for the big day.

"Let's pray," Calline says to the baffled party.

CHAPTER TWENTY-FOUR

THE GROOM'S MOTHER, Mildred Somers, polishes off her second martini. An ashtray next to her drink spills over. "I'm going to dock your allowance if you don't stand still," she warns, her hands trembling while trying to fasten her son's magenta cummerbund. Carl, the groom's best man, stands by making snide remarks so David will snap.

Margaret strains to get her daughter's veil to fasten, which is ridiculous, as Connie just refreshed her butch, spiked and gel-stiff.

"This damned thing is a symbol of male domination. We'll see who dominates." Connie rips off the veil and tosses it to David. He grabs it and throws it back. The couple plays keep-away from Carl, who crashes into a crystal lamp that hits the floor, almost shattering.

"Now! You three, stop it now!" Margaret leaps and twists to intercept the veil, catching her dress on the heel of her pale satin shoe. The couch cushions what could have been a worse tear to her once perfect satin sheen hemline. "Connie, you're wearing that veil if I have to duct tape it on." Margaret moans to see the tear in her dress, the scuffing on one shoe, and the irreparably shredded veil. For the umpteen-trillionth time Margaret has accepted her daughter's invitation into her drama.

Calline adjusts the microphone, stole and cross, and glances quickly into her Book of Worship to make sure of the order. Margaret, one shoe on and one off, joins Tendal who looks at the minister. "You ready for this?" Tendal can't help but smile; he leans in and elbows Calline like an accomplice before a prank.

"Rhetorical question," Calline says, sensing a bizarre numbness and aliveness all at once. She looks at her watch. "It's seven on the nose, are you ready Mother and Father of the Bride?"

Tendal, Connie and Margaret huddle and hug. For a moment Connie's emotions seem appropriate and fitting for a bride on the threshold of cleaving and leaving. Connie leaves streaks of mascara on her mother's cheek.

Margaret excuses herself for last minute primping and wardrobe reparations when Gertrude begins the prelude. Hoping to blunt the shock of Carly Simon just before Wagner's "Wedding March," she performs a medley of Baroque and modern. The sanctuary lights dim. The candles left over from Christmas bring warmth. Giant white bows and sprays of evergreens and red berries garnish the ends of the pews. Two arrangements of blood red and white roses awash in greens and baby's breath frame fresh candles on the altar. The unity candle whose lighting symbolizes David's and Connie's lives merging like two separate rivers into one, stands on the Christ candle stand at the center of the chancel. At Christmas it's hard to mistake the unity candle as symbolic of Christ's presence. His first public act was a wedding, turning water to wine, taking something ordinary and essential for life and enriching it. Suddenly, Calline feels a sense of mirth fill her spirit. "Dear God, turn something into something tonight. I'm not sure what, exactly. I just know you will."

Best man, Carl, leads the mothers down the aisle to seat them on opposite sides in the very front. He waits at the chancel. Calline stands with Tendal and the bride at the entrance. No groom, though. Gertrude looks over her shoulder from the keyboard, wondering when to shift gears. Calline offers her the familiar time-out signal, which means to stretch the prelude. She knows Gertrude is annoyed.

"Where's your husband-to-be?" Calline asks, suppressing annoyance. "It's getting late."

"He's peeing. Creep, he's never on time for anything. Not even his own darned wedding. We'll see how he behaves for his funeral.

May be earlier than he expects." Connie swigs on the butt of a dead cigarette she pulls from an ashtray, returns it, then wipes the cigarette hand on her dress sleeve, leaving a sizable soot streak. She doesn't care. "David. Get your puny butt out here, now. We're getting married," Connie hollers. The mothers look back to see what's not going on, smiling appropriately, lips stretched.

"I can't. I can't go through with this," David whines from the men's bathroom.

Tendal looks at Calline, a gaze of complete desperation. "Lord, help us now, deliver us in this moment. We've a wedding to do," Calline prays.

"I need a glass of milk first. Then maybe I'll marry you," says David, whimpering. Gertrude shrugs, looking back to Calline. Calline time-outs her again and shrugs back. No one knows when the ceremony will begin. Hell, maybe it won't.

"Where is milk, Cal? I'll get him some milk," Tendal says, disgusted, totally fed up.

"I know we have Coffee Mate in powder form that we use at coffee hour. You could mix that up, or there might be some sour milk in the fridge," Calline offers, shrugging, rubbing her knee.

"Anything." Tendal dashes to the kitchen. Refrigerator and cabinet doors, and drawers open and slam. Cussing and groaning, ripping and tearing, Tendal pours and stirs powder with cold water. Chalky lumps of Coffee Mate refuse to blend.

"That looks like shit, man." David whines.

"If you don't drink this, I will take your bride out of this building and you'll never see my daughter again. Now drink it, goddammit!"

There's a long stretch of quiet. Another minute goes by. Gertrude looks back again, red-faced and embarrassed. It's fifteen after seven. Tired of standing and waiting for the groom, best man, Carl, sits, forlorn. The formal anticipation of the small congregation changes to casual whispering and chatting neighbor-to-neighbor.

"I reckon 'here comes the bride', should read 'where went the bride'," Thomas chuckles over at Myrtle, who giggles.

"I didn't get this far in life being no wilting violet. I'm marrying David Somers tonight if I have to haul him," Connie announces, slapping her dress at the knee. She stomps to the bathroom, and heaves David like a 100-pound sack of grain over her shoulder and marches back to join the minister. Tendal follows with a glass of lumpy-watery Coffee Mate.

"Come on, Cal, we're having a wedding," growls Connie, leading the procession down the aisle. Gertrude is doing her best with "You're So Vain". The congregation stands laughing uproariously. Horror becomes the mothers of the bride and groom.

Connie drops her betrothed at the altar. He flips onto his back, raises hands and feet to the sky, bicycles and hollers, "Jesus, Lord God almighty, I'm marrying this woman NOW. Ain't she something else?" He hoots and howls, then kneels, brushes himself off, and extends his hands to his big butch bride, who reaches to haul him up beside her.

Whatever a father feels when his rearing of the likes of Connie is done, at least officially, is how Tendal must be feeling when he kisses his daughter and seals her hand with David's. Joining his wife of forty-two years, Tendal cries along with Margaret.

It's not smooth sailing. The best man drops both rings. David announces he has to pee again; Connie keeps trying to retie her bow that undid while she hauled David. Carl needs to lower his head between his knees so he won't faint. David wants to French kiss. Connie refuses him. A small tussle breaks out, but somehow Calline manages to guide them to face the congregation. "Ladies and gentlemen, I introduce you—after not a little drama—to Mr. and Mrs. David Somers." Calline nods to Gertrude to begin the recessional.

"I have to say," writes Calline in her journal that night. "I've never seen a congregation so broken up with unholy raucous joy. Or a couple so well-suited."

CHAPTER TWENTY-FIVE

WHEN DRIVING IN Michigan, it's plain bad form to let a winter storm call the shots and slow you down, but to Calline, Earl the limo driver is pressing his luck. Winds howl like mad wolves, sweeping the snow into high wispy drifts. It's zero visibility, except for the tail lights on the Mack in front. Calline can see the speedometer tipping forty miles an hour, breakneck speed in these conditions. She gnaws her cuticles, not worried they will be late, but that Ford International will close altogether. How can she stand to wait another second to be in paradise?

"We're halfway there, so why turn back now? Thank Jesus for the Mack. He's plowing the way," says the driver who shuttles passengers the one hour back and forth between Grand Rapids and the shoreline.

"You'll start to see stars in the clearing, the further east we get, I promise," Earl announces. All the passengers know they'll eventually be clear of Lake effect, but no matter, the nervous Calline wants to leave nothing to chance.

"I'll park and wait. You may need a ride home," says Earl who's driven more than a few disgruntled passengers to and immediately from the airport.

Sure enough, the boards are lit up like Vegas, blinking "delayed" and "canceled." Calline's heart sinks. Her nerves are frayed, and her patience spider web-thin.

"Yours was the last one to take off out of O'Hare. They'll land at eight o'clock and be off from here by nine. We're backed up, but it's clearing," the agent says, her eyes never leaving her keyboard. Calline's watch shows five-thirty. After a lingering dinner, a visit with a lonely gentleman who tells his uneventful life story, and a phone call to Patty, there is finally the glorious news that Flight 1264 to Bermuda is boarding, gate A-12.

The flight attendant offers a blanket the size of a pillow case and a pillow the size of a postage stamp. The view out the window distracts her from uncharitable feelings towards her neighbor, whose arm shoves hers from the rest. What must Heaven be like, she wonders, as she marvels at the countless stars, the swollen moon shining into infinity? They will land soon in Bermuda where centuries earlier coral reefs were so impossible for ships to pass, the island was dubbed "Isle of Devils," then renamed after Spanish explorer Juan de Bermudez. When a hurricane blew a British ship across the reefs a hundred years later, the explorers—originally headed for the American colonies—decided to settle.

Calline sleeps most of the flight over, works a cross-word, then hears the rote announcements in preparation to land. Over a hundred drowsy passengers off board while customs officers sleepily check passports and wave arriving passengers through. A large gentle woman in crisp white uniform with a shiny brass pin engraved with "Beach Lodge Resort," waits to help with the luggage of everyone going her way. She stoops to pick up Calline's carry-on, and shoves it in with the other luggage in the back of the resort van.

Weary van passengers offload at the cul-de-sac surrounded by bright bougainvillea, day lilies shut for the night, and peach roses that frame the brick walkway to the open air reception desk. A proper British lad locates the keys to her room, and carries Calline's bags under each arm. After turning on lamps, settling the bags, he glances around as if to make sure everything is in order. He pulls back the covers on the bed. As soon as the boy is satisfied with a tip and the door is shut, Calline leaps into the amply-fluffed queen-sized bed, lets out a loud "Hurray, we made it—thank you, God!" It's too late to call anyone, but first thing in the morning she will call Dad and Patty to share her glee that for a few glorious days her only responsibility will be to fashion a tan, and read fiction.

The room is simple and spacious. Speckled, cool terracotta terrazzo floors are warmed by spacious throw rugs that blend with the soft pastel walls accented by moldings and rafters of Bermuda cedar. A wide French door opens to a lanai. Through the half-opened doors, she can hear the ocean and feel the night breeze. Head barely to pillow, giving thanks for this, the exhausted pastor is off in dreamland, forgetting everything until she glances at the clock. "It's after eleven!" Calline bolts up, shading her eyes from a bright beam of light. "I told Dad I'd call when I got here."

"Honey, is that you? How's the place?" Bob sounds distant, tired.

"Well, so far, Pop, it's fabulous. It's a miracle I made it. We got into the typical weather on the way to the airport. I'm exhausted, but can't wait to hit the beach. You O.K.?" This is their ritual conversation, held at least every other day, back and forth, two lone family members missing the woman who made hearth and home, and who, in spite of how different she was from them both, devoted herself to their happiness.

"Dad, the surf is waiting, and I'm already missing half the day's sun. Well, sort of. It's balmy and cloudy. Talk soon?" Calline suppresses a yawn.

"Sure, honey. Now, be careful. I love you!"

The lanai is the perfect place to break her fast after stale pretzels swished back with watery soda on the flight over. The Lodge offers a simple continental breakfast brought to the rooms every day, as late as noon. Just in time, Calline orders a carafe of coffee with the cheese croissants, mixed fruit, and plain yogurt. While she nibbles dreamily, her slippered feet on the table, she watches the sun, almost at mid-sky, peeking from behind a cloud. It is windy and cool for the region, but gracious and plenty warm by her standards. Birds and clouds form undulating shadows on the ocean's spectacular deep blue greens. The wind whips up white caps. A lifeguard rearranges his station, a giant red high chair off which a solid blue flag shimmers and snaps. He pulls the flag down and hoists another that is white with a green cross. *It must be some kind of warning*, she thinks. *It looks pretty choppy out there.* After prayers of heartfelt thanks, intercessions for Vee, Dad, Rachael, and the Dixons, Calline is only too eager to get to the ocean to sun and swim. "Let 'er rip, baby!" she says with the confidence of someone who spent her childhood taking on whatever surf nature could bring.

The Lodge provides chaises lounges and umbrellas. Though the sun appears to want to hide, an umbrella will offer shade while she reads. Calline and an elderly woman reading the "Paris Match" are the only beach combers. The lifeguard preens his body, angular and taught like he's recently pumped some serious iron. Following his example, Calline rubs ample measure of UVP lotion over pale skin that she hopes will transform to bronze tones to show off back home. By the time she has examined maps, researched restaurants, and read the local newspaper, her thoughts wander to Sorrel and Elizabeth, romantically tucked in somewhere on the same patch of earth as she. But they might as well be on the other side of the world. She prays, more from obligation, that this time is healing for Elizabeth and for the couple, and for sweet Billy, whom she imagines is having a ball exploring the island on a moped. Yet her body betrays her. How can she suppress romantic urges, a growing anguish for his warmth next to her, his lips on her, all over her, for that matter? "Please dear God keep my Sorrel thoughts with you," Calline prays as she walks by the guard stand toward the water.

The soft breezes sweep across her cheeks, as if God is touching her with tender care. Shadows and light dance on the crystal water that chops angrily from the strong winds. Just like Lake

Michigan on most days. Cocky as she approaches, she knows she'll be challenged out there.

"Careful, lady," says the adolescent guard, wrestling with his umbrella. "It's strong out there. All I can do is warn you." The wind catches the umbrella and blows it inside out, then rips the flimsy canvas from its ribs. Disgusted, the boy tosses the whole thing to the ground, and climbs down the ladder, watching the woman with the pale skin walk confidently into the frothing waves.

Calline finds enough depth to dive over waves that come in closer repetitions and their swells grow. A handsome young surfer seizes the opportunity; he paddles like a mill wheel through the choppy surf to the waves furthest out. Calline begins a strong crawl, straight off the shoreline, still confident there's not much the ocean can deliver that she has not met. The sea water is cold, but not colder than Lake Michigan at the height of summer. In no time, her body thermostat adjusts. What a thrill to float, to dive into the cool, deep clear. The current tugs at her body, but from experience, she knows that—like in living—beneath the churning water, if she just goes deeper, there she will find stillness and peace. She fills her lungs with air and dives, lightly brushing the bottom with her chin, stroking the soft coral sand as if it were the skin of a newborn. There, the water rocks her gently; all is quiet. And she waits. She thinks of the sperm whale who can stay submerged for two hours, when her lungs begin to ache.

She shoves off the bottom and rockets to the surface, her lungs hungry for air. Against the current that pulls her further away from her put-in point, she paddles hard to get beyond the first wall of surf-sized waves. Now she is out with the slowly-mounting swells, chopping her way through white caps. Nothing will stop this reverie, her trusting the magnificent energy and force of the water that occupies seventy-five percent of Mother Earth. Why fight it? She can't fight it. *Just go with it*, she hears from within.

From the corner of her eye, she sees the surfer's head popping over a swelling wall of wave. He paddles furiously, and then stands. *A good catch*, she thinks, *a wonderful ride he's got coming.* The suction of the mounting wave pulls her to the wall. The wave builds its power, raises itself to a peak, then curls with a crash. Like a bullet shot through the white water of the crashing crest comes the surfer.

"Oh my God, lady, watch—!" screams the surfer, on the bullet-like trajectory of the swimmer's head.

All she feels and hears is a popping, like a hand grenade thrown to the ground and exploding. And then, no feeling but a covering of intense brightness. It's just like they tell you it is, Heaven that is. All that can be desired is to be forever bathed in this perfect Light. Yes, there is a tunnel, and, for eternity or for a nanosecond, Calline's tunnel is a Cinemax theater. She sees everything projected as big as life, she and her best friend Carly at ages twelve and thirteen. They are riding horses, like they had done together since they were five. Calline challenges Carly to a race. They both know that running her young horse could be dicey, even dangerous. "Let's do it!" Carly says, her body and her mare's trembling with fear and anticipation.

Who could resist the chill in the air of a late winter day, the mounting energy beneath of horses bred to run, heads shaking, feet pawing to go. With a click from his rider, Calline's gelding bolts forward, in seconds collected into a strong gallop. Carly's mare follows, eating the dust of the horse in front. In no time, both thoroughbred ex-race horses charge in a dead heat, head-to-head, down a dirt road. Feeling the power, the force of the animal beneath her, of being one with the breath, the sweat, the energy, is all Calline had dreamed. "Go, Mick, pick it up, boy," she calls to him, urging him on, looking back over her shoulder to see Carly not far behind, her mare lathered with sweat. Carley's face is stretched in terror. She is no longer the rider, but merely the holder-on.

Calline doesn't see the deer dart from behind a palmetto. Carly's bay jams her front feet into the sand, the halting force so powerful, Carly catapults from her saddle over the mare's head. Calline's gelding brakes hard and shies right, throwing Calline to the left into a ditch of soft sand. A pine stump catches her left leg, crushing her knee and shattering her femur. As her leg cracks, Calline watches Carly fold and crumple on the ground beneath the pine tree, hit head-on. Calline passes out. They tell her later that Carly didn't feel a thing. Carly's funeral was two days later.

As peaceful as she feels, as beautiful her surroundings, she wonders, "Why am I shown this when I spent so many years trying to forget?" An indescribably loving voice, neither male nor female says, "*You condemn yourself mercilessly. You can release this now. You must go back. We are done here.*"

Floating above, Calline watches an emergency vehicle screech to a halt and its occupants, two women, tear to the rear door. They haul out a gurney. She watches her body, a crumpled rag needing to be squeezed out and hung to dry. One of the women leans over the body and blows into the mouth. The surfer stands by, bedraggled and shocked. Two men in uniform leap from a police vehicle and run to the body. Everyone rushes. Time is of the essence. After all, Calline is here and her body is there. But then she feels her lungs like a match was lit inside. The stabbing, pumping, needles pricking, voices, and rank breath in her face. The scurry and hurry around her is desperate, so it can't be good. Calline tries to shout, "What's the big deal, guys? It's beautiful, dying."

"Come on, lady, come on, you can make it. Try." More pumping, pushing. No question: she's joined her body now.

Ouch! God, her head. It still blinks on and off with light, but no great Light, like the one that beckoned her. Her lungs agonize. Her ribs crack under the pressure of compressions. She burps and spits up ocean and sand and God knows what else. Someone hollers, "We've got a pulse, she's back! Don't stop working!"

"Stop! Please stop!" but words won't come. They don't hear her screaming, begging to go back. More water gushes from her and then everything goes to blur. She and Carly are at the shore riding sea horses, floating and bobbing like on a carousel, arms spread like wings. Not a care in the world. They turn and race into the water, deeper and deeper and deeper. Their horses swim away. Carly and she hold each other, laughing, breathing under water. Laughing their heads off; they float to the surface and swim back to shore, walking hand-in-hand toward a magnificent Light.

"Honey, it's me, can you hear me?" it's her father, but he's spinning and she's spinning. Someone holds her head over a can and she vomits. Dad's familiar warm hand presses hers. Her body feels to her like glass shattered and shattering. She dreams again. She sees Sorrel and her dancing. She sees him standing over her. She blinks to see if it's really him. Blurring through shattered smoky lenses is all she sees.

"Sorrel? That you?" She thinks she says, wondering if the dream is punctured and she is awake.

"Hey, guys, she talked! She actually talked," says Sorrel, beaming like a father whose child has taken her first step.

Her lungs burn trying to get air deep into them; her head is splitting, and there are tubes and wires and gauze everywhere. She feels caged and desperate to be free. One wrist is taped to the bed rail. Why so confined? "Please help. Somebody, help me get loose," Calline begs. No one hears.

"There, there it's O.K. now, just relax." And then some white-garbed blur pricks her behind and she floats off again, this time with no Light beaming perfect peace. "I want to be back there, not here in this body tangled up, burning and aching. I want to go home."

You have work to do. It's the voice from the tunnel.

"Cal, it's Dad and Patty, Sorrel and Billy, honey. We're here, you hold on now, it's going to be O.K. The Doctor says you were lucky."

Are his cheeks streaked with tears, or is this a dream of her dad crying? Patty holds her feet, rubbing them. Sorrel stands next to Billy, by the nurse. "Some way to welcome the New Year, huh? Where am I? What happened?" Her mouth is all cottony while her eyes blink at high shutter speed to focus. So hot.

"Cal, you're in Hamilton, Bermuda, in the hospital. You almost drowned." Patty holds a mirror for Calline to see her head wrapped in gauze, one eye plum-sized. All exposed skin is eggplant-purple and brown. Her nose is taped. She remembers now, the surfer coming head-on, the cracking sound, the Light, the reel-to-reel replay of the accident. Carly dying instantly, then being released of the pain of guilt, floating. And the peace. God, the peace.

"Patty, you there?" Calline calls to her friend.

"Yeah, baby. I'm here." Patty comes to her head and leans over to whisper. "You got yourself a few extra days of R&R. Glad to have you here, girl. We were plenty worried." She places her palm on Calline's forehead and says something so softly no one can hear. "Your first word was his name."

CHAPTER TWENTY-SIX

BUT FOR THE surfer's quick, athletic moves, the Reverend Calline Simpson would be a statistic. Six days after the accident, Calline can sit up, converse, read mail, and collapse in exhaustion. "I took in plenty of water but mainly suffer from a concussion from the collision with the surfboard," Calline talks quietly to Thomas Dreiden who calls regularly from High Dunes for updates.

"Calline, you are in our daily prayers, it goes without saying," Thomas consoles.

"Tell everyone thanks for the cards. My room looks like Eden from all the flowers." She can't keep from focusing on Heaven where, in fact, it is paradise. There were flowers everywhere, their colors beyond anything on earth. The feeling is of a complete unhampered state, an airy timelessness—bodiless—a peace that surpasses all understanding. Any attempt to articulate it is like writing a letter with only half the letters of the alphabet. Each day sends the experience further away, like a train pulling away from a magical kingdom. *The day comes when you put away your pictures, stop trying to explain to friends what it was like there, and make peace again with the daily vicissitudes of life in a flattened reality. I'll never pray "On earth as it is in Heaven" the same again,* Calline reflects.

A knock at the door interrupts. It can't be staff, they're not that polite. For days, her body has been everybody's territory but hers. She's feeling restless and ready to be in her own bed, with Bingo next to her. She misses the dog's soft, whiskery flues, her sweet, dark eyes. *I must do something special for Dalia for hosting Bingo.*

Quickly, she adjusts the flimsy hospital gown over her breasts, accepting that here, modesty is a forgotten luxury. "Come in."

"Rev. Cal, it's Luke Skulty." An Australian lilt softens his deep, raspy voice.

"Well, whoever Luke Skulty is, come on in, I guess." She's bored, and doesn't know most of the folks who buzz around her, seen mostly in a blurry haze, so why not Luke? He is tall, blond and looks sculpted from bronze. She's seen him somewhere.

"I'm the guy who almost killed you, and I came to pay my respects." Luke is gorgeous, young, lean, and athletic. Courageous, too. She waves to a chair which he takes, sitting on the edge, looking wide-eyed and uncomfortable, poised to bolt at first provocation.

"I just didn't see you." He looks down at his nails and then wipes his hand through his long blond-streaked locks. Then he looks hard into her eyes and waits. Calline suspects he seeks absolution, as though it were hers to offer.

"No kidding." Calline realizes she's being too cavalier before this repentant young man. "Look, Luke. It was an accident. I had one heck of an experience rocketing to the Light. It was everything they say it is. Now I have a whole stash of great sermons, and a chance to rethink everything I've ever known or thought. It was exactly as it had to be. And you hauled me to shore. That couldn't have been your everyday swim experience. So, let it go. I have. It's all a gift. You are a gift. Thank you, son." She reaches out with her hand, hoping he will take it.

He stands and looks at the floor. Another tap at the door; it's Sorrel. Calline slides under the covers to make sure her chin is the only part of her body exposed.

Seeming relieved to have an excuse to leave, Luke excuses himself and slips past Sorrel at the door. Wearing baggy turquoise Hawaiian shorts, a pink polo shirt, and sandals, Sorrel looks anything but Michigan boy. Hair tussled, skin copper-toned, he looks delectable.

"I like your chin," Sorrel jokes.

"Patty brought that pretty pink flannel robe. Could you hand it to me and excuse me while I get a bit more presentable?" Calline feels hot and nervous. Her eyes ache. Her heart, too, seeing him alone like this.

Sorrel steps out while she changes into the bathrobe and pinches her cheeks for a little blush. After two shavings, her hair looks like a mohawk gone haywire. Her eyes and nose still look ghoulish. "If you can stand looking at me like this, Sorrel, come on in."

"I can stand looking at you any time, any way, dear Reverend." He steps to the side of the bed, takes her hand, blotched and spotted from needle pricks, and looks at her with an expression she has never seen. His gaze reminds her of the Light: all love. She's off the pain IVs but she might as well be on them, this feels so good. Her body is consumed with a kind of vibration she's never experienced. Not like this, in her earthly body, anyway. Totally unexpected, Calline begins to cry.

His eyes are so large with compassion, she lets the torrents come. An expert with crying women, Sorrel is quiet. He holds her hand, waiting while the first wave of emotions subside. The complement of medications and weakness remove her defenses, and she says, without thinking of possible ramifications, "Do you remember when Billy was at my house you came with flowers, and I walked with you to your car?"

"Yep, what about it?" He seems clueless as his eyes roam her body, large and voluptuous like he likes.

"When you drove away, your hand had big red letters spelling 'wait'. What did that mean? God, I feel stupid asking you this, like it has something to do with me. How self-centered, presumptuous, how . . ." Sorrel touches her lips.

"How perfectly normal to be curious about something so, well, so potentially loaded." Sorrel backs away, and swallows hard. "Damn, it's the nurse." He takes Calline's hand and places a light kiss on it.

"I'm sorry, sir, you'll have to step out." The nurse rolls her cart to the bed.

Sorrel looks at the patient and shrugs. "Wait," he says smiling mysteriously, looking darling in his pink polo and tan. He seems relieved not to have to explain.

"Sorrel?"

"Yep."

"Never mind." She sniffs and wipes her sleeve over her eyes. "I want to thank you, but I'm not sure for what, and there is so much welling inside me that words can't contain." She sobs again, giving her arm to the nurse.

He winks, waves, and blows a kiss. The nurse looks at Calline, then at Sorrel and inquires without saying a word, "What is it between you two, anyway?"

"Near drowning," Calline says, entombing herself in sheets, knowing the accident—the vision—has propelled her life around a corner, off one highway of limited beliefs about herself, God, the world, onto another, where anything is possible, even a love that is forbidden.

Dr. Witherspoon knocks and enters without waiting. A man in his late sixties, balding and dignified, he smiles sweetly. Although he has applied pure science, his true healing balm has been a rare concoction of compassion and endearing humor.

"Ms. Simpson, you are out of the woods, my friend. Indeed, you've come a very long way in these few days, but I will warn you to go it easy. Do you hear me young lady?" He removes bandages that have wrapped her head like a nun's habit, reducing them to a single strip of gauze over the blade wound and the sutures that circle her left eye. He presses around the area where the blade of the surfboard just missed obliterating. "You look lovely in blues and purples, dear." He smiles and works with tenderness.

Calline is readier than her dog for a walk, to be sprung from this prison of bright lights, shoes squeaking on polished floors, starched nurses now-dearing her, neighbors snoring and retching, tubes, poking and prodding, forced medications, and watery food. The thought of signing release papers, going over insurance issues and flight changes, overwhelms.

Patty enters the room. Dr. Witherspoon says, "I'll be done in a minute, Patty, if you don't mind waiting. Your constant vigil has helped, dear. We docs know that it's not our science but your love that really does the work." After a brief lesson in wound cleaning and bandaging, the doctor says, "Done, now you two girls get to giggling. I'll be back tomorrow to check on you." He squeezes Calline's hand and looks into her eyes, a loving gaze full of hope for this patient whose life dangled so close to the precipice.

"Thanks for your science, Doc. Mainly, thanks for your love." Calline squeezes his hand and reaches for Patty's. "Sorrel held my hand, P., and looked at me with this look that was like seeing the Light. And you have to see the Light to know what I'm talking about; impossible to describe." Embarrassed, she pulls the sheet over her head.

Patty pours tropical juice into a cup of ice for herself and repeats the process for Calline. Her hair is frosted from the sun, her face red and freckled. She has always thanked God that she got most of her mother's genes, petite in stature, frizzy blonde hair, and freckles. The Frizzola genes went to her two older sisters, both with olive skin and big pear-shaped bottoms.

"You are cute as a button in that outfit," Calline admires.

"You don't look so shabby yourself, all lit up about Sorrel," Patty teases, taking off her madras blazer to hang and organize herself to help with discharge papers.

"I know you've given me warnings, dear; I can't stop myself. I . . ." Emotions have come so easily of late. Calline cries again while Patty sits and hands her tissue. "I think I'm in love with him, no return. Today, he gave me sort of a green light, unlike before. Don't be mad at me, P. Please."

Patty hands her a tissue. "Honey, I don't have the answers; I just know there's always been something between you two and maybe it's time to find out what the deal really is. Are you up to date on his situation with Elizabeth? Things could have shifted there, as well, you know." Patty reaches for another box of tissue. The phone light blinks. Calline blows, then trades it for the phone receiver. It's Sorrel.

"Cal, it's Elizabeth. Her meds got all screwed up and she's off beam, I mean really gone off somewhere, like I've never seen, ever. We called her doctor back home and he connected with a physician here, but we missed communications. What a mess. Elizabeth may have deliberately tangled the instructions. We're taking off tonight. Billy will go with us, kicking and screaming. Just wanted to let you know, I'm thinking of you and praying for you, and ask the same of you for us." The Sorrel she was just with sounds so far away, off on a tangent he seems now to resent.

"Oh Sorrel, of course. I'm making plans myself to be home by early next week. I feel like a hostage here, but these English are really being careful about letting me get up too soon. I'll call as soon as I get back, O.K.?" Oh God, poor Sorrel; she looks at Patty, thumbs down.

"About the 'wait' on the hand, Cal. If I could re-script that afternoon, it would have all been for you. The flowers were, stopping by to see you and Billy was. The hand, well, sounds silly, but it was for the goalie of the soccer team I coach. Bobby kept lunging way out into the field and leaving a hole a mile wide. I told him to look at my hand every time he had a notion to do that. The 'wait' was for Bobby Brown. I've got to run. Elizabeth is calling." The phone goes dead.

It would have all been for me. She swirls these words in her heart. Her head aches and her nose burns. Patty hands her a tissue and sips her drink, then says a soft prayer when Calline nods off to sleep. A volunteer delivers a post-card. Patty can't resist reading it.

"Cal, the Devil jus' about gotcha I hurd. We prayin' 4-U. Greens in the pot. Cum and gettem. Luv-U, Becky."

CHAPTER TWENTY-SEVEN

TRAVEL IS NEVER easy going, especially not during recovery from a concussion and a near-drowning.

"Don't even think of making the trip home, girlfriend, without me," Patty, intractable when she knows she's right, stares at Calline, who gingerly folds clean underwear.

"But what about . . ."

"But, nothing. My job can wait. Your dad and I will flank you on the trip." Patty lifts a tattered suitcase from the tiny storage locker in Calline's hospital home of the past ten days. Methodical and loving, Patty sorts, folds, and stacks each item of her friend's Bermuda wardrobe. "Your toiletries can go with you, just in case we get hung up somewhere." Patty's loving take charge feels as maternal as Calline can stand from anyone but her own mother. She can't admit that she will need her father and Patty to flank her all the way home.

As seamless as the trip, it is all Calline can do to muster the energy just to find a position to fall asleep until the next interruption. Her last recollection before arrival into the tiny limousine stand in High Dunes was arguing with Patty about how long her friend would stay as her caregiver. As soon as he was sure his daughter was safely tucked in, Bob Simpson, exhausted, would catch the 5 a.m. shuttle to Chicago, then back to Phoenix, his retirement home.

"Hey lady, are you the Reverend?" Are those your friends out there with the balloons?" The limo driver asks, nonchalant, as he pulls under the overhang at the curb marked "Grand Rapids-High Dunes Airport Limousine."

"WELCOME HOME, REV. CAL" the sign reads. People wave the banner with gestures of genuine delight. Most ecstatic is Bingo, attached at collar to four flying "welcome" balloons. When she sees her one true person exit the limo, she hauls like a freight train against the tugging Dalia, breaks free, and runs. Sorrel steps in just in time to intercept the leaping dog who would have tackled Calline hard to the ground. Lately, or always, it seems he's in the right place at the right time. Calline, just as eager to greet Bingo, kneels and allows the dog to place her front paws over her shoulders and lick her like an ice cream cone. Billy and Martha, Gertrude, Thomas and Myrtle, Dalia, David and Connie, Tendal, Smit, Kathy, Lilly Smith with husband—newborn and toddlers in tow—and George pushing Rachael in a wheelchair, comprise the welcome committee. Lo and behold, if Vee doesn't show too, accompanied by none other than Miss Becky. Calline feels light headed and dizzy, but manages to push the sensation away enough to climb atop two suitcases.

"Speech! Speech!" the greeters demand. Others in the terminal gather around to listen and observe. They must wonder what the bandaged prophet with the black and blue face has come to herald. Her message must have angered a few.

"Blessed are they who offer warm welcome, for they shall be called wonderful friends. Thank you all. I missed you. Bless you all for your concern and cards. I love you!" Dizziness overtakes her; she reaches out, wobbling. Sorrel steps over to offer a shoulder and a hand. His eyes warn. No one knows like he, Patty, and her father, the depth of the pastor's exhaustion, the near miss of it all.

"Billy, take these bags, would you, son? You and Martha take your car. I'll go with Bingo and the ladies." Sorrel helps Calline from her suitcase perch and takes her hand to steady. Sorrel stands protectively by as she hugs and thanks the well-wishers at the door, each one genuinely happy to see their shepherd. Patty finds an excuse to ride separately so Sorrel and Cal can have some alone time. The women glance knowingly; Calline is grateful.

Unsteady and faint, Calline takes Sorrel's hand. She doesn't know if it's that she nearly drowned from a collision with a surfboard or if it's seeing him again that dizzies her. By the side of the passenger door, Calline moans, "I don't feel hopeful that I'm going to make it home before . . ."

"You O.K.? You look . . ." Sorrel touches her shoulder.

"Never mind, no time." Calline buckles at her knees, kneels and vomits pretzels and tomato juice.

Sorrel feels her forehead. "Cal, you're on fire. We're going to the ER." Sorrel commands his Durango like the rapture is coming. Thankfully, the little hub of an airport is only seven minutes to the hospital if you hurry and evade the cops. Sorrel jumps from the car at the door to the ER entrance. "You sit tight, now you hear? Don't move. I think I can pull some strings to get you seen. An old college buddy of mine might be on duty; you remember Fred Martin?"

In spite of passive crowds of people of all stripes who wait to be seen, Sorrel's desperate concern alerts the gate keeper. "Dr. Martin, is he on tonight?" The receptionist resents these folks who drop names to get ahead of the line, but this very worried man has connections to the ER chief. She obliges with a call to the back, mentioning Sorrel Dixon. Dr. Martin appears through the doors, smiles and greets Sorrel with a warm hug.

Fred, my . . . I mean, The Reverend Calline Simpson is sitting in my car right now on fire with fever. Long Story. Accident in Bermuda. Almost drowned . . ." Sorrel's brow scrunches with worry. He pushes his hands deep into his pockets and waits for his friend's reply.

Dr. Martin calls to a near-by attendant, "Get a gurney to that Durango and meet me me in Bay 4."

Calline wobbles her body onto the gurney, then falls into a deep sleep. Dr. Martin coolly examines her face, listens to Sorrel report recent history, pulls off the bandage, and says methodically, "The wound is infected and it may be more widespread than that."

Sorrel leans in to her and whispers, "If it's any consolation dear, we've got the routine down. I'll post the Bermuda support team, and make sure to check in tomorrow. I think you're going to sleep fine tonight. Familiar environs—hospital." He plants a soft kiss on her forehead and follows the gurney to the elevator, his hand holding her right foot.

Her last words to him: "Please take Bingo to your house, Sorrel. Watch her for me? I love you."

Settled into Room 1620, Bed A, Calline passes in and out of a haze and dreams, of Carly and her on their seahorses, diving deeper and deeper, laughing, singing, talking, carefree. At times, she awakens in a sweat, crying, missing her, and hears her call in her soft southern lilting angel-voice how sorry she is that the accident happened. *"Move on, Cal. Forgive yourself. All is well."* It is the same voice she heard in the tunnel. *Perhaps after we die,* she thinks, *we become the mind and the voice of all that is and ever was; the soul liberated from the torments of the awful fruits of our fall: the human condition.*

Calline's dad canceled his flight home to keep vigil with Patty until his daughter recovers a second time. "Honey, you know I love you, but this hospital business is getting old." Bob adores his child, and his vigilance has been heroic. He's just old and tired.

She reaches to hold his hand, offering him solace. "Pops, you know you're my hero. I'll make this up to you, I promise." She smiles, and their eyes lock, saying everything words can't.

Sorrel drops by when he can take time from work and Elizabeth, back in the hospital detoxing from another overdose. Calline remembers how fetching he looked in Hawaiian shorts and pink polo. Now, he wears wool pants and a down vest over a dark wool sweater. He holds his gold and brown High Hopes cap and gloves. His tan has faded, but to her, he looks delicious. She quickly adjusts the blanket for warmth and modesty. He stands at the foot of her bed, rubbing her toes, looking into her eyes with an expression she doesn't recognize. "Rev., your flock misses you. Rev. V. has done a fine job filling in, but they want Elijah, not Elisha. I'm afraid we're getting too soft. Strangely, it's like we're in an eye of the storm. Things appear calm, anyway. I imagine as soon as the opposition senses you're back in the game, we'll be in . . . oh, hell, you don't need predictions of doom today." He works his way up the side of the bed to plant a light kiss on her bandaged face.

"Nice stall tactic, huh? A two week vacation turned into four?" Calline groans, then smiles and looks deeply into his eyes; how must the pink of her blush match the purples and browns of her bruises?

Sorrel takes her hand, black and blue from needles; his eyes fill with sorrow, more sorrow than the occasion warrants, since she is getting much better. But, there's Elizabeth. Of course, his fiancée. But no, it's not Elizabeth. It's about her precious Bingo.

"Bingo!" Calline bolts straight up, her sheet and blanket falling to reveal almost bare breasts. "God, Sorrel, what about her? What's happened to my dog? I asked you to take care of her. When did she disappear?" A wave of nausea hits, her head feels it's splitting open again.

Sorrel goes pale with worry. "Early this morning, Billy and Martha left out the front door. I found it unlocked and the bolt doesn't hold well. When I got downstairs the door was opened. I, of course, jumped in the car and scoured the neighborhood. A posse of kids went door knocking through the neighborhood. No luck. We posted an ad to run for five days starting this afternoon."

She knows Sorrel feels miserable with guilt, but the recovering patient cannot hide her fury. Her head in her hands, Calline weeps tears of a mother too overwrought to manage another crisis. There is nothing Sorrel or the hospital staff can say to console. "Just please help me with my things and get me out of here. I want to go home. I want to find my dog. Now!"

CHAPTER TWENTY-EIGHT

BED REST AT home with oversight by a visiting nurse is the pastor's fate until her next check-up in four days. Her obsession to find Bingo and tell Sister M.T. about Heaven is matched only by her fear that her long absence will give ammunition to Grimsley and her foot soldiers. They did honor the Christmas truce, and she opened sweet notes from many of the Petition-signers. Even Richard and Alexis let Christian charity prevail. They sent a card and flowers.

"Are you sure, Thomas? Things are fine till I get back in the saddle? I was given two weeks' vacation, with some grace for the accident. Is all this time away pushing the envelope? More fodder for the enemy, as much as I hate military metaphor." She picks at a scab next to her eyebrow. A brief visit with Thomas lifts her spirits.

"Not to worry, Cal. I've not picked up more than the usual petty rancor in the hallways. The truce seems to be holding. It's unseemly to wage battle against the leadership when the leader is down." Thomas laughs at the irony, sounding relaxed and cheerful. Surely the dam will hold with or without her, Calline imagines, but being back at the helm can't come soon enough. She's sick of counting ceiling tiles. Too much time to think, to let her imagination and her story-weaving set her into tail-spins of angst.

Calline posts another ad in "The Journal": *Fawn Boxer, age six, goes by name of 'Bingo' last seen in The Heights neighborhood. Nike swoosh mark between her ears with scar on right front shoulder,"* and adds contact information. Thankfully, Sister Marie Therese is willing to shift her calendar to fit Calline in earlier. Calline wants to tell her about Heaven. She wants to weave all the scattered pieces of the past weeks into a meaningful tapestry and present it for the sister's anointing. But what vocabulary will she use? Language is so inadequate.

The drive to Mercy Center is the first Calline has made alone since before vacation. No signs yet of spring. Bare branches reach their claws upward and over the Mercy Center drive lined by melting snow mounds, jagged and muddy. Calline's anticipation to see Sister M.T. outruns her body's readiness to move quickly. She almost trips and falls as she walks-limps-walks to the tiny chambers where Sr. Therese sits with a Bible and sips hot tea.

Sister M.T., seldom given to outbursts, is thrilled to see Calline. She rises with some difficulty and invites a hug. Calline wishes right now time would stop. Sister holds the embrace until Calline moves away to take her chair. Calline sits and begins to cry. "Here's more tissue, Cal. Take all you need." M.T. seems to have been ready for the pastor's effluence. The nun simply nods and closes her eyes. She knows near death experiences bring torrents of questions, and an ongoing need to appropriate the experience there and the process of re-entry to mere mortal existence here.

"I feel like I'm in a dream with a number two pencil to take a Life test at post-graduate level. I feel like a preschooler: near death, dog lost, the Petition going around." Calline blows her nose.

"Yea, graduate level Life seems to be what we're given, or rather thrown. It's like parenting. The kid comes and suddenly you're taking the final. Who prepared you? Prayer is not to change things, but to change us for things. When and how did you experience God then?" Marie Therese is always on the mark, the Source. Go back to the Source, and start from there.

"The tunnel, you mean? The Light. If you wanted to know the feeling of Jesus present, die. I mean flat line, like I did." Calline leans forward, excited. "Oh M.T., I never dreamed it could be so beautiful. Words fail, and I feel foolish to speak of this with anyone, except with someone who's been there, and you, of course." She knows M.T. will listen with the ears she has beyond the ears she has.

"Yes, I understand." The nun rubs her bony hands, nonchalant, as if encounters with Light and voices in tunnels are the norm, not the exception.

Calline recounts the details of the accident, the cracking sound when the surfer's board hit, and how she experienced being in a theater, showing every detail of the riding accident. "I did hear a voice, a kind of one-voice-fits-all. It told me I was not to blame for Carly's death. There was no physical body I could see, but it's like it reached out and lifted a two ton weight off my shoulders. Then it said I had work to do and that I couldn't stay. Who wants to leave Heaven and return to this mess? I know I didn't. That's the only time I felt sorrow." Calline cries.

Sister is silent. She hands more tissue.

"I was exonerated by God, by Carly, as if I'd been a prisoner on death row, given parole after a hundred rejections. What a relief. I've heard The Voice, and it's nothing like that mean preacher who planted in my head what I believed was an indelible image of God, a God who is judge and task master, quid pro quo. How freeing; so much so, I'm not sure what to do with this. I have this sensation of being a baby bird wired to fly, but still wobbling in the nest with its mouth open for a handout."

"Don't chide yourself, dear. It's like a tsunami of sorts, to have gone through what you've just been through. Your spiritual settings, if you will, will have to adjust to a new true north; you'll be appropriating new meaning from what God has shown you, new meaning about God. And life on this side. Oh, dear, be patient with yourself. A tall order, I know." M.T. smiles with love, and reaches to touch Calline's better knee.

The two women sit quietly as if silence is the only adequate container for all that Calline has entrusted. Sister comes in calmly. "I'm thinking of the Persian mystic, Kabir, his poem about prisons of doctrine. The teacher expounds on his doctrine of hell. He asks the student, 'So, what do you think of this doctrine?' The student says, 'Your hell sounds like an inhumane cage; no wonder the smart dogs ran off.' Sounds like maybe you are being freed from an inhumane cage that has condemned you. God has looked on all this time full of mercy. It took this dramatic event—this direct encounter—to convince you how intensely God loves and forgives."

"All the suffering I've inflicted on myself, on others. Why do we have to get walloped—literally, in my case—to come to our senses?" Calline rubs her eyebrow, and gazes out the window, pensive.

Sister rubs her frail hands together and smiles like someone has just whispered an enchanting secret to her. She looks at her watch and yawns, not bored, but just knowing she doesn't have to have all the answers. Those will be given in the fullness of time, all along the journey, when Calline is ready. Enough for today.

Leaving the Center down the long winding drive, the sun sparkling from the iced bare branches, Calline thanks God for this place where she can simply be with whatever comes to her. It's all fodder for healing and learning. Caught up in her reflections, she sees from the corner of her eye a stray animal limping along a stand of birch, sniffing and scratching for food. Her heart breaks to think this might be Bingo's fate, or worse. She sobs again, desperate to know if Bingo is safe, or even alive.

Lost animals are usually too frightened and confused to come, but it's in her instincts to try and help. She whispers to herself, "If I help this animal, perhaps the favor will extend to Bingo; I pray so." She pulls over and puts on the emergency blinkers, leaving the car running for heat. No one is coming behind; she gets out slowly and moves in the direction of the dog, scouring for food about fifty yards away. It tucks its rear and trots away.

"Come on, puppy," she calls loudly in her Bingo voice. The dog stops and spins to face her. It howls, bounding and limping, bounding and limping toward Calline. Is it attacking her? Then Calline sees her. "Bingo, it's you! Oh my God, it's you." Through convulsions of tears, she runs-limps to meet the injured, scruffy dog, hardly recognizable as her couch potato pet. The dog, barking a desperate whimper, leaps into Calline's arms. Together, they fall to the frozen ground. Bingo yelps, her whole body wriggling ecstasy. "Oh, girl, how I missed you. Dear God, thank you for bringing her back!"

Bingo pins her person to the ground, licking and baying the sweetest and most pathetic hello, like it's all she can do to tell everything, but mainly just to say, "I love you no matter what." Calline removes her jacket to cover the dog. Some power beyond her weakness gives her strength to lift and carry Bingo to the car, warm and full of familiar smells. Bingo submits to Calline's examination. She is thinner, but free of deep wounds or breaks. She might have pulled a muscle, causing her to limp. Where her collar once was are rub marks, like there was a struggle to break free from the hell of her confinement.

"Smart dog, Bingo! You ran off. Smart dog, girl!"

CHAPTER TWENTY-NINE

TO TRANSITION FROM four weeks away from church work is like changing out of old flannel pajamas and slippers into a new, heavily starched one-size smaller suit. Calline itches where stitches just came out. Her hair tries to fall in some direction toward normal. Her size-sixteens are looser and her appetite for sugary things has receded.

Dalia, knitting, doesn't look up or say hello. Instead, "Geeze, you look pretty awful, boss."

"Been a while, huh?" Calline says, touching the secretary's cold shoulder. She thumbs through stacked mail, wondering where Dalia is headed. "Got anything for me to do?" Dalia throws the ball of yarn more at Calline than to her.

"Hold this while I count." She nods over to the table next to the copier, where a box stuffed with scrap note paper and envelopes overflows. "Big pile over there for you to root through." She smacks and counts off. She is downright obnoxious.

"Don't pigs root? Dalia, are you mad at me?" Their relationship can stand up to bare bone honesty, but Calline is not sure she can handle this on her first day back after so long.

"Well, truth be known, I guess I am." She holds her hands still and looks at Calline for the first time. Dark purple liner and her afro-permed hair, colored a new shade of red, seem gross, really, but who is the pastor to critique hair after at least four buzz cuts of her own?

"Well, out with it. But don't be too hard on me. I've been through the mill." She feels tense and tired and it's not even ten o'clock.

"So has Bingo—been through it. You let Sorrel take care of her after you got back, when you knew she and Gofer Broke are best friends. When Bingo left, then disappeared, Broke was heartbroken. She wouldn't eat and she kept her head in her shell longer than I've ever seen. You know how attached she's become to Bingo." To laugh would humiliate her, but how not to?

"You can assure Miss Gofer Broke that her charge is home and doing fine." Calline touches Dalia's shoulder feeling a new tenderness toward this funny, eccentric woman upon whom the church depends for what? No one seems to be able to solve this central mystery.

"Next time you think of serious dog care, think of me and my turtle for the whole time. Promise? Broke would have never let Bingo out of her sight." Dalia huffs.

"Promise." Calline offers a Girl Scout salute. "Now, what should I look at first?" Calline throws the ball and it hits the floor and rolls under Dalia's chair.

"I quit counting your in-house messages after about twenty. Phone's been busy, a lot of sympathy calls, spying calls too—people checking up on how things are going with hiring that Peter guy—and folks just wanting attention. You know how they are. They call making you think they're on an important churchy-type mission when all they want to do is tell you about their aches and pains, how someone in the church is pissing them off, and they're always trying to wheedle something out of me about you. I swore the gag order, remember? My first day." Needles tap and gum pops. In this moment, Dalia's loyalty trumps all these objectionables.

"I see a lot of calls came asking for my address at the Hamilton Hilton," giggles Calline, more relaxed to be on even ground with Dalia.

"David and Connie left a message ten days ago to call ASAP. Vee called to ask how you were doing," says Dalia on a roll with pearl-one-knit-one.

"Smit wants to meet with the search committee as soon as I'm up to it." Calline thinks, *when I stop desiring the likes of Sorrel Dixon, then I'll be up to it.*

She reads that Rachael "called just to chat," which is code for "please call back."

Thomas says, "Call when you're up to it." Same response to him as to Smit: *as soon as I stop desiring.* "I have work to do. Guess I better get at it," she whispers to herself, "just like the Voice instructed." She settles in her office cubicle with a list of "to-dos", picks up the phone and dials the Dreiden's.

Myrtle Dreiden answers Calline's call for Thomas; she wants the scoop on the pastor's last bout of fever. Thomas takes the receiver in time for Calline to avoid having to give gossip fodder. He is cordial, happy that Reverend Simpson is back at the helm.

"Cal, Governance met a few times since you've been away. On the docket: your crisis, pulpit supply, bill-paying, and how to spend Willomena Brainard's sixty thousand. The show must go on. In the middle of handling all the survival issues, Gunther, with his mission and outreach hat on, posed an idea that got us thinking beyond just survival questions. By the way, we voted to move ahead with Peter's candidacy.

"See? Who needs a pastor when the parishioners are so capable and generous with time and talent? Thank you, Thomas, for the loving gifts of flowers and goodies. Your calls were medicine."

She knows better than to go into matters beyond practical with Thomas, but she can't help herself. "I've turned a corner in my journey of faith. I can't quite articulate it, but perhaps what I've received will spill forth to the congregation, what's left of it. Seeing the Light changes a person. It sure knocks the fear out of dying." Just as she expected, Thomas makes his awkward throat clearing sound and moves directly to business.

"We need to get the search committee pumped again, now that you're back. Grimsley is kicking up some dust again. I won't let us be held hostage by the prejudices that come packaged in anonymous mail, nasty phone calls, and you know what else. The more I think, Cal, the more I see it as our sinfulness, not Peter's, that we let this issue drag on like it has." Thomas opines with surprising resolve.

"My mother," said Calline, "made us kids memorize that text she said was like saying God has no grandchildren. From Romans: *'For there is no distinction between Jew and Greek; the same Lord is Lord of all and is generous to all who call on him.'*" Moderator and pastor schedule to meet together tomorrow. Calline hangs up and rubs her bristly-haired scalp. The wound itches. And so does she, to tackle church business and to see Vee; next stop, the Town High School.

"Dalia, I'm taking my lunch to the high school. Be back in about an hour." Dalia waves, abandoning her knitting momentarily, to work on the Sunday bulletin.

Throngs of teenage cliques move among the corridors of the Town High School, converted in the fifties from an industrial munitions factory. Calline approaches a young teen holding a baby, a girl she once saw Vee hanging out with. "You know Vee Morgan?"

"Yeah, she's right over there, by the Coke machine." The young woman snaps her fingers and trots over to meet her peers. In a flash, Vee is by Calline's side and talking up a storm. Her teen Ebonics is cryptic, fast, and might as well be a foreign language when the kids talk to each other.

"Rev. you 'kay? You was hurt real bad. Fer real, your hair's cool, I like it. I'm glad you're back and 'kay." Vee's pleasantries and real concern warm Calline on a cold, blustery day. Seeing Vee again brings joy.

"I was going to say the same thing to you. You look a whole lot better than when I last saw you. How are you? The baby?" Calline notices Vee is beginning to show. The two women walk hand-in-hand to a bench just outside the school's main entrance. Calline reaches for a banana and peanut butter sandwich from her purse. She hands Vee her apple. "For the baby."

"I got into some bad food and got that e-colly 'fection thing. Real dangerous for the baby with the high fever, but she 'kay. I spit up in the mornings. Doc says I have to get through first tri. Hey Rev. Cal, did you give some thought to putting the water on my baby?" Vee rubs the back of Calline's shoulder with her hand, a habit she picked up early in their friendship.

"You mean baptizing her?" Calline laughs and folds the girl's other hand into her lap. "Sure, child, I'll put the water on her. You say when. For now, let's ask God to give you a healthy baby." Calline and Vee hold hands in silence, until a gaggle of girls call to Vee. "Bye, sweetie. I love you," Calline calls to Vee's backside.

On her walk to the church, her thoughts go to Peter. How odd that it's the Christian community that excludes. "Love the sinner, hate the sin," say the well-meaning. Has anything changed since Jesus challenged exclusion? Menstruating women, lepers, Gentile, and Lord knows who else, were deemed by the most pious Jews in high positions unclean, beyond the pale of acknowledgment. She can hear the Holy Spirit whispering to the apostle Peter out on the rooftop. When Peter was instructed to eat everything lifted down in the net, most of it forbidden by Jewish law, it was as if God was saying, "Whatever it is that's different and scares the crap out of you, you must now accept." *Acceptance. Isn't that what it's about: acceptance of self, of differences, of other, of the manifold grace that extends far beneath, around, and over? To all God's children.* So absorbed in her thoughts, making notes for sermons to come, she walks past the turn onto the walkway to the front door.

"George Connors called. He sounds sad," Dalia announces as soon as Calline enters the building.

"Reverend Cal, Mom's back in the hospital. She's had another stroke. She's asking for you. Can you come?" George sounds open, not his usual bravado and arrogance. "You've been good to our family, Cal. You and I don't see eye-to-eye, but I'm grateful for your love for Mom. You've helped her feel necessary and important." He returns to stiff and formal, repressing a risky spill of vulnerability.

His mother is dying. How can Calline exclude this man she's rejected in her heart? "I'll drop everything, George, and come now." The thought of losing Rachael crushes her soul. But almost as hard is the thought she must accept her son, George, without condition.

Rachael will breathe her last breath in Room 436, Bed B. Her hair mats against her cheek, her skin ashen and sunken around her jaw. She breaths with a rasp. Every hint of strength gone, but the love in her eyes can meet the love in Calline's. Calline takes Rachael's well-worn Bible and turns to her favorite Psalm, 139. She knows Rachael trusts its promise, that no matter where we are from before conception to beyond this life, high or low, God is there. Always there. After reading, Calline whispers into her friend's good ear, "Thank you dear one, thank you for all you have been and meant to me and the congregation." Calline kisses Rachael's cheek, wipes a tear, certain this is good-bye, and makes room for George, his wife, and two children to keep vigil until the end.

On the drive back to the office, Calline rehearses the search committee decisions. Kathy will call Peter and Randy to see if they can fly out Friday week. Calline and Kathy will meet them at the airport, and everyone will meet at the Dreidens' Friday night. Peter and Pastor will spend Saturday together. He will play and direct the choir at Third Methodist on Sunday. If all goes well, Governance will vote on the recommendation from the search committee and recommend Peter to the congregation for their vote in a matter of weeks now. It is all happening so fast.

CHAPTER THIRTY

MONTHS HAVE PASSED since Calline has indulged herself and Bingo in an unhurried walk at Lake Michigan. The ice mounds that form a moonscape where water and sand meet grow smaller as the days lengthen. The vast expanse of water brings Calline's thoughts to her drowning, to the encounter with Light and Carly's pardon. She holds on to the details of the accident as if losing a single thread would move her further away from the vision and any hope of its manifesting in her world. Her leg seems to ache less and her spirits have warmed, like ice boulders in big chunks of unwelcome affliction have fallen away. The shift M.T. was talking about seems to reflect all around. The Spirit seems to have embraced the congregation with something new, something that might alter its own sense of true north. She wishes on the first evening star, a planet perhaps, and maybe as big as the one that led those first worshipers to the manger. She reviews her recent conversation with Thomas.

"We voted to designate half of Willomena Brainard's money, thirty grand, to serve the people in the neighborhood: a free weekly breakfast, a latchkey program, elder daycare, to name a few ideas that came to the table. We'd find some clever way to invite people to come one Sunday right before Easter. Gunther and his missions team volunteered to organize the walk and talk about the overall plan this Sunday, if you don't mind." Calline knows that during unsure and anxious times, the natural instinct is to grasp, to hoard, and to hold. She is delighted and surprised by this sudden act of largess from a church frightened and fighting.

"You'd think, Thomas, just the opposite would happen. We'd cling to that money for dear life, and here we are designating half in a daring venture of faith." To the evening star she calls, "Lord, let this open hand to the neighborhood be just the impetus we need to move to the next level of trust in You and love of neighbor. Thank you! Thank you!"

Bingo drops a piece of driftwood at Calline's feet. Calline notices her head isn't aching and the breeze doesn't burn her cheeks. Bingo is back. In the midst of tempests brewing comes a vision, something positive and hopeful for a change. She hums, *"There's a Wideness In God's Mercy"* all the way home, repeating, *"For the love of God is broader than the measures of our minds; and the heart of the Eternal is most wonderfully kind."*

The heat of her tiny house feels good after their walk. Calline changes into flannels, pours Earl Grey, fills Bingo's water, and settles before the fire, its cinders still glowing from the morning. A tap to one log ignites a smaller log. She dials into messages and hears, "She's gone, Cal." It's George. And then, "Oh, and Cal? I called Alexis Grimsley and asked her to take me off the Petition. You know Mother would haunt me forever if I don't stay in the fold." He snickers and coughs.

Calline says, as if he were standing there, "Forever is a long time, George. Welcome back to the fold." She brings her legs to her chest and hugs them to her. "The very one I wanted to exclude has returned. And I have returned to love him just the way he is. Hmm."

But still, there's her nemesis, Grimsley. Is she changing?

"Call."

"And say what?" Calline responds to the Voice that speaks more discernibly since the accident.

"I'll give you the words, just call."

"It's no use arguing," she says, fearful, dialing, and praying to sound official. Just that.

On the second ring, the old woman picks up, recognizing the pastor's voice as though she's been poised for this call. "Well, good evening, Pastor."

Calline clears her throat. "How are you? I know your sister..."

Are you kowtowing? If you think I'm going to back off, you've got another thing coming. If you called to soften me, to spy, forget it. My signature is set in stone." Alexis hrumphs and sneezes.

Calline feels all power dripping away. Almost whimpering, "You don't sound so good, Alexis." She really does care, but nothing works. Alexis is dug in. The pastor is the enemy.

"I don't need a pastor. I want a change in direction for this church and I intend to see that that happens when we vote against the godforsaken." Click.

"Did we accomplish anything?" Calline inquires, then takes a call from Vee.

"Vee, love. What's up?" Calline is rattled.

"Doc says I have to stay flat till the baby come."

Usually Vee is stoic, but now she cries. "Oh, honey, I'm so sorry. I can't imagine you flat on your back at your house with all those kids around and your mom away so much. How's that going to work?"

Then it occurs to Calline she's set herself up for the dunk.

"That's why I'm calling. Can I stay witchoo?" She sounds perky now, hopeful.

Oh brother, it's one thing to love your neighbor during office hours. It's quite another to love her under your own roof. Yet, "Of course, Vee, you will stay flat on your back at my house. But when? Will your mother approve? You should know that I'll fuss over you and insist you follow doctor's orders. Do you understand, young lady?"

"Sunday. Mama say fine by her. Can Bingo sleep in my room? You got one of those TV games they come out with?" Her familiarity and assumptions might irritate, but tonight it feels familial and just right.

"Room service, too, I suppose?" Calline teases. A little life in the house might do her good. The chance to be nurse and mother a youngster, albeit pregnant, might fill a vacant place in her spirit. She goes upstairs to inspect the extra room. Cluttered, cobwebs in every corner, it will take hours to excavate, dust, vacuum, and add a young teen's touches. She'll need to drag her old trunk from the attic to place next to the bed and find a lamp and dresser at a garage sale. The bathroom, no larger than a ship's head, has Dad's things scattered about. She and Vee will have to share her shower. Then there's food. Vee will have a strong voice for her tastes while Calline will voice the needs of the baby. Coke or milk?

Settled in her chair in front of the fireplace, she reaches for her journal and holds it close like an old familiar friend she's offended by letting it get in hostile hands. Not knowing the fallout from Grimsley's capture, stealing it back gives her the creeps and a profound sense of weariness and powerlessness. She smells it, reads some past entries, and takes up from where she wrote at the Hamilton Hospital. "Rachael Connors died. How many church members are truly out for others' best interest? Rachael took the bullets, listened . . ." She stops to blow her nose. "I stay with the Kabir poem, how most of us live in an inhumane cage of self-condemnation. If I must continue on this side of the pass, I hope to do so from the eternal glow of love and pardon shown me in the tunnel. Wouldn't it have been easier just to have traveled to the Light, to have remained face-to-face with God? I wonder what remains to do on this side? She scribes words from the poet Rilke whose advice seems best for the moment: *Do not now seek the answers, which cannot be given you because you would not be able to live them. And the point is, to live everything. Live the questions now. Perhaps you will then gradually, without noticing it, live along some distant day into the answer.*

CHAPTER THIRTY-ONE

"BOO! GOTCHA!"

It's before nine, cold as a freezer. Calline wrestles with the stubborn lock of the church door when from nowhere, this onslaught. She drops the keys and turns to face the newlyweds, Connie and David Somers. Both wear t-shirts, and sawn-off sweatpants. David looks heavier and Connie's hair looks less like the collar of a fighting bulldog, less spiked; floppier.

The shock of the couple's sudden appearance after the blast of sub-freezing wind on the walk over, and that she agreed to let Vee take the guest room, brings her to question her sanity. She does this a lot lately.

"Quick, come in and get warm. I'll get water boiling for tea; you guys take a seat in my office." The pastor sets the thermostat on seventy, turns on the stove, and thanks the Lord for the charity she exhibits, because she certainly does not *feel* charitable. Dalia has left a message on Calline's desk that she will be sick today, euphemism for shopping and lunch with mother. Calline feels vulnerable and alone.

"How was the honeymoon? Good trip?" Connie and David take a cup of tea from the tray Calline brings to her little office cubby. She takes her chair behind her desk and sorts mail. The couple jam together on the tiny love seat.

"We were in bed, like eighty hours straight," says Connie, chewing one of her nails to the quick. David giggles and turns red.

"You might have set a world record." Calline giggles in spite of her grim mood.

"We're preggo," they say in unison, high-fiving and doing their bounce-on-the-couch thing.

"Actually, Cal, just between you and us, I was throwing up on the honeymoon and we went to the doctor. She said I was twelve weeks along. The babies were at the wedding and we didn't even know it. We wanted you to be the first to know, because we want you to baptize them."

"Them?" She slips down into her chair and prays her eyes don't betray judgment.

Another high five and frantic bouncing.

"Yep," says David, "Twins, Bee and Bop."

"Bee and Bop? You're going to call them Bee and Bop?"

"Would you, Rev. Cal? Wait till Mom and Dad find out. We're telling them at dinner," says the newlywed, patting her stomach.

Calline hopes Tendal and Margaret eat something that goes down easy. Chasing it with this news could flatten them right out.

"Hey Cal, Dad said you ran into a surfboard, or something like that." She points to the pastor's head.

Calline feels for her scar and rubs the bristle of new hair growth.

"Your hair looks like mine," says Connie, proud.

"Yeah, I could do a lot worse," says Calline, swallowing a laugh.

Connie and David get up to leave, nothing said, letting the wind catch the door behind them. Slam.

The pastor's attention goes to the file that has collected poems and notes, scribbles and songs, letters, photographs, and all the correspondence with the church that form a patchwork quilt of Rachael Rigley Connors' eight decades of life. Calline is tempted to let the phone ring, but defers.

"Jack here," flat and business-like as usual. "The Connors' service will be Thursday. Ten."

The day before Peter and Randy arrive, Calline thinks, knowing she's powerless to rearrange Jack's schedule. "Like airplanes circling to land, huh, Jack?" Calline and Jack laugh. Even though they annoy each other, they know that every runway will be cleared to make room for the homecoming of Rachael R. Connors. Jack and his boys will do a fine job, and Calline will be glad when her dear friend, free of all suffering, is laid to rest with the richest honors she deserves. She blows her nose again and blankly flips through the scrapbook of Rachael's life. There are pieces missing, pieces that, if completed, would help the pastor honor more completely this woman of substance. Everyone knows she has a sister rarely mentioned. The photograph Calline examines identifies her as Gloria—third from the left. Curious to find where this all might lead, she calls George.

"George, it's Cal. I'm thinking about your mom's service, honoring her life as fully as I can. Her sister Gloria—is she still living?"

"Barely. She lives in Detroit; I'm not sure she wants contact. Don't expect much. She's over eighty herself, and still pretty angry." George is easy these days. Sorrow has blunted his edges and his return to the fold might have humbled him as well.

"Thanks. I'll call her, see if she might shed some light and come to the funeral. Thanks, George. I know this time is difficult." Calline hangs up from George, and dials Gloria Rigley's number.

"This is Gloria. And with whom am I speaking?" Her voice is soft and jittery.

"Miss Rigley, this is Rev. Calline Simpson in High Dunes. I'm calling about your sister, Rachael Connors." Calline waits, not expecting much from her, wondering if the old woman will hang up after a long second's pause.

"Mrs. Simpson, er, Reverend, I think it's time to let you in my side of life with Rachael. I can't talk right now. Can we talk tonight? I'll call you?" She seems genuine. Perhaps with mortality on her mind, she's convinced it is time to clean the slate, to release the pain of something long festered. Afraid Gloria might dodge, or simply forget, Calline offers, "I'd be happy to call you at a time convenient for you. Tonight?"

"7:30, then. Good-bye."

No less surprising than the willingness of Rachael's sister to talk is a sudden sharp stab of unwillingness of the pastor to continue her duties. The images of profound and otherworldly beauty, and tranquility of Heaven, resound in her heart as the songbird's calls after a sunrise walk. She will be forever drawn there, while the future here, even with glimmers of hope, seems negligible. Let someone else hire an out gay man, let someone else bury a pillar of the church, let someone else host a poor pregnant teenager, let someone else . . .

The cross-stitch next to her Certificate of Ordination draws her attention to the words of St. Augustine: "Do what you can do and pray for what you cannot do."

"O.K., I can welcome Bee and Bop into this crazy world, and pray for help with all the rest," she says, rubbing Bingo's neck while the dog snores on the floor next to her.

A renewing late afternoon walk at lakefront, followed by takeout from Curley's, bolster Calline for her talk with Rachael's sister. At 7:30 pm on the nose, she dials the phone. The frail woman answers; Gloria goes right to the story, as if running for a train pulling out.

"What I can tell you about my sister, Rachael," she says with mild sarcasm, "is she got it all, the good genes. From infancy, it was as if Ma and Pa could only see her. There was John and George and myself, but most of the family estate went to Sister. Her story pours out like lines spoken a thousand times. "I drowned my resentment in alcohol and prescription medications. I blamed Rachael for all my problems, imagined and real. She reached out, but I drove her away." Calline holds the receiver away while Gloria blows her nose.

"Rachael talked vaguely of something like survivor's guilt. Now I understand," said Calline judiciously. "'Why was I so special to the exclusion of the others?' she would ask. I think of the story Jesus told of the two sons, the one who spent his inheritance in squalor, the other who stayed home, did everything right. Yet, the father threw a big party for the wayward son when he returned. It's a story about unfairness, but if you dig deeper, you see that . . ."

"Your preaching eludes me, Reverend, and I will try to make the service. Thursday, ten?" She sounds sad and very tired. Defeated.

Calline hangs up, scratches some notes, and dials Patty. "Hey girl. Two things: Remember the saying that holding resentments is like drinking poison and expecting the other person to die? I just spoke with a woman who has poisoned herself most of her adult life, expecting her sister to die."

"I relate. And?" Patty exhales.

"The Prodigal son story; what do you make of it? Lately, I've been able to get my focus off the good brother-bad brother competition for the father's blessing, and onto the goodness of the father. That's what I saw in Heaven, Patty. The goodness of that father who was just glad to have me home, no matter my stubbornness, my indifference, self-will. You name it."

"Excellent pre-bed reflection, girlfriend. Why the dad didn't whoop the heck out of that younger son. You know that dad had both kids' pictures on his refrigerator. That's God for you, so crazy in love with us, prodigals and all." Patty yawns. Sometimes the two friends just hang silently on the phone, waiting for the other to come out with last ruminations before lights out.

"Peter and Randy come tomorrow. Pray. Bye, dear. Love you." Click. The phone rings. It's Sorrel. Calline feels dizzy and lightheaded.

"Hey, Cal, I have difficult news and wondered if I could come by, share stuff in front of the fire?" Sorrel cries, an alarming recognition of his vulnerability with her. She must rally for him, as tired to the bone as she feels. She will rally for him, for Sorrel Dixon. Yes, she will.

"Sure, come." In front of her mirror, she chides her reflection. "I'm pale and my cheeks are fat; the extra pound must go, and the grays in my hair. New grays. Ugh." *Now might be a good time to dab on some Chanel.*

Bingo bounds to the door. Sorrel lets himself in, kicks off his boots; water pools from ice thawing. He wears a faded red cashmere sweater and dark corduroy pants. She loves him unshaven. She loves him no matter what. In silence, Calline pulls two chairs together in front of the fire, hot coals hissing; the teapot whistles. A fresh log raises the flame. Sorrel, clearly upset, settles into his chair. He reaches for her hand and holds it. Now it is she who anchors him.

Sorrel sighs. "I don't know where to even begin. It's Elizabeth. God, it's always Elizabeth. She wants to leave and live up at Forest Glen in Ironwood, at some rehab facility. That's eight hours from here. I remember, Cal, if I could talk some . . ." Cal welcomes Sorrel's heart-spills, she calls them. Rarely does he seem so undone and clear at the same time. "I don't talk about her much, I know. It may be that she's more of a habit for me, than either a romantic, or a spiritual pull, if you know what I mean."

Calline remembers how Elizabeth cried that night at the Rehab center. Sorrel does the same, blowing, wadding the tissue and throwing it into the fire, and repeating the process until the energy behind the words is spent. He puts his head back and exhales a breath he's perhaps held for ages. "I don't think I've been very honest with either of us, Elizabeth or myself. These past weeks—in fact, since I've known her—she shows little resolve to invest in her life, never mind in a life with me and Billy. The lie

I've told myself is that I could really deeply love her, look away from her frailty and shallow endeavors. It feels like I've done all the paddling for both of us. I'm tired, Cal. I've lived most of my life more from obligation than true desire. Obligation here, obligation there. When is it *my* turn? Okay, I'm whining. Hell, I don't care." He looks over at Calline and brushes her cheek with the back of his fingers. He stretches and yawns and leans toward her, taking both her hands in his. "Look at me, woman." His deep green eyes reflect the flames from the fireplace and shine like polished glass.

As much as her love and admiration for him occupy her, she knows this is a man embroiled in grief. As much as she feels the warm fluids of lust fill her body, this is no time to make a move. *There is never a good time!* her conscience screams. This man is in pain. He doesn't need the complication of the two of them. He may be erasing Elizabeth from his life, but Elizabeth will occupy Sorrel's conscience and attention for months to come. Even still.... the Code.

Yet, she reaches to take his hand, gazes into the fire, then back to meet his eyes. "Sorrel, it's late. It's been a long day. You've got a lot to process about Elizabeth. How difficult this is for you." But reason cannot avert the call, the desire to engage body, mind, and spirit with this sweet, wonderful, painfully vulnerable man. Sorrel leans closer and takes her chin in his soft palm. He turns her face to his and plants a kiss; he holds his lips to hers for seconds and breathes deeply. With every ounce of will, she pulls away, touching his lips with her index finger, nodding no. In the glow of the fire, his hair shines, his eyes glisten from tears, his aftershave smells sweet and smoky. The only thing right to say is "good-bye" when her heart beats, "hello, Sorrel, hello forever." As he rises, he pulls her up and holds her to him. At the door, she hands him his coat and plants a soft kiss on his forehead. His hand, the one that said "wait", can't seem to release its grasp on hers. Or is it hers that can't release from his?

CHAPTER THIRTY-TWO

CALLINE WRITES IN her journal, "I wonder what I am leaving undone—like Rachael's sister—to regret when it's too late. Is it ever too late?" She rubs her knee, the place that holds shame, shame diminishing. Yet, as she writes, the grief of losing Rachael compounds with the sorrow of losing her mother. "The world is bereft of the elders who have let life teach them, like Rachael and Mom. They have stirred the swill of suffering and loss and made it into something beautiful. I will miss you dear friend. I miss you, Mom." She closes her journal, blows her nose, and knows that true wizening is not an automatic gratuity of getting old. Grimsley, for example, is eighty-five and mean as hell when things aren't going her way. "Okay, God, she has a generous streak, even though she is hard on people that aren't just like her, homosexuals in particular. I'll grant her that." Calline feels a smile come to her, not an expression she associates with thoughts of Grimsley. A hint of an attitude of tolerance and kindness catches her by surprise. But so does everything else that seems to be shifting within and around her.

The morning alarm startles her from a dead sleep after hours of awakening from a recurring dream of falling off a cliff and riding the air currents with magical wings. Calline's morning routine is rushed. She's late. Blustery lake winds cut, but not enough to require her brutal wear, she calls it. She dresses in layers while Bingo cocks her head as if maybe this time her person will let her go, too. Calline is sure her leg aches more than usual with the anticipation of meeting Peter and Randy. Dalia is gone for the day, so the building is quiet until the phone rings.

"Hi Cal. Today's the day. I'm excited, you?" Kathy is referring, of course, to meeting Peter and Randy. The sun always shines for Kathy, even when snow swirls in the graying sky.

"As I'll ever be, Kath. How 'bout I meet you at the Dodge place and we'll ride together?" Calline checks her calendar and her watch. The two men arrive at eleven, on the Chicago shuttle that flies in twice daily.

Plans solidified with Kathy, Calline takes a call from Thomas. "Hey Cal, just called to wish you luck. Please tell Peter and Randy that Governance and Smit's group look forward to meeting them. Come around six to our house. Oh yes, and this Sunday I'm going to announce our 'Open and Welcoming' campaign to the congregation. That cuts me out of hearing Peter play, but I trust the others. I'm about as musical as a dead bird." Except about his music talents, Thomas sure sounds confident about next steps.

"These are first steps for us, Thomas. I appreciate your resolve, just when mine is thinning a bit. I'll admit, I am nervous about all this." Calline swallows a lump of fear, hoping Thomas doesn't notice.

"These aren't steps we've ever taken, but babies must eventually walk. And walk we shall. Or fall flat on our faces," says Thomas. *At least faith is still alive, if only as big as a mustard seed*, she thinks, as she measures her own of late.

The airport is a small fly-in for the few commuter planes with access to High Dunes from cities east and west. Randy does well as a designer in San Francisco, so the men were happy to pick up the extra expense for the sake of convenience. Kathy and Calline linger at the huge viewing window to chat and watch landings and take-offs. Right at eleven o'clock, a commuter prop plane gently glides to touchdown and taxis to the gate.

Kathy touches Calline's shoulder for reassurance. Their gazes into each other's eyes seem to seal a sisters' bond in a daring mission, too late to retreat, too early to predict outcomes. As if needing something to do before the men enter the waiting area, the women hug. Calline turns and points.

Two handsome, tanned men appear side-by-side from the gate. Peter looks like his photograph. He's blond and balding. The large blue eyes in his photograph hide behind Ray-Bans. His smile is broad, his teeth straight and shining. He looks thinner than his pictures, like a twig that could easily snap. Randy, with black close-cut hair, wears a Lakers t-shirt and tightly fitting black jeans that reveal every curve in his toned, muscled body. Randy pulls a carry-on with one hand and secures a *N.Y. Times* and *Wall Street Journal* with the other. The two women smile and wave and walk toward them, a confluence of four lives, future unknown.

"Peter? Randy? It's you, I can tell from the photo you sent," Calline says nervously as she approaches Peter with one hand extended.

"You must be Calline. And you're Kathy?" Peter leans over and hugs the pastor like a long-lost sister, putting her immediately at ease. Calline notices how bony he feels. It never occurred to her that he might have A.I.D.S.. Kathy laughs and chatters obsequiously as Peter extends a hug to her. Randy hugs with a crushing strength, introducing himself with etiquette-school aplomb. In no time, luggage is collected and the four find their way through a light flurry. High Dunes' temperatures bring the two men quickly from sandals into boots, from short sleeves to flannel, vests, scarves and hats, fastidiously fashionable. They seem prepared, more than the pastor feels she will ever be.

The men will stay at The Ten Gables, a small B&B, just a walking distance from Curley's. The drive from the airport is brief, kept interesting with Peter's and Randy's talking like two boys fresh from a Boy Scout excursion. Obviously at ease with each other, their ability to put others at ease is notable. For that, Calline is grateful.

Kathy keeps the car warmed while Calline accompanies the men into the fashionably appointed reception area of the Inn. Calline wonders if Sally will meet them without staring or trying too hard. "This is on us, guys. You were generous to save us a drive to Grand Rapids." Calline shoos Randy away from trying to cover the bill, and gently chides, "Get yourself rested; Kathy will come around six to take you to the Dreidens'. I'll see you there! So glad you're here." Calline leans over to squeeze her knee, watching Peter watch her.

She'll only have a few minutes at home to bathe, unwind, and get a quick walk with Bingo before the evening at the Dreidens'. A quick review of phone messages brings up acid. It's Grimsley. Calline's gut says not to pick it up, and her head says that to not pay attention to her gut is a bad idea. But her head prevails. "I know he's arriving this weekend. This is not a threat, but a promise. Thirty of us will walk. We've just met to affirm the sinful and blatant stubbornness of this." Click.

Another one from Dalia. "Vee came by to remind you to pick her up Sunday at four. Her house. Good luck with the interview." Calline doesn't remember telling Dalia anything about the interview.

Not without deep inhales and holding her stomach in, does she get the zipper of her tweed pants to close. Bingo licks Calline's face while she tugs at heavy boots over thick gray wool socks. Enough outdoor wear covers her to walk to the Dreidens' in relative comfort. Bingo whines to go along, but defeated, creeps her way to her chair looking forlorn while Calline seals the door and locks it. She notices that, though her breath is frosted, her heart feels warm for reasons inexplicable. A full moon lights the night sky free of clouds, its light dancing on the shrinking snow banks that rise from snow-powdered sidewalks and streets.

"Come in everyone, and get comfortable." Thomas' tone is relaxed and welcoming. Is this because the anticipation is so much worse than the actual event? Interviewing an out gay man to run the music program—the elephant in the living room—is now actually in the living room.

What Calline had feared most, and no doubt, the two men as well: everyone is painfully conscientious. Calline remembers how once her mother was so focused on the bulbous over-sized nose of a stranger next to her in the grocery store, Mother approached the lady and asked, "Do you knows where the mayonnaise is?" What if the well-intentioned and proper Myrtle blurted out, "Is everyone having a gay time?" But Peter and Randy are seasoned social elephants.

"Come, for things are now ready," Myrtle intones the sacrament invitation. Each of the ten place settings exhibit her English Pembroke china, King Richard sterling, and crystal stemware. Big pink peonies float in a Waterford bowl in the center. The smells of roast ham, pie, and burning wood could discourage any thought that the evening could bring anything but a spirit of unity and cordiality. Thomas lights candles that float in four bowls that circle the flower bowl. Gunther, Sorrel, Kathy, Smit, Myrtle and Thomas, Calline, Lilly, and the two guests find their seats. J.B. Johnson, still on the Petition, is absent, to no one's surprise. Clerk Nancy Dobbs is said to be ill, but probably is not. Sorrel sits next to Calline, his hand settled on her knee. Unnerving, yet exciting, she can't help but smile as she places her hand over his. The forbidden excites her. Peter spontaneously offers to teach a prayer sung to the tune of "Amazing Grace". He and Randy demonstrate how the song is sung in a round. The group catches on quickly. What a brilliant move. Not only does music melt barriers, but it relaxes tensions. Tucked in with a heartfelt prayer by Thomas, how can discomfort survive?

Dinner conversation is easy, largely because of Kathy's upbeat ways, and Randy's obvious gifts of repartee. The two banter about life in California, Kathy's home state. When plates are emptied of Myrtle's specialty, shepherd's pie, Thomas rises to clear, a job he assumed when the two were first married. Gunther joins him, seeming relieved to have something to do. "Hot toddies in the living room," Myrtle announces as everyone pushes from the dining table to get more comfortable. If there is any edge on anyone's nerves at this point, the toddies will smooth them right out. Myrtle pours a hot sweet drink—her mother's favorite recipe—hot milk with peppermint and Kahlua. Randy and Peter pass, each sitting with hands folded, looking ethereally serene.

Smit goes to his briefcase to retrieve papers to hand to each person present. He and committee members have prepared questions that each will ask of the candidate. Randy offers graciously, "I'll step out if you all would like me to."

"If you want, Randy, although it would be fine if you stay," says Smit looking around the room, confident all will concur. The two men glance warmly at each other, to offer encouragement. From years of exclusion and hiding, both know to never become complacent. Tonight, certainly, is no exception, as genuinely gracious the company, and as warm and elegant the Dreiden's hospitality. Peter clears his throat, nervously squares away his bow tie which is already perfect, crosses his long, skinny legs, and folds his hands in his lap. "Fire away," he smiles, facing each inquisitor with a confident, rehearsed gaze.

"Peter, each of us has a question. Please take your time and don't hesitate to interject your questions along the way. Kathy will start us out." Smit says this with genuine kindness and respect. Peter simply nods ascent, coughs into a fisted right hand, and waits.

Some of the questions are whimsical, like "Who is your favorite cartoon character and why?" Some are pragmatic: "What's in High Dunes that attracts you?" Each offers Peter a platform from which to exhibit his sense of humor, his theological depth, and vast knowledge and experience as musician and choir director. After Peter addresses the last questions, the group seems so enamored and enchanted, how could any objection withstand? The man would be a Godsend. *Yet,* Calline thinks, *surely Peter must wonder if the church would be a Godsend to him.* It's now the committee's turn to answer his questions.

"We are wondering if Randy will be able to find employment in this area." Peter and Randy turn to face each other. "Even more important, can you all allow us to be ourselves here?" It is bold and risky to ask. The man has nothing to lose; jobs are plentiful, he's brilliant. Anyone applying for any job wants to know this. Of course, Peter means as a couple, as a married couple, a gay married couple, married in the eyes of God, but not in the eyes of the state. *Would we be comfortable?* Friends of his have been exiled, treated like pariahs, abused, abandoned, shot, left alone to die. Lepers.

Calline's heart swells for both men. *Why, God, why should they have to worry?* Such gifts, such devotion between them, such an offering to little old High Dunes First United Congregational Church; can anyone see the grace in this beautiful offering that a man of such faith and talent would endow upon their church? Or do they just see condemnation, judgment, and hatred? She lauds Peter for his courage to get to the crux of the matter.

Thomas speaks. "Peter, there's no sense beating around the bush. The idea of bringing you here is causing a stir in our congregation. Okay, a big divide is forming as we speak. Some have promised to leave if we call the right person for the job, who happens to be gay. I imagine this is nothing new for you." A long silence fills the room. Bodies shift and Myrtle rises to pour more warm liquor.

Peter, with a gentle sternness in his voice, says, "First, I thank you all for this most cordial and lovely reception of me and Randy. Really, I do. I think we've both shared our interest in coming." Randy nods affirmation. "There are too many congregations who say they are open, but when you get there, they dare you to be yourself. Of course, that wouldn't be fair to you, me, or Randy. Yet, here we are. Why?" A sense of deflation and disappointment fill the faces in the room. Have they come this far and fought so hard, stuck their necks out and now Peter is implying, *Forget it. It's too much for this little backwater church to handle? Yes? No?*

Peter lifts his face to each of their gazes. "Yet, there's so much that draws me here. I can't really explain. Well, there's your pastor with whom I think I'd work well; I've mentioned I grew up around the corner from here, my aging parents, a major consideration." Peter seems easy with his reasons for coming to this point with this particular church, not one he'd typically pursue. He looks to Randy who nods and turns the gold band on his left finger.

Thomas says, square on, "Then you should know a petition has circulated and thirty folks have signed, saying they'll walk if we call you. Some have changed their minds, though," Thomas offers, not so sure about anything. "You also should know, Peter, that precisely because of the resistance and the reasoning for which it is difficult for us to find a convincing basis, we here tonight, and many others, feel emboldened to press on. To me, it feels like it's our duty, our obligation, dare I say calling, to establish this course for our benefit, and we pray God, for yours and Randy's. No, it's not fun or easy, yet we maintain that true discipleship bears a price. Would others concur?" All heads nod vigorously.

Peter, expressionless, glances at Randy and rises. Everyone stands with him, except Calline who is caught up in thought that the fish might have just slipped back into the water. *Pray not, but why not? The committee has no solid proof to convince Peter that High Dunes First United Congregational Church isn't just another congregation full of fraidy-cats splitting over his back?*

"It's been a long day for these two. Perhaps we should circle up and say a closing prayer, or song, and call it a day," Calline says yawning, covering a smile that comes out of nowhere. Sorrel smiles and looks her way. He winks and she returns same. She thinks she sees Thomas watching them and doesn't really care.

Smit chimes in. "The search committee will host Peter and Randy for brunch at my place tomorrow. Then we'll pass him over to you, Cal, then to the Methodists on Sunday." Smit throws an invisible football.

"Feel like a football, Peter?" asks Kathy, laughing at Smit.

Peter laughs, exhausted, and hands Randy his hat and scarf. Randy helps Peter into his coat. They both turn to hug Myrtle, her hands held out to keep from getting dishwater on the men. She looks into Peter's eyes, voting for him with a broad smile and a light touch to his cheek. In no time, the house is empty, except for the delicious smells and the afterglow of an evening that ended with truth spoken, yet outcomes about as clear as the unwashed crystal.

Uninvited, Sorrel walks Calline back to her house. "Well, I'd say we've appropriately welcomed the two gays. I mean guys," giggles Sorrel. They laugh all the way back to the front door.

"Can you stay the night?" The reverend hears herself say, holding the door open for Sorrel to cross the threshold.

CHAPTER THIRTY-THREE

THE "OPEN AND Welcoming to All God's Children" initiative, voted by Governance as the best way to spend a portion of the gift from Willomena Brainard, might be a silver lining even though the vision's timing seems questionable. Thirty-or-so pledging units have withdrawn, and no telling if they will be restored. The Petition-signers are holding their ground, except for George Connors, who is sure his mother would hound him to an early grave if he didn't. J.B. is too habitual and principled to bail altogether. He is happy to keep his hands on the money-counting. Alexis Grimsley drops an occasional bomb on the pastor's message machine, threatening, "The troops await!" while husband Richard drops a much-diminished check into the offering plate.

"Richard Kellogg Grimsley's conscience won't allow him to sever the church's financial jugular entirely," Sorrel says on a recent surprise visit to the pastor's residence, a visit that follows the one the night before.

"I guess that's better than no check and no attendance on Sundays. What now?" Calline raises sad eyes to meet his, more dependent now than ever on his tenderness and understanding.

At the next Governance meeting, Treasurer, J.B., offers his grim and always practical assessment. "You all are aware that money is going south?" J.B. fires an inhospitable gaze at the pastor, then at Thomas. The rest of the folks avoid eye contact with the stern banker and financier.

"J.B., we knew winds would blow pretty hard over this, and we've decided, based on the unanimous recommendation of Smit's search committee, based on the applications of reason and faith and plain hard work, to call Peter. So, that's pretty much that." Moderator Thomas taps his fingers on the table and scratches his new beard, much less gray and thicker than his thinning hair. Everyone looks poker-faced, like they're ready to put a hefty stack of chips on the line in pure faith that the opponent is bluffing. "It's a go, then. Right? To call Peter?" All heads nod again, but J.B.'s. "You in or out, Johnson?" Thomas is also poker-faced and not a little aggravated with the starchy bean counter.

"What does it matter how I vote? By next year, there won't be any organ to play or choir to direct, because there won't be any church." J.B. pushes his printed financial report copies toward Thomas and excuses himself. He pats his hips and makes a funny guttural sound on his way out the door.

Thomas pounds his fist. "Then Peter it will be if all of us are in, right? Nancy, as Clerk, you'll have to notify the congregation of the vote to be taken directly after worship, Sunday after this one. Gunther, how's it going for Saturday's outreach to the neighbors and the mailings?" Thomas fidgets with a pencil, eager to get things on paper, sealed, and delivered, like firing a rocket on a launching pad that's sat there way too long.

Chair of Missions, Gunther, offers, "A few approached me after your announcement, Thomas, willing to work on what Missions is calling **WOW**, *We are Open and Welcoming—to All God's Children.* Clever, huh?" The group claps. Puffed up and commanding, Gunther continues, "As you all know, we've called everyone to meet here Saturday at 9:00 for continental breakfast, and then to go door-to-door introducing ourselves, giving discount coupons to area restaurants, and free fresh foods from the Food Gleaners. We want to invite anyone and everyone to come to church first Sunday in March. Any who come will get a good meal; hopefully Rev., you'll preach a fine sermon—not too hard on us—and the music will be full tilt." Calline nods, promising her best. The others mechanically rise to circle. All pray and call it an evening.

Sorrel and the pastor remain to check the back doors and to double lock the front. The delay is intentional; to be sure all have driven away, leaving the two in the front walkway standing face-to-face, a full moon rising behind a low cloud. It's hovering at freezing, after nine. Calline sighs from weariness, and Sorrel offers, "How 'bout some hot chocolate or something stronger for you, at the Pub?"

"Sure." She's too tired to resist and wouldn't if she could. He opens the door to the Durango. They sit while the car heats. His hand reaches to her knee and he turns to face her. A wave of electricity goes through her body, more intense each time they touch and, yes, they have touched. Calline's brakes are broken. Sorrel and she have turned a corner onto a one way street.

"I told you Elizabeth signed herself in at Forrest Glen. It's like the Elizabeth I once knew, presuming I knew her at all, left her body. I don't know who lives there now. She was so unconcerned when she left. She put herself on a bus, wouldn't even let me drive her. Said the wedding was off indefinitely. I have to admit, I felt relief." Sorrel looks down at Calline's hand and massages her fingers, looking like there's little else to feel or do where Elizabeth is concerned. Then he places his free hand on her cheek and gazes into her eyes with a penetration that frightens her. He can see her at some level no one has; just by the way he smiles and looks and touches, and smiles and looks again.

She does not avert her gaze. She feels warm tingling in her hands and in places that have been neglected for too long. He leans into her and she meets him. A long, lingering sweet kiss sends them to a place she remembers having gone, like returning to a childhood hideout, but it's been so long, it's hardly recognizable. She gently pulls away, places her hand on his shoulder, and offers to make a mean cup of cocoa to share in front of her fireplace. "Let's skip the Pub tonight, baby. My place." She winks.

Sorrel pulls her back to him, his eyes glazed with that man-I'm-hungry look. Calline pulls away, suddenly aware they are fraternizing in the church parking lot under a street lamp. "Can we go now? I think we've managed to escape the kissing police, but I don't want to push my luck. It probably wouldn't go over too big, the pastor getting busted for necking with a parishioner." She does her habitual survey to see if anyone is looking.

"Nope. But it sure goes over big with me—the pastor getting it on with this parishioner." Sorrel revs the engine. The Durango fishtails from the parking lot. They laugh like two school kids who just discovered their bodies and the freedom to go with.

Warm drinks at the fire and flirtatious talk is for Sorrel the prelude to hoped-for intimacy with this woman who's become more and more a part of him. But he meets with a strong arm that pushes him to the front door. "Sorrel, honey, it's late. I'm tired."

"Then when? I'm crazy about you, you must know." Sorrel presses against her, obviously aroused. For a flash, she feels afraid and pushes him off. He pulls away suddenly and straightens his jacket, looking coy. "I'm sorry, Cal. Forgive me. I'm always lecturing Billy about using restraint with women. Look at me." He blushes and turns to leave.

She is overcome with tenderness and desire for him. "Sorrel?" He turns back.

"Yes?" He sighs a pathetic sigh.

"I love you. Now, get your tail home and get some rest. Tomorrow's a big day. See you there." She cracks the door and Bingo bounds out and runs to Sorrel. While they romp, she disappears into the house, door slammed tight before she changes her mind.

CHAPTER THIRTY-FOUR

ON HER WALK to join the Saturday **WOW** walkers, Calline's focus is upon anything and everything Sorrel Dixon; like she's taken a medication, the side effect of which is obsession. The enthusiastic turn-out for the neighborhood outreach is a pleasant distraction from the Peter controversy. The Lord only knows what will come of it as far as new people coming, to fill the gaps as disgruntled members leave. Walkers gather around for donuts, bagels, coffee, and hot cider, more people than worship attenders of late.

Miss Becky joins in, too, warmly greeting Calline. "I like we can do missions together, Reverend. Something be on you, I can tell. It's a good something this time, not that mean ol' Devil." She sees and teases as only Miss Becky can. Calline squeezes Becky's hand, knowing Becky knows. Becky winks and hollers out, "Y'all'll be cold and thirsty fo' sho after you knock on all those doors. Come by the Eatery for hot chocolate and goodies. I mean it now."

Melinda Suarez, mother of the Three Jesuses, has her entire brood in tow, five in all. David Somers, without his pregnant Connie, arrives with two buddies. Billy and Martha come with two college friends. Mims Smith from a new neighborhood community organization that supports people with developmental challenges, introduces herself again to Calline. "Reverend, do you mind if I come, too?" Calline recollects their conversation by phone a week ago. "We want to rent the brown building across the street to use as a community gathering place. We'd call it 'The

Lemonade Stand'. That's because life has given most of us lemons, but we've decided to make lemonade."

"That'd be fine by me, Mims. Welcome to the hood," Calline says with less conviction than her voice portrays. She doubts the neighbors will roll out the red carpet for the likes of Mims's crowd.

Gunther, clad in army pants, black turtleneck, and an orange hunting vest, unpacks boxes of printed doorknob fliers in church colors, brown and gold. Each one is designed to hang neatly on a door knob like a "don't disturb" sign in hotels. It says *High Dunes First United Congregational Church is Open and Welcoming to All God's Children* and lists worship times. A flier extends an invitation to a free breakfast, children's activities and "fun" church, first Sunday in March. Restaurant coupons and Gleaners certificates are stuffed into envelopes with "compliments of HDFUCC". Nancy and helpers stuff brightly-colored lunch bags with sweet homemade goodies. The youth pack fliers, goodies, and helpful information into backpacks.

Gunther rises with portable megaphone, ringing the bell used to call worshipers to the sanctuary. "Welcome to our first *Open and Welcoming* outreach event and thanks, all of you, for coming! Calline, would you offer a prayer?" Gunther seems in rare form, this new mission giving him energy and pep unfamiliar to all who know the man. No doubt this event helps get everyone's mind off troubles, and onto what might bring the congregation renewed vitality. It surely can't hurt, even if the neighborhood walk is just that, a walk. Gunther's enthusiasm is infectious. Calline's prayer flies to the ones whose lives the walkers will touch, on a day that offers a warmer sun and a joyful spirit. "Grant us traveling mercies, merciful God. Amen."

Gunther's voice rises with his hands, "Amen, may we be the voices, hands and feet of our Lord." Nancy distributes maps that divide the neighborhood into four sections. Gunther instructs, "We'll get into four groups and work the places marked on the maps. They are all a walking distance from our starting point, a little east of the high school. We'll drive to there and park. We won't reach the full potential of possible visitors, but it's a good start. I figure at least two hundred houses and apartment units are drawn in our circle. Team leaders, raise your hands, please, Kathy, Sorrel, Smit, and Thomas. Let's count off one-to-four. Join up with the leader who has your number. We'll role-play a typical visit, and answer questions you might have."

"One." Gunther points to Billy and Martha who walk to stand by Smit. "Two," he points to two of Billy's friends. "Three," he points to Myrtle; "Four," he points to Dalia. The enthusiasm and energy in the room are palpable. This warms Calline's heart as much as Sorrel does. Almost.

It's a circus act getting everyone into six automobiles. Calline locks the building, checks her watch, and gets into the passenger front seat of Thomas's huge Dodge van, back seats flattened to make a platform large enough to squeeze in David with his two friends, and Mims from the Lemonade Stand. Calline giggles at the sight; she notices she's generally giddy, wondering at every inhale and exhale what Sorrel is doing as she watches his Durango pull behind. *See if you cannot think about elephants flying*, she tells herself and laughs.

Thomas takes each turn gently in deference to the cargo passengers. David Somers growls, "Someone's foot is jamming into my private parts; keep it up, I'll hunt you down." Through the visor mirror, Calline sees that the someone, and only, is Mims's foot doing the job on David. She looks to be having some sort of serious face tremor and ticking.

"Mims, you O.K.?" Calline isn't sure how strong Mims is, wedged between David's two friends, men over six feet tall. Mims is clearly stressed. Calline turns to lock David's gaze. He knows by that look, he'll be singing soprano if he says another word. He makes a hard shift to the left and appears relieved. So does

Mims. Thomas says, "Here we are. We'll start here. Everybody out and wait until I can park and get to you with your supplies." Like circus clowns, people pile from their cars and vans, awaiting instructions. David walks and leans against a tree, lowering his head between his knees.

"Mims, would you care to walk with me? I'd like to get to know you," Calline offers to a woman she genuinely hopes to befriend. After all, they could be neighbors soon. Mims could use friends, and her Lemonade Stand will face a battle to claim a space in a neighborhood where the folks like folks that look just like themselves. Mims's hands tremble, but she nods yes and seems relieved.

Gunther joins up with the gathering crowd. "Each of us gets a backpack and there are two carry-alls for each group. Each group has a different map that charts your general path in your quadrant." Gunther thrives in his role as platoon leader.

"I don't want to go with her," protests Pequita Suarez who is twelve and doesn't want to walk with her mother and screaming siblings. Embarrassing.

"Come with us, Pequita," Gunther hollers. "If your mother doesn't mind." Melinda waves to Gunther with thanks while she shoves the three-pod stroller forward, an impressive concert emanating from the triplets.

"O.K., traveling mercies, everyone," Gunther hollers. "Do just as we practiced, and you'll be fine. Let's all set our watches for 11:10 and meet at Miss Becky's at 1:00. Miss Becky's is marked on your maps as 'MBE' with a phone number. If you get into trouble, stay together, call Miss Becky's, and stay put until we can get to you. We won't start worrying until we don't see you after 2:00 or so."

David and his two friends take off down a narrow street like three sailors on furlough, back packs flying from their shoulders. David yells, "See you at Miss Becky's!"

CHAPTER THIRTY-FIVE

WALKING STREETS NOT shown on any map, climbing stairs to four-story apartments, exploring alleys and tree-lined drives can wear a person plumb out. When Mims and Calline discover their common roots in the South, Thomas decides to split off and follow along with Melinda and kids. So it's just the pastor and Mims for the two hour effort to draw a circle large enough to welcome strangers to a church grabbing at straws. Handshakes and bribes with sweets don't keep some doors from slamming. "Religious fanatics!" they holler. They greet children playing in the streets who just want to talk. Old ladies and men, alone and fragile, are happy for a visit, any visit. A blind man, at least seventy-five, invites the two women in. They enter, even though the dog threatens. At least fifteen cats, six dogs, some kind of rodent and its babies, a large exotic bird, and six rabbits, live in the blind man's zoo.

"Folks call me Critter. Critter Friend," he says while petting the bird perched on his shoulder. "Tell these nice folks what you think, Tweeter."

"Ya'll come back ya hea'? Ya'll come back ya hea'?" The bird's diction is superb, low and resonant on the "y'all come back" and high and sonorous on the "ya hea'?" If you weren't looking, you'd swear it was a refined Southern lady bidding her guests' return. Of course, Mims and Calline are thrilled by this touch of the old South, etched so deeply in their bones.

Critter gives Tweeter a dollop of peanut butter and orders the dogs to go to the corner. They circle, sniffing the women's feet and then do as they're told, slinking where a pile of dirty laundry mounts. There's something about Critter that Calline likes, but she can't put her finger on it. Mims seems comfortable too, which says a lot. No doubt, people like Mims have been society's canaries, hyper sensitive and aware at levels that most aren't.

"We hope you will come to our Welcome and Open Sunday. Call if you need a ride. Might have to leave the critters here, though. We're not that open. Yet. Trust me, we're working on it." Calline laughs, knowing how much she loves her critter. A warm good-bye gives the women new zeal to carry on.

"Brother, my feet are killing me. How about you?" Mims stutters and rubs her hands to make heat. She forgot her mittens. Her hat, torn and holey, covers her ears.

"Miss Becky makes the best hot chocolate and sweet potato pie in the world. Can we place these last ten hangers, Mims? You up for it?" Calline is all too eager to get some warm drink in and some liquid out. As their last target, they choose the doorknobs of a little row of subsidized apartments. Old rusted out cars, bikes without chains, and turned-over trash barrels clutter yards. Christmas lights dangle from the roof that connects each of the units. A tiny pair of eyes peers alongside another pair of eyes from a window with a bullet hole and an outline of a snow-sprayed snow man. Calline knocks on that door, a faded brick color, kicked in and rusting.

"Yea? Who the hell is it?" It's a voice that comes from a big man.

"The church." Calline considers running. Mims fidgets.

"The who? Hell, Ain't no chooch been to this house evah." He softens a bit.

Mims fires a nervous look and fidgets with her coat buttons. The door opens just as the women turn to get away.

"Yea? Whatchoo want?" A man the size of a small refrigerator looks them up and down. He is on crutches and has a stub for a leg. Calline's eyes fix on that leg, not to stare, but because his stub is at eye level, almost.

"What's yo bidness? Chooch you say? Make it quick. It's cold." He shifts back and forth on the crutches. One child, all eyes, about three, clings to the good leg; the other boy, five maybe, hangs onto the stub staring, wide-eyed.

Mims breaks the ice. "We just want to leave you some goodies and invite you and the children to come visit us in two weeks." Mims has one bag of sweets left and a couple of fliers. She hands them to him. "Directions, and what we are about, are all here to read at your leisure." Mims really has the touch with people.

The children look up to the man, as up to the peak of a mountain, hoping he'll be benevolent and hand them the bag. Calline doubts they've eaten a square meal in weeks. She invites them to come for the delicious meal to be served and hands them plenty of food coupons. The boys dive for the bag when their father drops it.

"I doubt we'll make it to no white chooch, but O.K., thanks anyway." He turns away and then looks back and points to his leg. "Leg rotted from an accident and they had to cut it off." Then he whistles to the kids, the same whistle old Critter gave to his pack of mutts, and slams the door. Two tiny mouths fog the glass. This household haunts Calline.

"Ya'll come on in now and get those cold covers off you," says Miss Becky, her usual bold, loving self. "Hey Rev., come on in girl and get yo'self some cocoa 'n pie. Who's your friend there?" Miss Becky smiles and holds her arms wide to Mims.

Calline lets Becky press her to her large, doughy bosom.

"This is Mims from the Lemonade Stand, Becky."

"Here's a hug for you, too, Mims, cause if you a friend of the Reverent, you my friend." Miss Becky gives that from-Heaven laugh. Mims smiles. Who can't be calmed by such love? And the smells? Straight from Heaven's kitchen.

Soon, the little restaurant is packed with church folks. No one seems ruffled or the worse for the experience. Gunther arrives kicking his boots. He calls through the megaphone, "Everybody alive?"

Someone wisecracks, "Who would answer if we were dead?"

"I darned near got killed out there," says Lilly who is interrupted by another, another, and another, each eager to one-up the last story. Miss Becky stands at the stove, stirring a giant pot of her killer hot chocolate. Soon, a giant ladle spills hot cocoa into large mugs reaching toward the pot. Becky ladles a hefty dollop of homemade whipped cream with a sprinkle of nutmeg. Any who won't imbibe in a slice of the best pie in the world will surely be bereft of a spot of heaven.

"Hey, where's David and his buddies? It's almost two-thirty." Gunther feels responsible for every detail of the outing. No one seems concerned; all are so busy with pie and hot chocolate and tales getting loftier by the telling. Gunther collects the empty tote bags to count the fliers and door hangers remaining. "Hey, everyone! Listen up! We carried over two hundred door hangers and fliers and envelopes of coupons. I count thirteen fliers, ten door hangers, and six envelopes left. Way to go. Give yourselves a big pat on the back."

Whipped cream-mustached, Gunther beams. Soon, everyone makes a mustache and someone shouts, "They're back!" The bell on the door rings, announcing three very drunk men. In they pile, collapsing on the floor at the feet of one very cross proprietor.

"Well, it looks like our sailors on furlough are back," Gunther says over the whooping and clapping. All three roll on the floor, giggle, and then get still. Miss Becky looks down, stirring her pot like a witch preparing a brew. "My, my, the devil done his thing with those three. I'll give 'em some of my devil potion. That'll get 'em goin' strong. Hold 'em down while I whip it up." She laughs, returning to the counter to mix and stir, licking her lips with a vengeance.

"If it's strong enough for the devil, it might kill the boys, but when Miss Becky gets her mind on chasing off the devil, you might as well just step aside and pray along with her," Calline whispers to Gunther who isn't so sure. The crowd circles the men who blink and cough, rise up then fall again, flat. All are silent while Miss Becky leans down and pours into each mouth something blistering hot, as in spicy hot.

"Holy shit, mother of God!" screams one, leaping to his feet and running out the door. The other runs out, collapses in the snow to shovel hard flakes of ice into his mouth. He ignores the yellows of it. David stares up from the floor, covering his mouth, refusing to let Miss Becky deliver her devil-beating recipe.

"Good Lord, how many times now have I seen David Somers in this pose?" Calline asks of no one.

David pushes hard to stand up. "Dear Lord, I'm sorry. I'm so sorry," he cries. "I promise, I'll never do it again, I promise. Just don't make me eat the devil's fire, please, Miss Becky." Then he blacks out. People laugh, then get real quiet. Is he dead?

"He'll be back, ya'll. Lawd's working on him. That boy needs some work," assures Miss Becky. All heads nod agreement and laughter fills the room, the kind that salves sorrows that linger way down deep.

CHAPTER THIRTY-SIX

THOMAS NOTICES IT first. "Where's that smoke coming from?" He steers wildly over the curb, flooring it. The van screeches around the next corner and heads straight until, in no time, the smoke curling out from under the front door of the church building comes to full view. Sorrel's Durango gets to the parking lot first. His car still running, passengers frozen with fright, Sorrel runs to the door. Thomas and Calline chase after.

"I've seen enough fire movies to know there are flames behind that door just waiting to burst," says Sorrel, holding his arm out as a gate to anyone who tries to get too close. "Calline, stay back, please! The door could explode." Calline runs into the bushes to a tiny rose window at the side of the entrance foyer to survey. She yells, "It's just smoke. I don't see flames. The extinguisher box is right next to the bench in the entrance hall."

While Thomas and Sorrel decide to open the door and step into the smoke, others crowd around, careening to see. But all that's there is smoke, thick billows of it. Sorrel and Thomas cover their noses and mouths with handkerchiefs.

"You guys stay back," shouts Sorrel, who's already in. Coughing and banging at the glass to get to the extinguisher and axe, Sorrel smashes hard one more time and dashes out of the building, gasping for fresh air. He holds the fire extinguisher canister like a baby under his arm and, without thinking, yanks the round lever.

"Sorrel, don't! Dalia and I just studied how to use this thing. You have to get a good grip first, aim, and then pull the thing," shouts Calline. Too late, though. What's gotten into him? He's usually so level headed about these things? A shaving cream spray spews from the head. It slips from Sorrel's hold and hits the ground, spinning like a garden hose on full blast. The crowds jump back. Sorrel dives and grabs the tank, fights to get off the ground, and runs into the building again.

"Better be enough juice left to do any good. I'll go in and back him up," shouts Thomas. Both men disappear into the smoke. Sirens and engines grind and roar, their sounds banging and piercing as they come closer. To get as close as he can, the driver smashes the lovingly-tended hedges near the entrance platform. The light pole bends from the impact. Five masked men suited in bright yellow slicks leap from the truck.

Calline imagines flames curling around each pew, the ancient chapel beams like the logs in her fireplace, the entire place a barren heap of ash, fit for no one but the devil himself. How will they welcome friends to a house of worship that smells like a forest after a fire, that is, if the place is still standing? *We are open and welcoming to all God's children—it may smell and look like hell, but we promise Heaven.* The pastor rehearses worst case scenarios. She coughs to clear her lungs of the smoke. A tear draws a white line through the soot on her cheeks.

"It's suffocating in there. I saw flames coming from the kitchen, pointed the guys to there, and got the heck out," Sorrel says, breathing like he's been snorkeling for a day without surfacing. His face smeared with soot, he looks Vaudevillian. Tears streak his cheeks; his eyes strain to cool themselves from the searing smoke. Thomas stands by him, uttering senseless words, trying to catch oxygen, coughing, and rubbing his eyes with sooty hands.

Calline can't help but think how foolish the two men were to dash into a burning building, but she puts her hands on their shoulders, proud of them. "All we can do is wait and let the pros tell us the extent of the damage." She thinks *what a stupid thing to say,* as if just because she's the reverend it's her job to say something, anything to feel in control of an otherwise unmanageable circumstance.

The fire Chief, Chief Landon, stands outside by the cab, barking orders into a hand-held device to the guys inside. Loud calls through scratches and blips emanate from the small speaker. He looks over to the gathered crowd, then climbs into the cab and shuts the door. He doesn't look too happy. It seems hours before the first fighter, and then another, appears at the door. They come to get water, get air, and to consult with the Chief. More time passes before the other three emerge from the damage.

Chief Landon approaches Calline. Ten onlookers push closer to hear. The sun is long gone and it's well below freezing.

"Aren't you the lady pastor?" Chief Landon, asks, skeptical that a lady of any persuasion can understand fire-talk.

"That's me, yes, sir. But these folks around you are the church. Could you kindly speak loudly enough for everyone to hear?" Calline, scared, shivers. Sorrel puts his sooty hands around her shoulders, a bold move in front of everyone to see.

The Chief speaks through the megaphone. "The fire started in the kitchen. You two men did the right thing, dangerous though." He points to Sorrel and Thomas. "The kitchen is pretty much gone. You'll have to do some major repairs. Getting the smell out can be a bear. The doors to chapel, sanctuary, office, and classrooms were closed, so no smoke damage there, just a strong smell. Good of you to keep those doors closed." Everyone sighs relief. Chief looks down at his feet, raises some phlegm, and covers his mouth. "The bad news is, we think someone started the fire. Show 'em, Johnny." Everyone turns to look at the young volunteer fighter standing on the front fender of the truck. He raises, for all to see, a crowbar and an empty jar.

Johnny says, "I found the crowbar under the front of the refrigerator and the jar still has gas fumes. Fresh." He tosses the jar in the air and catches it.

"Not a whole lot of evidence, but something we sure should investigate, you think?" The Chief looks over to Calline and Sorrel who look at each other in sheer disbelief.

Sorrel groans. "Chief, it's been a tinder box here for the past few months. Doesn't surprise me if someone *was* up to no good today, but what an unbelievably lousy hand to play." Sorrel boxes the air with clenched fists.

"Let's nail their asses," shouts David, his buddies hooting. The crowd, stirred with anger, follows suit.

"Now everyone, settle down. Revenge is sweet, but it's not the way of our Lord. You know that, I know that. We don't have all the facts. Let's thank the crew for the fine show of courage and skill. I'm sure they'd like to get home." Thomas's Christian sensibilities settle the revolt. Folks clap, slap backs.

Gunther steps up. "It's cold, time to go home, get warm. It's been a heck of a day, ending with this, but onward and upward. Come tomorrow if you can to help tidy up best we can for coffee hour. I'll be here at seven." Good Gunther.

Sorrel, Thomas, and Calline stay to peruse the damage. Walls, refrigerator, and cabinets are streaked with black soot, the floor tiles ruined, and the dishwasher and stove shot. Like red ink in a glass of water smoke permeates he entire building. "Who on earth is going to feel welcomed in this ashtray?" Calline offers, disgusted.

Thomas waves a hasty farewell to Sorrel and Calline at the sooted door and dashes to his car. "Well, here we are again. I think we are the official door lockers," says Sorrel who looks comical covered in soot.

"Ashes to ashes, dust to dust," the pastor intones as she draws the sign of the cross on Sorrel's dusted forehead. He glances around to see they are alone, then leans over to press his cheek against hers. "Turn the other cheek, dear. So I can match one sooted one to the other." Laughing, they get carried away, smudging and arm wrestling, then holding each other as if on a raft in high seas.

"Now that we're both covered in smoke, you got any ideas what next?" Calline flirts.

"Where there's smoke, there's fire," he says, looking ridiculous, looking hard into her eyes, holding her chin.

"Where's it burning tonight?" she asks, flirting and burning.

CHAPTER THIRTY-SEVEN

IT'S ONE THING to talk God's vision of love and justice; it's quite another to walk it. Figure one African American pregnant teen in residence with a middle class white woman who has never parented. Mix the two together for less than a fortnight, and what you have is—well, you decide.

When mother Reverend deigns to straighten Vee's room, towels hung, shoes placed in neat rows, bed made, the pregnant teen looks at her like the woman has gone mad. "You messin' with my crap again, Rev. I don't like it." Vee rubs some coconut-smelling grease on her legs. "My skin gets nappy," she says, seeming to wear a look of disgust more indelibly since she moved in.

Well-rounded meals get the same treatment. "OOOhhhhh, this is nasty! Ain't you got no fries and hot sauce?" She sits and sulks, the baby going hungry again.

Calline is ready to fling boiling hot broccoli.

"Vee, honey, it's 2:00 a.m. You're keeping the entire neighborhood awake with that music." Boom, boom, booms and vibration defy any resemblance to actual music. She ignores Calline's pathetic observations, but turns the music down long enough to call the baby's father. Calline careens to the door to hear, "I'm going to kill it if it's a boy."

In the morning, when Vee usually lumbers in for coffee and donuts, the only breakfast she'll eat, she is nowhere to be found. Calline, worried sick, does the only thing she knows to do. Call her mother. "Vee has left and I don't know where to." She might have said, "Might rain tomorrow."

Mrs. Morgan replies, sounding besotted. "She run off with that boy. His people stay in Ionia. Rev, you done a lot. She'll come around. Kids." Frankly, the pastor hopes she won't come around for a while. She makes no bones that she's pretty fed up, her privacy violated, and her emotions spent with caring and concern, mostly for the unborn. The high school attendance officer confirms that Vee Morgan is AWOL.

On her walk to the church, spring announces itself as a balmy fifty degrees and a sun ray that cracks through a cloud. Calline prays to surrender Vee to her Protector and for willingness to go the distance to the big day, the day of the vote on Peter. It seems weeks since the neighborhood walk. Calline is aware of Dalia in the building, probably working her weekly crossword with an earnestness that far exceeds her dedication to the work of the church.

"How's the smoke in here for you, Dal?"

"It's kicking my ass," she says flatly, popping a bubble.

Calline is startled by the secretary's bluntness and her hair, dyed jet black and frizzed to beat the band.

"Nice 'do, Dalia. Did you forget your eyebrows? Or did you mean to contrast?"

"I like the contrast, if you don't mind. Hey, boss, what's a major city on the Ganges River? She's completely riveted on her crossword. The phone rings. "Would you mind getting that? If I don't get seven across, I can't finish the section." *Pop!*

"Don't let me interfere," the pastor says, irritated. She does have her limits, but they don't faze Dalia. "Hello?" It's Mims Smith.

Calline settles at her desk and takes the receiver. "Hey, Mims. It's great to hear from you. How've you been since our outing Saturday? Yep, I feel like I work in a pair of smoker's lungs. It's pretty bad in here. Thanks for asking. What can I do for you today?" The women bonded on their walk together. Calline knows life for Mims has not been easy. Born into a family where if good genes were money, they'd be destitute. Mims has struggled all her forty-eight years to master the simplest functions, to feel understood, and to desire to go on.

Mims laughs and talks to someone in the room with her. Is there someone in the room with her? "The Lemonade Stand is lobbying before the Zoning Commission Wednesday, so we can use the house across from you all as our meeting place and a shelter for our homeless. We're passing a petition and hope your church folks will sign." Mims sounds like she's on the higher end of the bi-polar spectrum.

"You can rest assured, I'm not one of those *not-in-my backyard* people, Mims, but I can't speak for the surrounding neighbors or my church folks. Already, I've heard some griping. You can count on my support and feel free to bring the Petition on Sundays. Just tell any naysayers I said it was okay for you to circulate for signatures. Sure, Wednesday at 3:00 at City Hall, you bet. Stand Lemonade Stand. Bye." Calline hopes Mims and her unusual and challenging mix of friends will prevail in spite of likely protests. She can just hear old Mr. Jax, self-coroneted king of the neighborhood. "You telling me a bunch of sicko nobodies are moving across the street? Those weirdos hang out at the Day Labor place, loiter at the mall, beg, talk to themselves? One is one thing, but a whole houseful—not in my backyard!" And so it goes.

"NIMBY," Calline speaks, loud enough for Dalia to perk up at her crossword.

"Nimby? Is that a city on the Ganges, Cal?"

"No, silly, those are our new neighbors." She howls, and answers the phone.

"High Dunes First. This is Rev. Simpson."

"Rev. Simpson, this is Officer Jensen, Crime Scene Investigator over at the police department. What Chief Landon found in your kitchen is evidence for possible arson. We've sent the jar and crowbar to a lab in Detroit. For now, I'd like to ask you a few questions if you don't mind."

Calline is stunned; the building is a mess due to evil intent. "Should I come in, Officer? And bring an officer of the church with?" She wants Sorrel with her, although it would be appropriate for Trustee Tendal Harris to come.

"Bring your team. 1:30 if you can." Jensen says, hurried.

"Thanks, Mr. Jensen. I and a church member will see you today at 1:30. We want to get to the bottom of this and we're glad you're on it."

A quick call to Tendal confirms his unavailability to meet with Jensen.

"Hey, you." Sorrel asks Calline to hold while he talks to someone. She hears him say, "Hold my calls and clear the decks for this afternoon." *For me*, she wonders?

"I was thinking about you this morning," she says. "How much I want to be with you all the time." Such candor is way out there for her, but it's come to this now. Calline is sure Dalia is too wrapped up in some project not related to church work to hear. "Can you go with me to the police station? 1:30?"

"Better yet, why don't I swing by and get you for lunch? Earl's. I'll nail the S.O.B. who did this." Sorrel hangs up abruptly, probably another call. She's sick to her stomach with anticipation.

Dalia hollers from her work space. "The electrician is coming at 1:45. Do you want me to handle him while you're out with Sorrel? *How much of the conversation did Dalia hear, anyway?* She droops over her desk, head in hands. It's hopeless. Yet, never has she felt so hopeful in a long while.

CHAPTER THIRTY-EIGHT

THROUGH THE TINY port hole Calline watches Sorrel wheel into the parking lot. The way he springs from his car, bounding like a school boy to the front door, turns her on. He looks dashing in a dark suit and orange tie with tiny patterns of dark blue. He's letting his hair grow so his natural curls fall over his ears and down his neck. She bunches her sweater cuffs into her hands and leans to rub her knee, a habitual gesture both of anticipation and worry. Sorrel's smile, his boyishness, is emotional sunshine. "I'm out to see the detective. Be back around 4:00," Calline mumbles as she tries not to appear excited like a girl on her first date.

"You know I'll be gone by then," Dalia says, folding bulletins. "Don't forget to call Lilly. Something about classrooms. And Kathy left a message. Search committee business." Calline is too eager to have the door between her and the secretary.

Scanning to see if anyone is around, the two exchange a luscious kiss. Sorrel looks at Calline as if truly in love, and reaches his hand to hers to lead her to his car.

"I'm glad you called. I needed out of that office for an hour or two, or three, or . . ."

"I understand. I really do." Calline reaches for his hand and squeezes it. "Where to, Prince?" Not a name she's called him, but today she feels like royalty, a label she would seldom, if ever, give herself.

"Earl's?" Sorrel sounds like he did on the way to the Grimsley mansion break-in. Mischievous.

"Great, Max. Let's go." They laugh uproariously, like two teens skipping school.

Earl's is a tiny hamburger and fries joint that competes directly with Curley's Diner. It's hard to find a seat on weekday lunches. While Sorrel finds a parking place, Calline looks for a place to sit. She immediately sees him sitting in a corner booth. It's Richard Grimsley and a friend. Richard does not see the couple until the waitress seats them in the only booth available, right behind the one where Richard dines. Richard gives a discreet salute to Sorrel who salutes back. Richard and his friend lean over their food to hear over the noise.

"That's the Reverend and Sorrel Dixon from my church. My wife, you know Alexis, is leading the charge against hiring a queer," says Richard matter-of-factly.

Calline leans into Sorrel, "Richard thinks we can't hear him? He might as well have a megaphone."

"Cal, he wants us to hear. Hiring a queer? My God!" Sorrel hails the waitress for a Mountain Dew and hot tea for Calline.

Richard's friend, unknown to either the pastor or Sorrel, replies, "Honest now, Richard. What is your stance on this issue?"

Richard Grimsley fists his hands and slides them across the table, leaning in, eyes set squarely on his friend's. "Based on all I learned as a kid, my automatic answer is to lock them all up and throw out the key. This is certainly how Alexis feels. Don't cross Alexis. But the more I listen I think this old dog should be learning some new tricks. I'm learning to use those damned computers, why not master a new viewpoint while I'm at it?" He looks over to Sorrel's and Calline's booth.

"But, Rich, if it weren't for queers, there'd be no church music. So what's the big deal? They're like no-see-ums. You know they're there, you slap at them, and they keep showing up. Why, really, is Alexis and her crowd so stirred up?" His friend takes a swig of his Pabst Blue Ribbon.

Richard doesn't hesitate. "Because the candidate, to be voted on in a couple of weeks, refuses to be a no-see-um. He is partnered with another no-see-um. Together, everyone will see 'em. Plus, Alexis—my dear, contentious Alexis—loves a good fight. Give her a scrap of something, anything, and she's all over it. The gay organist is one helluva bone. Alexis is pushing eighty-five, but she's in there like a pissed-off rat terrier." The men laugh and swig down their beers.

Sorrel touches Calline's good knee under the table and sighs. "What do you say we get out of here?"

"They're not done yet. Sorrel, I need to hear the rest of this bull." Sorrel knows she's dug in to the bitter conclusion of this nonsense.

The friend continues. "Are you with Alexis, Rich? Or will you vote for the guy?" The men settle up with the waitress, who chomps gum and slaps change into Richard's palm.

"Since Great Granddaddy built the company, hence the church, I won't cut off my pledge, although I've come damned close. I think we old fogies need to open our minds some. If you tell Alexis I'm even equivocating, there will be a double murder: yours, then mine." Richard gets up and walks right past Calline and Sorrel, looking lost in thought.

"A good church musician, sissy or not, is nearly impossible to find. Send him over to us if Alexis defeats the cause, would you?" The friend takes his hat from the rack and waves. Richard looks at Sorrel and Calline, more through them than anything, and goes to pay.

Calline acknowledges Richard with a nod, and looks at Sorrel, "You know he wanted us to hear all this."

"Richard defecting from the cause would be stranger than fiction, if you ask me." Sorrel leaves a ten dollar bill and thanks the waitress.

The couple crosses the street to meet Officer Jensen in the front lobby. He stands next to none other than Wonder-Full Counselor, upon whom Calline has not laid eyes since Christmas day. "Why is he here?" she whispers to Sorrel.

"Well, Reverend, if you aren't a sight for sore eyes," says the man, still dread-locked and wearing the old brogans and long green scissor-hemmed coat, eyes still shining. Calline smiles up at him, reaches to shake his hand. The man then turns, waves, and walks from the building. He steps onto a bus that pulls away and heads east. To Calline, the way the man leaves is more like an evaporation of a figure with lightness of being, like she experienced him in the cemetery.

"If you all could take a seat in my office, I'll be right with you," says Jensen, skipping formalities. Calline and Sorrel take the two gray chairs and wait, touching each other's knees, holding each other's gaze, silent.

Investigator Jensen enters the cold office, decorated in hues of gray and metal, like an officer's barracks on a retired war ship. He pulls up the one empty chair. "That man you just saw. Do you know him?" Jensen, a short, stocky man with thick, dark strawberry blond hair waits, chewing on a toothpick. A photograph of him, much younger, with a woman and a litter of kids sits on his desk.

"I know him. Sort of," says Calline, utterly taken aback that a man like the stranger with the incandescent eyes could be suspect in any way. Sure, he loved surprising people, but he swore he was not out to cause harm anymore. She believed him then. She believes him now.

"He was around our building a lot at Christmas. I actually talked to him at the Cemetery for Indigents. I'm convinced he is a beautiful person who fell on some hard times, and is trying to get clean and make up for bad choices in the past. Why do you ask?" Calline looks to Sorrel for support.

"We think he might be your man." Jensen looks at his nails and picks a cuticle. "His family name is Kettle Jones. He's lived under several identities and we've traced all of them. He moved around a lot, switched names when trouble found him. He lives in The Mansion retirement home out east at the county line. The director said he just appeared on a freezing night and the night watchman felt sorry for him, fed him, and gave him a cot in an empty storage closet. They give him odd jobs and find him genuinely lovable. The residents are growing attached to him. They call him Hair."

"How could he possibly be the guy?" Calline, amused by the moniker, "Hair," is incredulous. The man struck her as so otherworldly, transparent, out to do only good as the fruits of much suffering.

"Based on his record, he's a viable suspect. He was arraigned in Texas for building fires in a no-fires designated area where he made camp and lived for months. We can't arrest him on a hunch, but you can bet if the lab work matches, 'ol Hair will be cut short for good." Jensen gestures the axe at his neckline.

"So, Officer, what do you need from us?" Sorrel asks, wondering Hair's fate.

"Nothing, now. Just thought you'd like to know we have a suspect and that we're on the case. How's the smoke? Jensen puts his feet on the desk.

"It smells like an incinerator, but we think we can carry out business while the insurance people assess the damage. We were lucky." This from Sorrel, who sees it's after 2:30 and has to attend some personal fires of his own. He gets up and reaches for Calline's hand.

"I was hoping you had opened the afternoon for us, sweet," she whispers in his ear as they walk down the polished hallway of the station. "If I have to stay on this side of the veil, I'd like you

BETSY P. SKINNER

for a travel companion." She looks at Sorrel and smiles, surprising herself and him with such a direct admission.

"Thanks, really. But to be respectable, I have got to check on a new site we're prepping." He leans over to kiss her cheek as she buckles up and he revs the engine.

Calline feels lightheaded and nauseous. "Sorrel, I think I'm coming down with something."

"Me too." he says, half-grinning.

"No. Serious." Then she catches his drift.

"The love bug, you think?" he says. Their laughter is so loud and the engine so revved, the dogs down the street start up.

CHAPTER THIRTY-NINE

AFTER DINNER, SNUGGLED under the comforter with Bingo salivating over a piece of meringue pie, Calline complains to Patty. "It's like they are organizing the offense from some secret outpost. There's nothing creepier than a stealth operation. I rarely see Alexis or the Petition-signers between Sundays, and only a few then. J.B.—you know, the stiff-necked banker—gripes about drawing down reserves to pay me and Dalia. That man would toss me to the dogs in a blink to keep the zany secretary and the lights on. I'm gnawing on all the bones here. Are we going the right way with Peter, with the outreach campaign, blah, blah . . ." Calline's stomach swirls and dizziness overcomes. Not the love kind, but the sick kind. She gives Bingo the rest of the pie and the fork to lick clean.

"And you're pretty much ignoring the petitioners? And they're ignoring you?" Patty asks, interested as always.

"Yep, stand-off, I guess. We haven't tried to meet or reason since the three guys came to the Dreidens'." She can't help but giggle, remembering Lilly's water breaking and everyone scattering like flushed birds.

"Was that a God-thing or what? Lots of babies at your place, Cal: triplets, Bee and Bop, Vee's baby, Lilly's." Comedy feels better than specters in the night.

"Can we change the subject? Tell me about this Ray guy you mentioned." Calline is happy to share man-talk with her friend who's been pretty much single since her divorce.

"We met at a contra-dance. I like this man, Cal. I think he could be the one. Can you slow me down?" She sips and exhales.

"How can I hit your brakes, when my own are plain broken? Trust me; it's not easy to avoid the cart before the horse when the hormones are firing.

"How far ahead is the cart with you and Sorrel, huh?" Patty gets dead quiet.

"Let's just say—to switch metaphors—restraint is melting with the ice."

"Why so vague? Hey, it's me, Patty." Patty listens intently, hoping not a sound will distract her friend from confessing. Everything.

"I don't know. It's weird; ridiculous, actually. If I spill the details to myself, and to my best friend, it will be real and I'll have to deal with the shame around it, like the illusion when I was a kid: if I cover myself with my sheets, the boogie-man can't see me. Plus, I know you feel obliged to speak the voice of the Code. Of course you have to. It's precisely that voice that makes this difficult for me. I want carte blanche acceptance, while at the same time I . . . I . . ." Calline can feel the heat rise to her cheeks, and tears coming. "Am I awful to get it on with this man, with Elizabeth sick, even if Sorrel assures me, in no uncertain terms, Elizabeth isn't available, physically or emotionally? The wedding is off. She's up at some sanitarium in the U.P., indefinitely, he tells me. Should Sorrel and I just cut it off? Like that? I'm in love. I believe the feeling is mutual. I don't believe at this point I *can* cut it off. O.K., I said it, minus the details." Calline feels like a huge log just rolled off her back.

"You said 'get it on' . . . and?" Patty persists. She wants more. Everything. "Is he a good lover, Cal? Wait, back up. Did you consummate the thing? You haven't even divulged that detail!" Patty pushes hard for more.

"Gawwd, Patty. Why?" Calline blushes again, remembering the unleashed passion just the other night, Sorrel pushing himself against her at her bedroom door, her locking her mouth to his, laughing, crying, no and yes, then letting him take her onto her bed, his heat and hardness against her, his nakedness, hers, his raw hunger to have all of her, and her complete and abandoned yes. "I can't, Patty. I just can't talk about this. It's as if to say 'it' would make it true. How stupid is that?" Withholding like this from her closest friend feels totally absurd. But she does.

"O.K., I won't insist. Tonight, anyway." Patty exaggerates a moan and blows smoke. After a stretched-out whine about weather, work, and worries, she says, "This Sunday, isn't it the Open and Welcoming day?"

"I love that you care so much, P. I love you. I promise I'll give you more, some day. Some day when . . . when. Oh hell, soon, I promise. Anyway, yes, this Sunday is the day we'll see if all the door knocking did any good. The one I'm anxious about is the Sunday we vote for Peter. He needs at least sixty percent of the votes, but just winning isn't the point. Peter, I'm sure, would back out—if he hasn't already—if the vote isn't decisive. I can't imagine why he'd want to put up with our crap. If our door knocking yields zero, what with a third of the congregation threatening to bolt, the church might as well burn down."

"You say that with such a full heart, I know," says Patty, totally in sync with the weight of the situation for her friend. "I wish I could just pick you up and carry you off to some paradise. Oops, bad metaphor. Just carry you off somewhere safe and nurturing."

Calline laughs, waiting to hear if Patty wants to offer another jewel of comfort. "It's like the church is a baby bird ready to leap from the edge of the nest." Patty waxes poetic. "Hang onto your feathers," Patty laughs and blows a kiss into the receiver.

The turbulence of worry, the distraction of romance, the daily-ness of it all can so deafen. Now, more than ever, the pastor needs the everlasting arms to lean on, the blessed assurance.

"Bye, babe. Thanks for the bird metaphor. Pray." Calline hangs up from Patty to take a call from Sorrel.

"Hey love. Yes, I'm feeling worried, sad, and giddy all bundled into a tangle of nerves. I just talked to Patty. That helps." She feels the chemicals of love and lust enflame her to heightened awareness and desire. There's no turning back now. She knows this.

"You're not going to believe this. Are you sitting down?"

"Sorrel, I'm not sure I'm ready for any more news." Calline pulls the covers to her chin. "I'm lying down. What?"

"Billy and Martha called last night from Bermuda. They tied the knot at that little chapel where we rode bikes to pray for you. Can you believe it?" Sorrel sounds more shocked than pleasantly surprised.

"I'm not so surprised, just jealous I don't get to tie their knot. Let's have a big shebang for them when they get back. How long are they staying over there?" Calline stretches and yawns.

"They just left things open. They'll miss out on our big Sundays. By the way, J.B. was able to get his guys from the bank to scrub soot from walls and clean carpets. Miss Becky said she'd lend her catering equipment until the kitchen is re-done. The Hall and the sanctuary should be fully usable, though still smelling like the inside of a coal mine. Gunther and his team are making a banner that reads "WOW! Open and Welcoming to All God's Children."

"Oh, Sorrel, this all sounds so wonderful." As practical and down-to-earth as he is, for which she is glad, still she wishes for sweet nothings when she feels this small and vulnerable. In love.

"There's more. Balloons will fly on the flag poles and steeple; Miss Becky says she'll put on some mean vittles for our guests." Sorrel's enthusiasm is infections.

Calline sits up, wide awake, enchanted by this exciting plan for Sunday.

"I wonder who'll come, Sorrel, how many? I am so afraid if few come, the naysayers will naysay. What do you think?" Calline chews on a cuticle.

"I think the Lord has it all under control. Hey, who's the minister here?" Sorrel teases.

"You are," giggles the pastor. "You sure minister to me, anyway, boyfriend!"

He chides, "You're the one always laying that Romans text on us about all things coming to good; listen to your own best sermon. I'd be there now to do some laying on of hands." Sorrel sounds lighter than he has in weeks.

"Sorrel Dixon, I love you. I need those hands of yours on me, you know that. Tomorrow's a big day. I need to be rested." She wants him. There are no words. Just sensations.

"Yup. I'm glad. I'm so glad. Now, hold your head up, Rev. Look up to the place from whence the help comes. I've got a call coming in. So long?" Sorrel hangs up before he can hear her longing words.

"So long?"

Wide awake now, Calline grabs her pad and pen to scratch notes for Sunday's sermon. What word would soothe and encourage? What word would invite and attract? What word would ignite and excite peoples' deepest longings for truth that endures and brings hope? Who might be there to hear? The man whose leg rotted off from a work accident, or old Critter and all his pets, or Hair, Mims, and her Lemonade Stand? And Vee and Roscoe? The doors will swing wide to welcome the likes of them all. All God's children. Will they come and actually feel welcome? Would they want to come back after they've been courted and fed and loved? What of all those of different sexual orientation, all those of color, all those . . .

"Jesus equals love personified," she quotes, "the church equals love organized." Is High Dunes First United Congregational Church organized to impart love to all who enter? No matter where they are on life's journey.

CHAPTER FORTY

FANTASIES OF HER and Sorrel out of their minds with passion, worries about a vacant sanctuary filled with smoke and ashes, Bingo wanting out more than once—destroy a good night's sleep. Crumpled papers carpet the bedroom floor; her pad full of scratched notes offer a mish-mash of admonitions, consolations, the gospel. Wide awake at 4:30, she makes tea and toast, and listens to the silence of the pre-dawn morning. The phone rings.

"Hi Dad. It's five. I know you're an early bird, but, this hour?" She's thrilled it's him.

"I knew you'd be up, Sweetie. This is the big day, huh? The Open and Welcoming Sunday?" His voice sounds raspy.

"You are a love, Pop. Thanks for calling, for remembering. I've been up all night. You know me when I worry."

"Too much. Not good for my little girl."

"I feel sick, frankly." She hopes the tea and toast will settle her some.

"You got your mother's stomach. Pepto. It always worked for her, and no orange juice." Calline can hear the sadness whenever he mentions his deceased wife. Bob Simpson is over eighty and still on the ball. Old age will claim him, but she knows he'll never slip when it comes to his only daughter. For her whole life, Calline has leaned on her father who would have gladly drowned to save her that fateful day in Bermuda. For so long she took for granted his steadfastness and help, but after hearing so many stories of fathers absent, violent, unaware, this gift is one she wants to enshrine and take with her when she crosses over again.

"Is your hair growing O.K., honey?"

"It's kind of funny looking, Pop. I think it's my heart that's acting up now. It's Sorrel. Don't get me started, but I promise to update you soon. I do have to run. Run away, maybe." She laughs. "I love you, Pop. Bye." Her heart is warmed, her mind full, her gut in need of something soothing.

The sun barely cracks the horizon, and the breeze off the lake smells like summer might one day come to thaw things out. The fading stars dot a sky painted with dawn's pale purples and pinks. The sky at dawn and dusk appear surreal in the light reflected from the lake, like off a huge mirror.

Miss Becky and two of her children carry items from their station wagon loaded with heating trays and boxes of delectable brunch foods. Gunther and Nancy Dobbs have arrived early enough to open and warm the building, and to count and sort bulletins. Others arrive to help set up the welcome station, the children's area, and to decorate. A banner hangs between the two columns over the entrance. In bright gold letters outlined in brown, it reads, "WOW! WELCOME! OPEN TO ALL GOD'S CHILDREN. Worship at 10:00." The banner ripples in the breeze. Bright yellow helium balloons fly from the yard sign and mailbox.

The building smells like a picnic ground with a thousand barbecue grills. Thanks to J.B.'s bank, though, the interior is as sparkling clean as it could possibly be. Fresh banners, large plants, newly fashioned bulletin boards, and spot-paint disguise smoke-damaged areas. The Hall will accommodate tables and chairs to seat fifty. Miss Becky's inventions for cooking, washing, and serving substitute for the kitchen rendered useless.

Except for the odor, the sanctuary is in fine shape. Calline enters the sacristy to gather items to prepare the Lord's Table. Today, her church goes to the highways and byways to invite everyone to the banquet. "Lord, bring them in, Critter Friend, anybody. Your lambs," she prays while unfolding the ancient cloth that miraculously survived the first church fire. As it has always done since the founding of the church, it will cover the altar. She feels its worn softness and holds it to her nostrils to sniff the faint hint of bleach and softener. She remembers the love poured into the care of the linens and silver by Helen Mellbridge and Rachael Connors. Gone.

"Mornin' Rev," Gertrude Rudders nods from the organ bench. She and choir warm aging voices, except for Kathy, the sole alto, who waves to Calline, all glee. Richard Grimsley occasionally steps into the choir, and today he offers a generous presence. *Should I be suspicious?* Calline wonders, but instead, she waves back to Gertrude and the choir, and steps into the chancel to finish preparations. On the altar beneath the large brass cross sits a vase stuffed with a bright array of tulips.

"Things do grow somewhere," said Dalia as she put them out on Friday. "Just not here. Yet."

The pastor reviews service details. One of Lilly's girls will carry the taper and light the candles. Thomas, lay leader, will greet and introduce guests. Calline steps back to examine the table, making sure the elements are arranged in a way she can easily tend. She checks her watch and fidgets, then takes her note pad covered with pen and scratch marks to the pulpit, praying something will deliver through her, God's prophet, God's vessel. The service begins in half an hour.

Gunther hollers from the Hall, "If you were on Saturday's neighborhood walk, please meet me here in the Hall."

Robed and prepared for worship, whispering a silent prayer, "Help and thanks," Calline joins Gunther and the others.

"O.K. everyone, this is the day we've worked so hard for. Hospitality is a gift and that gift must shine in each of us, Spirit willing. Let's not overwhelm the folks, but by all means, don't be shy. Do what you would do if guests came to your house."

"Order out!" mumbles J.B., looking at his watch.

"Now, Miss Becky and her son and daughter have gone overboard to prepare a great meal." Everyone claps. Miss Becky stirs and grins ear-to-ear to be a part of the spectacle, one of the ministers of the congregation. Gunther waves to her. "So, I sure hope you stay and welcome folks to stay for a bite. Let's not hurt Miss Becky's feelings."

"Lawd, chil', you can't hurt this ol' lady's feelins. It's for the Lawd, and that's all that matters. Ya'll jes bring 'em. We'll feed 'em." Calline's and her eyes meet. Calline's heart bursts with love and gratitude for her friend, this immense offering.

Suddenly, *Bam!* from behind. Calline goes down to the floor on her good knee, thank God; her other heel slides on the floor, stretching her bad leg straight out. "Ouch!" She twists around to see just two inches from her face, the face of the same little guy she saw on Saturday, the boy who clung to his daddy's stump. Next to him is his father and the other son. The man puts out one of his crutches like a tree branch. Calline grabs it and the man, so strong, pulls her up like a rag doll.

"We decided to come see yo' chooch," he says, quietly. His two boys flank him just like they did at their apartment. Mims appears and hugs the two boys, and guides them to the children's table manned by Melinda Suarez and her daughters. The triplets stayed home with Abuela—grandmother.

"I'm Timmy Johns." He puts out his hand, the size of a brick, but otherwise soft and supple. "The boys is Micky and Ricky Johns." He points to the boys. "Their mama ran off with some no good, so it's just us men." His sadness consumes him.

"We are delighted you are here Timmy. Please make yourself at home." Calline notices the time: ten before the hour. "Excuse me, Mr. Johns. I have to get to my duties."

Mims steps in to visit with Timmy, embracing him like a brother.

Gertrude starts the pre-service music while Calline helps Lilly's four-year-old light the taper. Gertrude shifts into something peppy while folks enter, chat, and settle. Calline steps from the altar to take the chair next to the pulpit. No one is certain, but some say the founding pastor, Nehemiah, felled and carved the tree for the seat. Thomas, liturgist, sits across from Calline and fidgets nervously. Both face the congregation and watch the folks take their places. The typical crowd since the Petition circulated are those who are either totally indifferent to the conflict, or those who care but aren't protesting. Calline's thoughts go to the thirty who signed the Petition. The specialness of this day appears to not have moved the majority to act for love of neighbor and stranger. They are absent.

Right on the hour, Calline can't tell anyone has responded to Saturday's outreach but Mr. Johns, Micky, and Ricky. She tries not to let her disappointment show, after all, worship is a time for gratitude and praise of God, not to complain about outcomes of the efforts of fallen human beings. Just as Thomas goes forward to welcome the congregation, a young mother, who can't be much older than Vee, leads two little ones into the sanctuary. A couple in their thirties, maybe, pushing a stroller with an infant and trailed by two toddlers follows. Lilly intercepts them and ushers them into a pew, handing the two toddlers a bag full of things to distract them before the children leave for their classes. An old man in a wheelchair, pushed by a younger man, makes it painfully evident that this church's worship space is not as open and welcoming to the mobility-challenged. *How did they get up the stairs into the building?* Calline ponders, embarrassed by the insensitivities of people who build buildings only for people who can manage them. Then three women enter, all with red hair, each maybe in their sixties. Dalia invites them to sit with her.

"Way to go, Dalia." Calline waves and smiles. Mims welcomes three of her friends from the Lemonade Stand and invites them to sit with her. Gunther and Nancy do a fine job smiling and warmly greeting everyone, passing bulletins, and helping people find places.

"As far as I can count," whispers Gunther to Nancy, "with those folks and Mr. Johns' three, attendance just jumped one hundred percent from one Sunday ago, quite literally in a matter of seconds."

"Honey, I love you," Nancy, out of nowhere, hugs her husband of forty-seven years. "There's always a ram in the bush, my Sunday school teacher back home used to say. Just before old Abe chops off Isaac's head—out pops the ram, in case you forgot the story." She takes his hand in hers.

"The ram gets the axe, you mean, not the kid. In the nick of time! Now, shhhh. Let's see what happens next," orders Gunther, walking to greet another stranger like a soldier home from war.

CHAPTER FORTY-ONE

GUNTHER PRACTICALLY KNOCKS Calline over after the service. "Did you see that, Cal?" He rubs his beard and expects she has certainly seen the same phenomenon that clearly has him dazzled.

"What?" Calline asks, looking up to meet his gaze.

"The man on crutches with his two kids, three; the mother and two kids, three more; the three redheads; Mims's three friends and Mims; mom, dad with infant and toddlers, four. And the boy pushing the wheelchair. Melinda Suarez and her brood, add four, that's nineteen right there, well over a quarter of our regular Sunday attendance. Nance and I were twenty-eight bulletins short. We usually print eighty." Gunther tiptoes and bounces, smiling broadly.

The dinner bell rings. "Ya'll come. Vittles ready," Becky hollers from the Hall. For a moment, the delicious smells blunt the rancid odors from the fire.

"Hey Gunther, let's go greet the folks. God willing, if we're welcoming, they'll want to come back. What do you say?" Calline holds her elbow to Gunther's. Gunther, jubilant, leads Calline on his right and Nancy on his left.

"If the vittles don't get them, nothing will." He laughs like Calline hasn't heard Gunther laugh for years.

Waiting to fill her plate, Calline scans the room. Full. It seems unusually quiet as the strangers focus on eating. "I bet some haven't had a good square in a week," whispers Calline to Gunther and Nancy. Both nod.

"I'm darned proud of our folks, Cal. They welcomed our guests, and gave their all to make everyone feel as at home as possible," beams Gunther, filling his plate to overflow.

Mr. Johns approaches Calline as she serves her second helping. "Rev. Cal, what a nice chooch you have. We'd be right pleased to come back. The boys had fun and you're a right good preacher for a woman. No offense or nothin'." Timmy shifts his weight on his crutches.

"None taken." Calline looks up and grins broadly. She sees something in this man that shines of pure beauty, something that inspires compassion and respect. The boys' hands, all greasy after they've stuffed their pocket with cornbread and sausage, reach for Calline's.

As folks leave, Calline greets the young couple who introduce themselves as new to the neighborhood. The redheads—sisters—giggle and chortle some nonsense about having come for the food, but as devout Catholics, they don't want to spend eternity in purgatory. "Changing religions would condemn us forever," one of the sisters says. "Great grits and cornbread, though, thanks." They're out the door and well on their way before Calline can find out how she might followup.

"We're looking for a place Dad can get his wheelchair in without a major hassle," says the boy, who clearly has had it with buildings constructed for a world attuned only to the physically privileged.

Warmly, the pastor reaches for his hand, but he refuses, "Thank you for coming?" She hopes he'll offer his name.

"Jackson. Jackson Hewitt. This is my Pop. Mr. Hewitt." Mr. Hewitt seems in pain. Calline is embarrassed that Thomas and Smit must carry Mr. Hewitt in the wheelchair down the stairs. They have learned something very important today about including folks.

After the last guest has gone, Gunther thanks the stragglers for their hard work. The morning has been a huge success. Calline stays back to adjust thermostats and close doors. Sorrel left shortly after handing Miss Becky a hundred dollar bill. He said something earlier about going to Grand Rapids, but so many details cloud her mind, and she's already projecting for Peter's visit; she can't remember what he told her. All she can feel now is a huge letdown, like the yellow balloons that blow tangled and shriveled on the ground.

On her walk home, beneath a warming sun, she notices a strong and strange sensation in her stomach, different than romance, different than nerves. A warning sensation, like something forbidding lurks around the next bend. Bingo bounces wildly at the door and pushes by her to sniff the bushes and pee. Hanging her coat and scarf, gloves thrown on the bed, Calline notices the blinks on the message machine. Sorrel says he'll call later. Peter's message sends an alarm. "Please call at your earliest convenience."

She changes into her favorite sweats, overdue for a wash, lets Bingo in, and makes tea. "Off the chair girl, I have an important call." On the first ring, Peter answers. He sounds tired. Calline's anxiety spikes. Did something happen? What's going on?

Through a yawn, Peter says, "Hello Cal, thanks for calling back so soon. I have been a wreck the past twenty-four hours. Do you want the good news or the bad news first?"

"Good." She says without hesitation. Delaying gratification is not her long suit.

"The good news is that Randy's been offered a great job as design director at Rhoades Home Interiors in Grand Rapids."

Calline says, grudgingly, "The bad?"

"The bad news is I've just been offered my dream position as Choir Master and secondary organist at the American Church in Paris, the day after Smit extended a call to High Dunes. The American Church wants to hear from me in six days. This brings new meaning to being caught between two bales of hay."

"And to the word call. What side of the ocean is it coming from? How are you being led? And I imagine if you could answer that you would." Calline prays to be lovingly detached when she really wants to scream bloody murder. After all they've been through to respect and honor Peter as a person, as a great talent that could so bless the church. After all they've been through, period.

"Frankly, Cal, I promised myself a long time ago I'd not go again to places where I feel like a new species introduced at the local zoo. The dynamics before people get bored with the novelty of having a gay couple around or, until they one day just realize the truth that we're God's kids just like they are? That's why we moved out here to live. I know I'm preaching to the choir, but you get my drift." He sighs and sounds tired. Why wouldn't he be? Calline is almost ready to bless the man on his way to gay Paree.

"Peter, this is a crucible for you and Randy. I wish I had the answer. All I know is that I want you here. I believe I speak for the majority of our congregation. I don't know how you'd be treated. Sure, a real wrench has been thrown into the process, but what a learning time for all of us, Peter. I thank you for that, though you didn't ask for any of this. Those against are packing their bags now to leave. It looks like the Spirit might be building a whole new church, anyway. Would you concur, Peter?"

"Yes, Cal, I would. Hey, I've got another call. Pray. I will. Randy will. And we'll get back. All the best, Cal. I wish I could do more than this right now."

"Right now it's enough, Peter. God bless you. And Randy, too." She hangs the receiver and sighs, "Oh, Sorrel, how I wish you were here." The phone rings.

"Cal, honey, it's me. I'm in Grand Rapids meeting Billy and Martha. They decided to fly in tonight. I wish you'd join us. You O.K.?" Sorrel sounds happy, until she tells him about Peter's dream job.

"No, I'm not O.K."

"We're having dinner in an hour. I'll see you at your place, after. Two hours? Sooner, I wish." She can almost feel his grin.

"Hug Billy and Martha for me." She slams the receiver and wails into her pillow.

CHAPTER FORTY-TWO

"I SUPPOSE TONIGHT'S NOT the night either," Sorrel snaps, something he rarely does with Calline. Sorrel has done a good job of his recovery from years of drinking, and the work shows, overall. Tonight, though, he just wants what he wants, and Calline feels his pushiness; the pressure of the harsh edges in his voice she doesn't need. She knows his desire is strong, but she promised herself a long time ago, never to abandon herself to make it all right for a man's crazed sex drive, or for anything else, for that matter.

"I'm sorry, hon. I just, I just . . ." Calline puts her head into the pillow and sobs, her first open crying in front of Sorrel since the hospital. He curls her body into his and holds her, irritated that he cut dinner short with Billy and Martha and hurried from Grand Rapids, fantasizing a night of unleashed passion. Now this, and the crying which Calline does unabashedly, so unromantic! She once said to him, "When I let go with my tears like this—if you don't mind, could you just be there with me? This will move through. I promise." She doubts he will be patient enough, but prays he will be.

"I know you hate this, Sorrel. You came here with a plan, an expectation."

"Premeditated resentment, those plans, huh?" Sorrel seems surrendered.

"All the while you were driving I had a plan, too, to ravage you. But gawd, Sorrel, sometimes it's all just so sad. The world is in such a fix."

"Here you go again, globalizing. Cripe, Reverend, you can awfulize—your word—with the best of them. Could you think brighter thoughts so we can, you know?" He moves his hand between her thighs, then up to her crotch and hopes touching there will flip the switch of passion, but knows when she is overtaken by the ghoul, he calls it, to insist would only delay. "And?" Sorrel turns to her with eyes of profound compassion and unabated lust. Waiting.

"Just when I think our little Jesus enterprise might make a dent for good, things go all haywire. I feel like all we do is put out fires, literally, with little energy and passion to actually accomplish something. And when it looks like we might be going somewhere, like today, it all goes to crap." Sensing how deep her despair and discouragement, Sorrel puts his arms around her and pulls her to him, planting light kisses on her head. "When we pray the Our Father, 'let it be on earth as it is in heaven', I get so focused on the discrepancy."

"But, God is right here, mingling in this mess with us. I trust that God accepts us just as we really are, in all our blundering, commissions, and omissions. Don't you?" For the first time, it occurs to Sorrel that his pastor may be just arriving at that place of really trusting God's goodness, no matter what. This realization of her doubt, and his faith, startles him.

"Pretty darned good theology, dear. Who taught you that?" She sniffs, and presses his head into her chest, kissing his bald spot.

He pulls away to give his customary soft rub on her cheek and a kiss at the top of her ear. "Is it my imagination or have I arrived at my truth—the best kind, in my opinion—before my pastor has?"

Calline straightens up, and looks into his eyes, a look so deep, adoring, and appreciative, that words aren't needed. At times when she doubts, like now, she borrows his faith and trust: she the child, he the ancient oracle.

He kneads her bad knee the way she likes it. "For some reason, I never really have wanted to know about your limp. It's been hard to make my pastor human, a woman who limps, cusses, fraternizes with parishioners, sees the Light . . . and who is as unapologetic about doubt and uncertainty as she is absolute in any just cause."

"God, stop, Sorrel! I hate hearing this from you. Yes, I'm human. I'm frustrated a lot lately that I wear this mantle of ordination that reads like a neon sign: 'I'll be religious and righteous so you don't have to be. You can project your junk onto me to avoid the lonely trip required, the walk into and through the slough of despond, the Via Delarosa. After all, the story is one of the Passion, isn't it? Good Friday, then Easter. We all just want the banquet without having to take the hard, narrow road to get there. Who wants to have her skull cracked open to get it, really get it, about sin and grace, when it would be easier just to have a religious professional do it for you? Phew, you touched something there, man." She throws back the covers to cool herself. "One reason among many that I love you, Sorrel, is that I know I can be human and not get that 'but I never expected this of the pastor' look."

Sorrel laughs to think how rarely he has experienced her delivery consistent with his expectations; how profound and profane she can be, all at once.

"Are you listening?" She tugs on his ear. "You know what I'm talking about: how people would just as soon be told the rules to follow, when Salvation—used interchangeably with healing—is a process, not a product, and the process is not a trip to the Magic Kingdom. Boy, I'm profound tonight." She sighs deeply and looks sadly into his eyes.

Sorrel puts his finger on her lips. "I don't want to sound preachy, dear, but there are standards for your office, for all Christians. The bar is supposed to be higher for you. You can't get around that. You don't *want* to get around that. Do you?" He pinches her side and she laughs, then gets quiet. She knows he's right. But how can the Code trump this moment when she feels so held, so loved, like God has arms just for her. "I want to know and accept you just as you are, love. As a sexy, funny, smart woman who is—as you've said on more than one occasion—one beggar showing another where the well is. And you can preach like a stump on fire, girl. Since the accident, you speak more passionately of a God who accepts, not a cop-judge-tyrant God with arms crossed, tapping his—excuse me, her—toes, judgmental and allusive, waiting for us to mess up. Or else. You've said those words, but I hear you now as knowing these words. That's what preaches, sister. Believing it as firsthand knowledge instead of as something you read in a book."

Calline is amazed, never imagining a theological discussion could arouse her. But it does. "I think you've got me!" She cries again, blowing her nose, holding his hand to her lips and kissing every freckle. No restraints of thought or emotion—just Bingo who won't stay on the floor—the couple twist and turn to join their bodies as one. Sweating, limp, cuddled, and satisfied, Sorrel dares to ask Calline why she limps. She wonders if the telling will require more vulnerability than she expressed in their love-making. "It started when Carly and I met at church . . ." She tells him everything, even after his snoring begins. She just keeps telling it and telling it, holding his hand, listening to him breathe, knowing that simply in the telling and in his sleep, more healing comes to the wounds of a fierce injury to body and soul.

The note under her pillow reads, "I understand some things better now. I love you. S."

"Bingo, it's eleven! You must be going crazy to go out!" The dog stares out the door while Calline splashes water onto her face, noticing in the mirror dark circles that are more difficult to erase since she turned forty. The phone rings. It's Thomas sounding alarmed.

"There is not going to be any Peter Vanderlaan, Calline. He's going to Paris!" If words could describe Thomas's voice, it would be something like a groom jilted at the altar.

Calline had a feeling this would be Peter's decision, but to Thomas she says, "What on earth, Thomas? As it is in heaven?" This just spills out.

"What are you mumbling about, earth, heaven, Calline?" Thomas says, sounding raw, never comfortable with heaven-speak.

"On earth as it is in heaven, Thomas!" Calline almost shouts.

"When the hell does heaven come down here, Rev.? Tell me that, would you!" He hangs up, beloved Thomas Dreiden, heroic in carrying the strains of the past months on his shoulders, practically single-handedly, and now this. Calline can't help but want to join him in the complaint, one mere mortal next to another wondering if and when the vision she saw might someday be the vision realized. Here. Right now.

CHAPTER FORTY-THREE

Journal Entry—March 26, 1988:   AT PATTY'S HOUSE.

BINGO SLEEPS AT my feet. Patty's great about letting my pal come along. This girlfriend takes spring seriously. Countless trumpet lilies blast their scent. I had to push tulips and daffodils aside to find my cot to sleep on. Now, for the update on things church:

After Peter decided to go to Paris it felt like we were shipwrecked and the sea had swallowed everything. Precious treasures, the fruits of hard work and hope, had sunk to an unfathomable bottom. I came a bit unraveled. Edit: a lot unraveled. Dad came to console, cook, and clean—in his eighties, my hero—while I just tried to keep the church fires burning, so to speak. Gertrude, begrudgingly, agreed to keep playing until we could reorganize and start a new search. Kathy, Thomas, Gunther, and Smit all stepped up, tired, discouraged, but willing—bless their hearts—to begin again. I tried to fake hope in my heart so I could convey some thread of the same to the congregation.

The smell of the building keeps bringing to mind the Ash Wednesday and burial litany, "ashes to ashes, dust to dust," how ephemeral all things are, even the best laid plans. Speaking of fires burning, Officer Jensen told us Hair wasn't the culprit, thank goodness. He may have an arson background, but I sure didn't want to see this man locked up on our account. Jensen said it'd be a one-to-million chance we'd ever catch the person who did this. Grimsley was a suspect, but she was the one who made the new kitchen possible. One conflagration from her is enough, and I have to cut the woman some slack. She's like the church. Even when you wonder what good it ever does, you try to imagine the world without it.

After Peter backed out, would Alexis make us eat crow? I wondered. She just said to me one day on the phone, "I'm glad we can go back to being the church, the righteous church, not preparing for HELL." She said "hell" really loudly then slammed the phone. She might have been referring to Peter's destination for being gay, but probably to mine, too, for some of the things she read in my journal. What will she do with what she knows? What will I do with THAT she knows? The conversation went something like this:

"Let me just ask you one thing, Alexis. If Peter had come, would you really have withdrawn your membership? Left your friends?

"You guarandamntee I would have." I could see her boxing the air, like she does to make a POINT. Was she calling my bluff? Yes or no, it's always her job to agitate; I couldn't see her abdicating her role any time soon.

Vee called out of the blue.

"The doctor tol' me I was lucky, but the baby be full term." She said she wanted me to see the baby born so I'd know how to put the water on him or her.

While most of us could imagine only the bad when Peter backed out, God was working like fertilizer in ripped up soil. Folks acted like family members do after a bad fight. Some disappear for a while, some just don't speak; the regulars stay and do all the work, and most pretend everything is just fine. Next thing you know everybody is at the dining room table chatting and enjoying each other's company like nothing ever happened. Snow birds trickled back from the South. The majority of Petition-signers became regular attenders again. The neighbors from our Open and Welcoming Sunday weave themselves nicely into the expanding tapestry of the church, like new patches sewn into an old quilt. (stop—Patty and Ray back).

CHAPTER FORTY-FOUR

SETTLED BACK IN after a brief visit to Patty's to meet Ray and rest, Calline knows that no one expects a peppy Easter this year. *Make God laugh, have a plan*, she thinks, as she reflects again on all that has not happened in a compressed amount of time, basically, since Peter decided to go to Paris. She reaches for her pad to scratch notes for Easter when the phone rings.

"Cal, it's Peter."

"Peter. I thought you'd crossed the ocean days ago! How wonderful to hear your voice." *A slight prevarication*, she thinks, as she clears her throat and takes an extra big swig of Earl Grey and waits. *What now?*

"This is really bizarre, I know." Peter sounds on edge, like someone who's broken a window with a baseball and has returned to account for it. "I'll get to the point, Calline. I want to candidate at High Dunes, if it's not too late." Listen for the pen to drop. "Mom had a serious turn in her health. I just can't imagine taking off for Europe right now. My brother, John and his wife live in Oregon. Impossible for them to step in." He sighs deeply.

Calline rubs her belly and waits. Is there more to go with this explosion of news?

"Peter . . . I . . . uh. I don't know, well . . . yes, I guess. I'd have to call a meeting of Governance, like yesterday. Six days 'til Easter and that would be the Sunday to have you here, I think." Calline feels dizzy.

"I understand. I . . . uh." He laughs. "Hard to get our words out, wouldn't you say? I feel horrible to cause this stir, Cal. Yet, I want to come. Easter would be fabulous. I've composed a choral

Easter anthem for Paris, I can simplify for your choir if you like?" He stammers and clears his throat.

"It sounds like a fine idea; it's just righting the ship, and turning it to sail in a new direction, in lightening speed. Not easy. Not for me, anyway, and I imagine the others too. Calline's tone is more resigned than expectant. "I'll get back, or Thomas, perhaps. Sit tight." She hangs up, bows her head and holds silence and her breath for how long, she's not sure. *Call Thomas*, she hears.

Without ceremony or drama, Calline simply states,"Thomas, are you sitting down? Peter called. He wants to candidate Easter."

"Cripe, you're kidding, Cal. I'm playing nine holes this afternoon. Myrtle's meeting the kids at the airport." Plenty irritated, Thomas acts like a man who reeled his arms sore to bring in the big one, lost the fish, now has to stop the boat, turn around, re-rig tackle and bait, cast, and reel again, long after the sun has set and the Michelob has warmed.

"I feel ya," as the kids say. But . . . honestly, I don't know what to say. 'Want to pray and get back?" says Calline, sympathetic.

"The iron is cold, granted. But we've got to strike. I'll call and see who I can round up to meet tonight and get right back," Thomas acquiesces. The receiver goes blank. Calline sits quietly, prays, watching the logs in the fireplace smolder, wondering if any flames will pop for this totally unexpected surprise. Less than an hour later the phone rings. It's Thomas, faithful Thomas.

"Cal, seven sharp at our place. Kathy, Smit, Sorrel, me, Gunther, Tendal, Lilly can make it. J.B. and Nancy passed. To entice the others to drop everything and be here I offered Myrtle's cookies and lunch at the club. We have a quorum." Thomas sounds like another meeting will send him to a horror-filled netherworld. It very well could.

Calline feels knotted up. The human mind and soul can't respond to sudden turns like this, at least hers can't. That everyone "yesses" with comparatively little discussion, indicates either a confirmation of the Spirit, or a unanimous desire to get the whole ordeal done and over with, the sooner the better. Or both. Now it's just the practical issues. Who will call Peter, where will he and Randy stay? At this last minute can they suspend the By-laws stipulation that two-week's notice must be given before a congregational vote? Governance members will have to call active members: "We are taking a vote this Sunday, Easter, to yay or nay Peter Vanderlaan to serve as music director and choir master."

On Easter morning the sun shows itself like a shy child, who suddenly gains confidence to move from behind a curtain of clouds and shine into a sky of widening blue. The wind-chill hovers in the high forties. Green shoots from the daffodil bulbs appear at the front stoop of the pastor's house. Calline dresses in a bright orange and yellow light flannel dress with a wide pale yellow belt, looser since last worn. She presses her mother's cotton bonnet onto her head and ties the long purple satin sash under her chin, paying no mind to its fatigued or ill-matching style.

The "Open and Welcome to All God's Children" banner flies over the church entrance, flapping in the strengthening lake breeze, just like it did the Sunday the neighbors came.

As she enters the building, Calline feels a rising in her throat, tears welling in her eyes. Something wonderful, something mysterious is going to happen here today, she just feels it. Lilies line the narthex and the chancel steps, their scent mixed with smoke, but their scent nevertheless.

She greets Thomas and Myrtle stationed at the sanctuary entrance to hand out bulletins. Dalia printed an extra fifty. She had one of her "knowings," she calls them. "We'll need more than ever for this Sunday," says Dalia, all in now and maybe reformed enough to keep her job.

"'mornin' Rev," Thomas smiles broadly. "Just to remind you: Peter and Randy are with Smit. You just give us your best from the pulpit and we'll handle the rest." Calline tip-toes to peck Thomas's cheek with a kiss, and to squeeze his hands.

"Happy Easter Thomas. Feels like another one of God's surprises, like Christmas." She laughs, feeling joyful to the marrow of her bones.

Choir voices tune and croak. Peter's anthem is a simple two-part piece, four-beat number with lots of hallelujah harmonies and He-is-risens, arranged perfectly to encourage a small choir to sing their hearts out and to not worry.

"Let's do our best for Peter, our new . . . er . . . our candidate for my job," encourages Gertrude whose crankiness since the delay in her retirement seems in remission. Calline joins them in the chancel to place her notes in the pulpit, to check the alter draped with the traditional Easter linens. Tall trumpet lilies surround the base and line themselves along the chancel steps. Calline touches each element: the chalice, the plate, the fresh loaf of Nancy Dobbs's bread, as if this small gesture imbues them with the hope that rises in her spirit like never before.

Journal Entry—April 5, 1988   EASTER BLOW-OUT

Thanks to Mims Smith, who showed up with a busload from the Lemonade Stand, over sixty neighbors helped us sing our hallelujahs. Most who signed the Petition to quit the church, to pull their pledges if Peter were hired, were THERE. Even the Grimsleys. I don't understand it, except that it was Easter and you never try to figure out things that happen on Easter. Of course, I tried to analyze the situation. Were people bored with the fight over Peter? Were they in complete denial that we actually were going to vote to call an out married homosexual? Or was God just strutting her stuff, rolling away the stone, putting on a show? Just like the first Easter?

At first, I felt bold to reveal some of my story: why I limp, how my limp had taken on its own meaning and power, like a sacrament; it had become an outward sign of inward guilt and shame. It seemed I needed a surfboard to split my thinking in two, to open my heart to the way God was looking on—not how I was looking on at myself. I quoted Sister M.T. who must have said a thousand times, "If only you could see yourself the way the one who made you does. The disparity can be met and salved only by the presence and action of our Divine Therapist, God. If only we'd consent to that work."

"Why did Jesus come, anyway?" I asked again. Isaiah 61, Luke 4, etc. etc.. "God had to perform a show-and-tell of breaking down prejudice and hatred, shame, and ignorance, greed, pride. Had to show us a way to unite us, to unbind us, a way that says just your being is fine. I love you. Now go, be your gorgeous selves. Let (emphasis on "let") the stone be rolled away here, there, and everywhere."

Easter miracles don't cease. People clapped like it mattered after Peter was voted in, seventy-six votes "yea", five "nay", with three abstentions. Peter took a deep bow alongside Randy. He seemed happy that people liked the anthem the choir sang with Peter's accompaniment.

Becky came with her kids and their kids. She felt led to witness her love for the Lord, so we had two sermons. Becky grew up in the Jim Crow South, and no one has to hear again what that was like for any child with skin other than white. I couldn't clap loud enough for her courage, the person she is. Her largess over past weeks was rewarded with a generous gift from an anonymous donor. It was she who made peppermint ice cream for Peter (his favorite) and the congregation. Billy and Martha came from Bermuda to help with an Easter egg hunt that dissolved into egg-throwing and some bruises. Hair showed up, too, standing in the back, his crystal eyes gleaming, love in them to beat the band.

Prayer: Dear Jesus—I think of all the prayers your Easter has inspired. Will you take them all as mine today?

EPILOGUE

EASTER SUNDAY RESTORED to The Reverend Calline Simpson a step like a newborn filly first turned out to pasture to romp and to taste the tender new grass of early summer.

She is ecstatic to tell Sister M.T. about Easter, the filled pews, Miss Becky's moving testimony, the decisive vote for Peter. Before she can say a word she exhales, a sigh so deep to signify that a part of her, so patently missing for so long, had found its way back and taken its rightful place. "It's a sensation of warm fluids being poured into the hollow of my bones, fluids that have the DNA of my ancestors, that bring real healing, and a sense of completion," she tries to articulate. A long silence between them seems the best way to properly acknowledge the return of this essential part of herself. "It—what do you call it? It makes romantic love seem like the fizz on the real thing." Calline exhales deeply again, recognizing that romance feels good, but there's nothing like a return to one's truest self.

"There had better be something more abiding, more filling, more enduring—than fizz, the bubbles and froth of romance, you think?" Calline waits, wanting to trust that her words make sense.

Sister M.T. looks up and winks, like there's someone else in the room with them and the joke is on Calline. Then, M.T. leans in to show her keen interest, her delight that perhaps this woman who has talked and talked and talked over months and months, is finally onto something powerful and meaningful that proves the breadth and depth of Spirit's work when the human cooperates and persists.

"Oh, don't get me wrong, I've got it for Sorrel. Bad." Sister and Calline laugh. In contrast to the profundity of M.T.'s deep insights drawn from years listening in prayer, Calline gets it that her romantic narrative, by comparison, is trivial. Yet, to her amazement, M.T. takes it all in without judgment or advice. Calline knows now it's because God takes it all in. Everything: her foibles, her escapades, her doubts, her illusions. All of it is safe to be shared, fodder to be dismantled, composted, and turned into something rich and beautiful, the truest reflection of holy intention. Her authentic being.

With folded hands Sister twirls her thumbs. It seems forever for her to impart, "We all yearn for what's been there the whole time, a deep sense that we are never really alone, and that our truest selves are all God wants of us. Our hurry, our fears and cravings, draw us away from what is truly gratifying: a sense that right here, right now, the Presence is actually present and wants to assure us that all things will be well. Deep inner peace is achievable, not by muscle, but by....oh my I'm preaching." M.T. laughs and hands Calline a tissue.

Calline puts her head back on the chair and sighs again, as if for the first time she really hears M.T.'s words that have been repeated and repeated like an ancient liturgy, like a drip-drip of water until one day a discernible mark on the rock appears. "I suppose you have to really want it. I know I do, now that the realization has come to me that I am accepted and loved. What a delivery though. Wham!" Calline giggles and traces the line of the tiny scar that encircles her eye.

Calline and M.T. sit quietly, watching through the huge view window the water pop with silver, the sun's light play hide-and-seek behind a puffy thunderhead. The lake looks like the baptismal pool of the Atlantic where she died and rose, and in the stark Light she came to, seeing herself, not from her vantage point, but from God's. A new voice had penetrated the wall of separation, a whisper so sweet and gentle and full of love. "You are the beloved. With you I am pleased."

Back home, Calline changes into a flannel nightgown, heats a cup of Earl Grey, and settles in front of the fire, flames dancing behind a blackened log. Bingo curls up at her feet, belly exposed, begging for a scratch. Oh, the tearing apart and the mending, hearts broken and swelled with love, the near-death, the rising, the coming around again. She reaches to rub Bingo's belly. Her thoughts go to her great-grandmother. "There is no way, Grand, I could have figured all this out."

Thank God, you no longer think you have to! The pastor thinks she hears.